When do you need a

MOTIVE

for MURDER? Ask Joe Morgan.

To Susan,
Thanks for all your
help making this book
possible

Dennis M. Adams

NFB Publishing
Buffalo, New York

NFB
<<<>>>
NFB Publishing/Amelia Press
119 Dorchester Road
Buffalo, New York 14213

For more information visit
Nfbpublishing.com

DEDICATION

I actually have two dedications to note.

The first and foremost is for Evy who has supported me through all my endeavors, through all the good times and bad, and I know will be there for the remaining chapters of our lives. Thank you, Dear!

And secondly, I like to dedicate this book to the men and women who suit-up and put their lives on the line in every city across this nation. Whether they wear the Police, Fire, or Military uniform, they risk so much for so few who appreciate them.

COTERIE: (ko'de-rie, kot'-er-ie) noun
A small group of people with shared interests or tastes, especially one that is exclusive of other people.
ie: "a coterie of friends and advisers"

TABLE OF CONTENTS

CHAPTER 1
Saturday, March 16, 2019

DINNER, DISHES AND DESPAIR

As was Joe Morgan's routine, on Saturday he would have an early dinner with his son Mike, his daughter-in-law Chrissy, and his only grandson, Sean.

After saying grace, Mike declared, "Mom would be happy that we're all together."

Joe smiled and added, "But undoubtedly she would be telling Chrissy the *right way* to cook the ham." They all acknowledged with a respectful laugh.

The conversation around the table covered everything from current affairs to Mike and Chrissy's jobs, a police officer and ER nurse, respectively, to Joe's retirement from "the job."

After half clearing his plate, Sean reminded his grandfather, "Gramps, tomorrow is the 17th of March. You know what that is?" he asked excitedly.

"Of course, Sean. How could I forget?" he teased. "Yesterday was the Ides of March, today is Saturday dinner, and tomorrow is St. Patrick's Day."

"No Gramps!" Sean was emphatic. "Remember what you said? You said that you'd go to my next track meet. That's tomorrow, Gramps."

"Are you sure you don't want to go to the St. Paddy's Day parade?"

"No Gramps. The parade is downtown in the morning. And we have to be at Delaware Park by 9 o'clock for the track meet."

"Okay Sean," Joe relented. "I guess I can change my schedule around."

With a puzzled look, Sean asked, "And what is the Ides of March, anyway?"

Joe reflected for a moment. "It was a very bad day," he answered with a profound seriousness. Joe stared across the room and beyond, as he recalled one of the worst days of his life.

IT was March 15, 2008, going into the last hour of the tour. Sergeant Al Taylor Jr. knocked on Lt. Joe Morgan's door.

"Hey, Loot," the Sergeant announced as he poked his head into the Supervisor's Office, "I'm going to make the last check of the beat-men. You want to come along?"

That night, there were three officers assigned to walking posts: one on Ontario Street, another on Tonawanda Avenue, and the last on North Thames Street. It was only minutes after the Sergeant and Lieutenant stopped to speak with the first two beat-men and were on the way to the third, when Sgt. Taylor pulled the squad car up to the side of the Riverside Bodega. "If you don't mind Loot, I'll just run in for a pack of smokes." Taylor stated.

Before the Lieutenant's driver could exit the car, Morgan answered. "As a matter of fact, I was going to stop for a quart of milk and a loaf of bread on the way home. I may as well get them now. Go on in, Junior. I'll let the dispatcher know that we'll be out of service for a few."

"13-L to dispatch. We'll be out of service for a couple minutes at the Riverside Bodega, 1241 North Thames."

"Clear 13-L," the dispatcher acknowledged.

Morgan followed Taylor into the store. As Sgt. Taylor entered, he observed three black males grouped together at the counter facing a Hispanic male clerk. The clerk was drenched with fear and panic. One of the young men turned and displayed a handgun. Before Taylor could react, a single shot rang out.

Sgt. Taylor bent forward, grabbing his abdomen just below the bottom of his vest, but he remained on his feet.

At the same moment, another of the holdup men flashed a chrome plated revolver, scurried around the end of the counter, and grabbed the clerk around the neck. "Drop your gun or I'll shoot him. You hear me? Now!" he screamed.

As Junior Taylor struggled to stay on his feet, his body blocked the doorway, preventing the Lieutenant from entering. Morgan's only view of the suspects was over the staggering Sergeant's shoulder. Without hesitation, Morgan reached around the Sergeant and took his first shot, striking the man who was holding the clerk as a shield. The thug was hit dead center of his forehead causing him to fall backward, releasing his grip on the clerk, and dropping the silver revolver onto the counter as he collapsed to the floor. Morgan was surprised when he heard two more shots explode from Taylor's weapon. The Sergeant was still hunched forward as he pumped bullets into the floor.

Officer Billy Mullins was walking his beat when he heard the shots from the bodega, a half block away. He radioed to the dispatcher as he ran, "Shots fired at the bodega on North Thames. Beat 13-3 responding."

"You have officers out of service at that location," the dispatcher advised.

Just as Officer Mullins reached the entrance to the store, the second suspect let loose with a barrage of bullets from a small caliber automatic. One struck Taylor's vest on the left side of his chest, and another round hit the top of his head. As the Sergeant began to fall forward, Lt. Morgan grabbed him by the collar of his coat and swung him into a side aisle, out of the line of fire. Morgan then dove behind a display rack at the end of the next aisle.

Officer Mullins rushed through the entrance to catch one bullet in his upper thigh, but managed to return fire. The second gunman was hit but not down. The third robber rushed up to the counter, grabbed the chrome plated gun that was dropped by his now-deceased partner, and disappeared down the rear aisle of the store, throwing a couple shots back over his shoulder.

Lt. Morgan carefully made his way to the end of his aisle and peeked around the far corner. Clear. He cautiously moved down the adjoining end aisle. Peeking around the corner shelf he checked the next parallel aisle. Clear. He could hear some mumbling and a dragging noise coming from the last parallel aisle, which was along the rear wall of the store. Inch by inch he crept to the end of the shelving, bobbed his head around the corner and saw the second robber lying on his side in a fetal position. As the Lieutenant climbed to his feet, the wounded robber looked up toward Morgan. Neither spoke a word. Instinctively, the criminal and the cop knew that their survival depended on the next few seconds. There was no time for trust. The body on the floor started to roll to his other side, revealing a handgun that he raised and pointed in Morgan's direction. It was the last bad decision of the thug's short seventeen years.

By the time Morgan was able to clear the rest of the store, a half dozen backup units had arrived and flooded the street with flashing red and blue lights. The clerk stated that the last robber ran out the rear entrance with the chrome plated snub-nose revolver. A vague description of the suspect broadcast was broadcast: "Black male, 16 to 20 years old, 6 feet tall, medium build, armed with a chrome plated snub-nose revolver. Consider Armed and Dangerous." The third robber was never located that night, or any time since.

THEN Joe's dark reminiscence was broken by the sound of Sean asking repeatedly, "What Gramps? What was a bad day?"

Mike ignored his father's momentary distant stare. He laughed as he turned his attention to Sean. "I thought you were going to be the scholar of the family. It's from the play *Julius Caesar*. It means the 15th of March."

"Oh yeah. Now I remember from English class, Shakespeare. But we're running on the 17th, Gramps."

"Don't worry Sean. I'll be there." Joe assured with a smile.

After dinner Sean asked his grandfather, "Would you like to stay for a while and play rummy tonight?"

"Sure, kiddo," Joe agreed. Then nodding toward the other end of the table he asked Sean, "You think your Mom and Dad would like to play?"

"That sounds great," Mike volunteered. "But first we have to clean up. Sean, you can help your mother clear the table."

"Okay, Dad!" Sean answered enthusiastically. "And I'll clean off the dishes and put them in the dishwasher."

"Thanks, Sean." Mike approved. "And I'll wipe down the table and get the cards out."

Joe offered, "While you're all busy in the kitchen, I think I'll just run back to my apartment to feed Mitsy. She's probably wondering where her dinner is."

"Hey Gramps," Sean called from the kitchen, "If you want, I'll go and feed Mitsy."

"I forgot you're driving now," Joe answered. "It sounds good to me, but…" Joe glanced toward Mike. "What do you think Mike?"

Sean rushed back into the dining room. "Can I Dad? I've been driving after dark for a couple months. I promise I'll be careful."

"Our car is parked ahead of the City vehicle in the driveway, and I can't let you drive the City car. Even if it's only in the driveway," Mike explained.

"But my car is on the street," Joe offered. "That is, if you don't mind your son being seen driving an old beige Buick." Joe laughed.

"Okay, okay," Mike agreed, "But load the dishwasher first."

Joe tossed his keys to Sean and said, "Be careful, kiddo!"

"I will, Gramps. I promise!" Sean beamed as he quickly finished his kitchen chores and flew out the door.

As promised, Sean was diligent with his driving. He was fully compliant with the speed limit, made full stops at stop signs, and gave total concentration to his driving. He even turned the radio off so as not to be distracted by the "oldies" station that his grandfather always listened to. Sean stayed on the main roads, even though it was the long way to Gramp's place. The roads were well lit, until Sean turned southbound onto Parkside Drive. Here the residential street had fewer streetlights, with most of their light obstructed by the huge maple trees that lined the street. He slowed down to 20 mph until he came across a large open length of curb across from Joe's apartment building. Carefully he backed the Buick into the generous space. When Sean turned off the headlights he switched on the dome light, so that he could separate the building and apartment keys from the rest of the keys on the ring. A moment later he bounded from the driver's seat. In his enthusiasm, he dropped the key ring as he turned to lock the driver's door. He looked in the direction of the sound where the keys had fallen, but could not see them. He resorted to moving his foot back and forth along the surface of the asphalt. As he moved closer to the middle of the street, he heard the roar of an engine start up, and then the clink of the keys he had been searching for. Looking toward where he thought the keys were, he was oblivious to the vehicle that sped out from the curb on the opposite side of the street.

The vehicle swerved across Parkside Drive and struck Sean while he stood frozen in a half-bent position. The thudding impact threw his body twenty feet into the air, arcing gracelessly until he landed face-first, well ahead of the vehicle. The vehicle stopped momentarily and then sped forward again, striking Sean's crumpled body a second time, as it fled north on Parkside. It wasn't until the vehicle roared into second gear that the headlights went on, and the taillights disappeared around the next corner.

CHAPTER 2

AIN'T NO SECOND CHANCE

THE MORNING SUN created a blinding glare across the windshield as the truck turned eastbound onto Main Street. The driver pulled to the curb and picked up his cellphone, scrolled to the name "T-Bone" and activated the auto dialer. The call was into the fifth ring when a sleepy voice answered.

"Where you at T-Bone?" the caller asked frantically. "I been lookin' all over for you. You on the strip?"

"Shit no, man. I'm still at the crib. How come you rousting my ass at this time of morning?"

"You got the TV on? You screwed up big time, m'man," declared the caller. "You were supposed to scare the shit out of the bastard. Boss said to mess him up bad. Not kill him." Then there was a long silence. "You listening?"

The trembling T-Bone answered, "Yeah, yeah, I'm listening. I told you last night that I got him good, and you said that I did a good job. How would I know he was killed? What we gonna do now?"

The caller advised, "Bax wants to meet with the two of us. He's really pissed. But I think the boss will cool down. Don't worry, brother."

"What do you mean don't worry, Tyrell. You're the one who told me to do the guy. You gave me the type of car and plate number. It all matched up. I didn't think I ran over him that bad, but I couldn't tell 'cause it was so dark. I just did what you told me to do!" Now panicking, T-Bone pleaded, "What we do now?"

"I will pick you up in a half hour at your crib. We gonna have to talk. We gotta get our stories straight and then we'll meet up with Bax. So, chill. Okay?"

"Yeah, man. Okay. I'll be waiting on the corner."

As the black pickup truck dressed up with chrome trim and dual wheels approached the corner, T-Bone paced back and forth. He climbed up into the truck and asked, "You talk to Bax yet?"

"No," the driver responded. "I told you that we have to talk first, get our stories straight. So, we're gonna go where we can have some privacy. Somewhere I can get these wheels off the street. Where do you suggest?" Tyrell knew that he was only a few blocks from the abandoned warehouses at the foot of Dutton Street, where he had taken T-Bone many times to deliver his supply of coke and heroin.

T-Bone thought for a moment and responded, as Tyrell hoped he would, "What about at that warehouse on Dutton Street?"

During the short drive T-Bone sought Tyrell's guidance. "You don't think he'd be pissed so much that he'd have me disappear? You know what I mean?"

The driver snickered, "You think he don't appreciate the business you do for him? You're a good earner, man. When it comes to business, he's all about the bottom line. As long as you're producing... Shit, I wouldn't worry if I was you. We're both probably gonna get our asses chewed. That's all. But we're gonna have to get our stories straight."

The truck turned onto Dutton, travelled down to the dead-end, and then continued onto a beaten path of tire ruts that twisted around the shells of several buildings. Then Tyrell finally pulled into one structure that was pretty much intact. As soon as Tyrell cut the engine he suggested, "C'mon, T-Bone. Let's sit on the tailgate and figure this out." He then stepped out and headed toward the back of the truck.

After letting out a long breath of relief, T-Bone jumped out of the truck and walked along the passenger side to the rear of the bed. There was no time for shock to register on his face. He never heard the explosion or saw the flash, before the bullet smashed through his forehead and took out the back side of his skull. He was dead before he hit the ground.

"Sorry, T-Bone. You goin' to a better place now." Tyrell announced and almost sounded like he meant it.

CHAPTER 3

Sorrow, Anger, and Reunion

For the second time in four years, tragedy brought the Morgan family together to hurt and mourn. The wake drew in the extended family of friends and professional acquaintances. Even those long-estranged were compelled to attend, if only to make an obligatory appearance. The last time, the wake had been for Joe's wife, Amy, after she lost a bitter battle with cancer. He recalled standing helplessly in the very same spot as people filed by. This time it was worse. Much worse.

Joe stood at the side of the coffin, eyes closed, with a scowl etched into his face. Fighting the weight of emptiness, his right hand motioned the sign of the cross - touching his forehead, then chest, and shoulder to shoulder. Gathering himself, Joe took a sturdy step back, as if standing guard over his son and daughter-in-law, who remained in prayer on the kneeler.

Mike had his arm draped around Chrissy, supporting her during their deepest hours of suffering. Mike's strength was bolstered by his father, standing at his side, and from the crowd of blue uniforms that monopolized the rear of the room and filled the rows behind the seated family, classmates, and close personal friends. Joe scanned the crowd, taking note of the faces and the purpose that each face expressed. Some sat in silence, drained of emotion, reflecting the realization that life is fragile, and too easily lost. Some showed unfeigned compassion as they struggled to comfort others with recounted memories. Yet others appeared out of obligation, and milled in small clusters around the projected photos on the wall in the long hallway. But they all came.

Joe knew that family friends were there to offer whatever support they could for Mike and Chrissy. He suspected that most of the young people that arrived, and departed in haste, were upset with the loss of a friend and classmate. It was apparent that few of the youngsters had ever experienced death this personal, outside their own family.

The majority of uniformed officers that passed through the doors, from the Police Commissioner down to the newly appointed, approached Mike for a moment, voiced their contempt for the manner of his son's death, and pledged to do whatever they could to apprehend the hit-and-run driver. They covered a wide range of ages, ethnicities and backgrounds, but the sentiment was the same. Joe stood aside, taking in all the emotion of others, yet stifling his own pain. That changed when a slouch-shouldered, white-haired figure appeared at his side.

The voice was gruff and gravelly and took Joe by surprise. Though he could not recall the last time he heard the voice of Harry Doyle, it was unmistakable. Joe turned to catch full view of the heavyset man. His face was set with a half smile. Harry had an extremely receded hairline, and as always, a pair of readers that capped the outcrop of his remaining white hair.

"My deepest sympathy, Joe. I remember when Mike brought Chris and Sean home from the hospital. I was the first to take a picture of him with his Dad and Granddad. Both of you in uniform, and you had your shield pinned on his blanket."

"Yeah. I thought he was going to be the fourth generation of Morgans in the Department." Joe's head sank with the evaporation of that dream. "You know, Harry, I haven't thought about that day since... Oh God, you would have to bring that up!" Joe heaved a deep sigh and looked toward the ceiling to control the tears that began to well up in his eyes. His thumb and forefinger pinched away the moisture as he barked back to Harry, "Jesus, it's so good to see you. What's it been? Four years since Amy was here."

"It's been about that long," Harry responded. "You never joined any of the retirement groups. That's where all of us dinosaurs keep in touch with each other."

"And how's Ella?" Joe asked.

"Well," Harry grumbled. "She stuck with me through 36 years of the job, but the marriage didn't survive my retirement. To think that she put up with me being a cop for all those years, then after a couple years, she couldn't stand me being home all the time. She's living with her sister in Arizona. Now, we're just good friends. We keep in touch. I talk with her almost every week." Sensing that Joe didn't want to be bothered with small talk, Harry offered, "Well enough of me. I was just concerned for you, Mike, and Chris. I wanted to express my sympathy and ask if maybe you'd like to get together for coffee in the next few days?"

Joe's eyes ceased scanning the room and fell back on his old friend.

"That would be marvelous, Harry. It's been way too long. I'll call you and we can set something up. Okay?"

"Sure Joe, sure!" Harry responded in a reassuring voice, but he knew Joe, and didn't believe that he would call. Harry filed a mental note - *one week, call Morgan.* He shook Joe's hand as though it might be the last time, and slapped him on the back before slowly turning and melting into the crowd.

The last two hours of the wake seemed to last an eternity, answering the same questions with the same optimistic responses, now more rehearsed than spontaneous. It was difficult for Joe to explain over and over how after dinner at his son's house, he had sent his grandson to his apartment to feed his dog. He had left in Joe's car and never returned.

Most of the faces wearing uniforms were unfamiliar, but the show of support offered a warm feeling of solidarity. It showed the respect that he and Mike had earned from his peers. That was how it should be. Joe was so proud of his son, and especially proud of Chrissy, for being such a good wife. He, of all people, knew how difficult it was for the wives of cops -

good cops. He envied all those who could make both their job and their marriage work.

Commissioner George Howes entered the room with the Chief of Detectives, Howard Smyth, in tow. Joe greeted the PC and then tried to feel grateful for the words of encouragement from the Chief of Ds, who updated Joe on the ongoing search for the hit-and-run driver. Joe had to bite his tongue while Smyth noted the cost of the increased manpower for the past five days. By the time the near-weeping, half-drunk Police Chaplain, Monsignor Herberger approached, Joe had reached his fill of diplomacy. "Monsignor, I do not mean to be disrespectful, but could you please get on with leading us with a few prayers so we can keep this program moving?"

"Joseph," the Monsignor responded in a confiding manner, "would you mind if I kept it short? I'm really not feeling too good right now." He rested his arm on Joe's shoulder as much for balance as to offer emotional support. "You know, I think it's this absurd swing of emotions. I just left a wedding reception, such a joyous event and rushed right over here, to such a sad occasion. I can't express how bad I feel for you, Joseph. You…and Mike!"

Joe nodded his agreement as he ushered the Monsignor to the front of the room and the podium situated near the casket. "Thank you ever so much, Monsignor." Joe raised his arms to get the attention of the overflowing room. "Everyone! Please, everyone! Monsignor Herberger would like to say a few words and lead us in prayer for my grandson, and Mike and Chrissy."

After the minute or two that it took for silence to overtake the room, the Monsignor began to address the crowd. "Lord, our God. You are always faithful and quick to show mercy. Our brother, Sean Patrick Michael Morgan, was suddenly taken from us. Come swiftly to his aid, and have mercy on him, and comfort his family and friends by the power and protection of your love."

The wake had finally come to a close. By 9:30 the people had all drifted out of the funeral home, and Mike and Chris had spent their final moments with their son. Joe was the last to share his thoughts and prayers with Sean, before leaving. Joe couldn't help but think ahead to tomorrow morning. It would be worse for Mike and Chrissy, as funerals usually are for parents. Their final farewell to their child.

As he walked from the building toward his vehicle, Joe noticed a shadow behind the wheel of the only other car in the parking lot. Joe squinted to get a better view as he approached the car, then stopped dead in his tracks as the glow of a cigarette dimly illuminated the face of the driver.

The voice from within the vehicle was strong, yet apologetic. "I didn't know if I would be welcome, Cap. I waited, thought about it, and before I figured what I should do, people were already leaving. I thought I'd wait out here for you."

"You didn't have to wait outside," Joe replied, as he spied nearly a dozen cigarette butts below the driver's window of the Dodge Charger. "You should've come in, Chuck. I'm sure that Mike would have liked to see you again. If I recall correctly, you both were in the same Academy class."

"Yeah. We were." Then the voice became more personal. "I just didn't know if there were any hard feelings. You know... with the way I left the job, and how I let you down."

"Chuck, I was your Captain. I tried to keep you on track, but you decided to do things your way. Then I did what a Captain is supposed to do. If I couldn't straighten out the problem, then I had to eliminate the problem. I don't apologize for doing my job, but I feel like I failed at turning you around."

"No, no, no, Cap. I have no bad feelings on that. And you were right to do what you did. I appreciate what you tried to do for me. Really! I do. You were the one that stopped the Commissioner from pressing charges, and allowed me to resign. For that, I will always be in your debt. As a matter of fact, it allowed me to get to where I am now. And for that I thank you."

"Thanks for what?" Morgan asked. "You don't owe me anything."

"You may not know it, Cap, but I owe you a lot. You kept telling me that

I'd get jammed up if I didn't change my ways. And...well...you were right about a lot of things. It just took me a little longer to get my act together. So, when I heard about your grandson, I had to come to see you."

Joe stood quiet for a moment. "Chuck, I am happy that you seem to have put your life back together. I'm glad that you stopped by to say what you did. I've often wondered whatever became of you. I'm glad it all worked out for the best."

"Better than you can imagine, Cap. Please tell Mike that I stopped by and extend my deepest sympathy to him and his wife."

"Why don't you stop by St. Catherine's tomorrow morning before the funeral? Tell him yourself."

"I would if I could, Cap. But I have an early flight to catch in the morning. It's business."

"Business?" Morgan asked.

"Yeah. I'm with the Feds now. Have been since Nine-Eleven." Chuck proudly announced.

"FBI?" Joe queried.

"I'd rather not say, Cap. You know how it is with us Feds," he laughed. "Let's just say it is somewhere between DHS and the CIA," Chuck said as he handed a business card to Joe. On the card were just a name and phone number - *Charles Mason 202-912-9855 ext. 666.* Then Chuck offered, "If you need anything, and I mean *ANYTHING* at all - just call me. It does my heart good knowing that you are well, and we're on good terms. Again, I am so sorry to hear about Mike's boy."

"Thanks, Chuck. But please, give me a call some time. I'd like to talk more when we have time." Joe was curious about which agency would have hired him, but he would not press the issue. "Have a safe flight." Joe watched as Chuck drove out of the parking lot. Typical of Chuck, the Charger fishtailed as he sped into the darkness. Chuck had always been hard to read. Joe typically wondered how much of what he said was true.

THE next morning came too soon. Joe hadn't slept half the night, and he looked like it. No sooner had he entered the bathroom, than the phone rang.

It was Mike. "How are you holding up, Dad?"

Joe responded as he usually did, "Fine. Although I've had better nights. How are you and Chrissy doing?"

There was a meaningful silence before Mike answered, "I have an empty, hollow feeling in the pit of my stomach. Chris has been crying and throwing up all night. It's really taking a toll on her."

Joe knew all too well that the emptiness would linger for years after the tears. "Is there anything I can do, son?" he asked.

"No Dad. There's nothing anybody can do. We're just going to have to get through today, and then take it a day at a time."

"Okay then. I'll see you at the church at ten."

As usual, Joe considered himself to be late if he was not at least ten minutes early, no matter what the occasion. He stood shoulder to shoulder with Father Sullivan, his parish priest, to meet Mike and Chrissy as they arrived at Saint Catherine's. The arrangements had been finalized, vehicles were being situated in the procession order, and there was a heavy air of sorrow filling the church. People dressed in black, or dress blues filled the pews, while still more were crowded around the rear walls and flowed out onto the steps.

Father Sullivan, the pastor of Saint Catherine of Sienna, where Sean had been baptized, celebrated his First Communion, and Confirmation, spoke eloquently. He continued to cite how this young man, Sean Morgan, had contributed so much to other people's lives in his brief span of seventeen years.

Afterward, a somber and now sober, Monsignor Herberger spoke about the brave men and women putting their lives on the line each day to protect other people, their children, and their loved ones. He asked the gathering, "Who watches over the protectors and their families?" After a perfectly timed pause, "Our Lord," he answered. "And we must believe that in the scheme of the larger Universe and Heaven above, there is a plan set for us all. That plan is on a need-to-know basis. And when something like this happens there is not a need for us to know *WHY*, but the *NEED* is for us to *KNOW… HIM*. And to *KNOW* that there is a better place waiting for us all."

Joe listened attentively, but couldn't help to think that it was all meaningless. At this moment he felt so cynical that the priest's platitudes might as well have been the rhetoric and promises of a politician. Although sounding lofty and impressive, the words couldn't be absorbed with any rational meaning. He thought that a sermon of "We're all left here to fend for ourselves and try not to kill our neighbors," would have been a more brutally honest homily.

Two of Sean's classmates spoke briefly of how he showed leadership ability and was always compassionate to others, and how he was always at the center of a crowd.

Finally, Mike spoke. He admitted that he was feeling selfish pity over his loss of a son, and not for Sean's loss of life and his future. He acknowledged that Sean was one of the main threads of a woven cloth they called "family," and questioned if he and Chrissy could pull together the tattered ends of that fabric. He spoke of the three loves in his life: his wife Chrissy, his son Sean, and his chosen profession as a Police Officer. They all had their value, and in his heart, none had any less purpose than the others. Each made him cherish life. Now one was gone.

Joe began to choke up as he listened attentively and recalled when he felt that strongly about the job. He remembered a time when he was so absorbed in his career that he drifted away from his wife and son. He knew that his depression was the result of his past priorities and choices. When Mike married Chrissy, it felt like he had lost Mike. Then when Amy took ill and needed full time attention, he left his career. He retired and tried to make amends with her. But then, she passed away. Joe then attempted to devote his time to the remnants of his family, drawing ever closer to Mike and Chrissy, and treating Sean as he should have treated his own son. But his choices caught up with him as he felt the full weight of his losses: his wife, his career, and now his grandson. Joe was damned if he would let go of what was left - Mike and Chrissy. They were now his only reason to get out of bed each day.

The procession of sixty-seven vehicles snaked through the city's south side, past Police Headquarters, through downtown, and finally stopped inside the gates of Forest Lawn Cemetery. It was the hallowed ground for a President, a Governor, several Mayors, business tycoons, a rock star, military heroes, and now Joe's grandson. As all gathered at the graveside, two short prayers were read, roses were placed on the coffin by each mourner as they filed by, and the parents stood embracing each other and sobbing. Joe proceeded past the coffin after pausing for a final pat on the top of Sean's casket. Then Mike and Chrissy stood frozen at the edge of the grave, lingering not enough to recall a lifetime of memories, yet wishing they could just run away, leaving all this sorrow behind. Funerals are such a cataclysmic entanglement of love and hate, hope and despair, fulfillment and emptiness.

Upon conclusion of the graveside service Father Sullivan announced, "The Morgan family would like to welcome all friends and guests to a brunch at the Pierpont Café on Hertel Avenue immediately after the service. They would appreciate your attendance."

Afterward, as Joe made his way back to his car, Father Sullivan hurriedly approached calling, "Oh, Joe. Joe!" Morgan looked back toward the priest.

Father Sullivan was waving a paper folded in quarters. "I forgot to give you this note. The man wanted me to give it to you after the service at the church this morning, but I forgot. I'm sorry." He handed the paper to Joe and began walking away.

Suddenly Joe called out to the priest, "Who gave you this note?"

Surprised by Joe's agitated tone, Father Sullivan turned to see Joe clutching the open paper in his fist. He answered, "I don't know the man, Joe. He acted like he was a friend of yours. He told me that he was delivering a message for another friend and that you two go way back. He asked if I could give you that note."

"And you waited until now? You didn't think that THIS was more important?"

Father Sullivan was taken aback by the cold anger in Joe's voice. "I have no idea what you're talking about, Joe. I didn't read that note. I wouldn't. It was for you."

Joe took a deep breath and asked more calmly, "Sully, can you please tell me who this person is… or at least what this guy looked like? It's important, Sully."

Father Sullivan closed his eyes and carefully chose his words. "He looked like a broken man. Old. Worn out and bent over to one side. The man handed me the note as I was entering the church… but I don't recall seeing him go in. He had an uncombed mop of gray hair and wore sloppy clothes. I hadn't seen him before, and he didn't look much like the other retired cops that came to the funeral home yesterday, or to the church today. He had a weak voice with a bit of an accent. Italian, I think. That's about all I recall. Although I do remember one other thing. He did have a strange odor about him. Like he hadn't bathed in a while. I wish I could tell you more, Joe."

"No," Joe mumbled, staring at the note again. Joe dragged his eyes up to meet those of the concerned priest, and with an apologetic look he offered, "Sorry for snapping at you. It's just that I don't know who this guy is, or what…" Joe stopped mid-sentence to search for words. "I'm sorry, Sully."

Father Sullivan waved his hand forgivingly in the air as he walked away.

Joe opened his car door and backed into the driver's seat, again studying the folded paper and its message. On the top front of the folded paper was scribbled, "**To Captain Joseph Morgan.**" When opened, the inside message read, "**NOW, your family can suffer like mine did. You only have yourself to blame. Burn in HELL you bastard!**"

Joe arrived at Pierpont's well after everyone else. He tried not to dwell on the sadistic note, but he found that he couldn't stop looking at it every so often.

Mike spotted his Dad as he entered. "You okay? I was getting worried. Where were you?"

"Just thinking things over," Joe answered. "It seems the older I get the less I understand."

With a gentle hand on Joe's shoulder Mike guided him toward a long table on the far side of the restaurant. "Some of your old buddies were asking for you. I told them I'd bring you over as soon as you arrived. Chrissy and I saved you a place at the main table up at the front, but take your time with your friends."

Joe nodded in appreciation before Mike headed to where Chrissy was seated. Joe maneuvered through the tangle of people to the table of old compatriots. His friends rose in a gesture of respect until "Captain Joe" took his seat.

"Thank you, guys. I can't tell you how much it means to me to have you all here. Really. Thank you!" As Joe settled in his seat near the middle of the table, he gazed at the faces of the retired cops he had known, worked for, and with. This was the coterie of friends that Joe had known and trusted his life to for many decades. All but embarrassed by his distraction, Joe anxiously looked through the crowd for anyone wearing sloppy clothes, having an unkempt head of gray hair, a bent over posture, and a weak voice with an Italian accent. Nobody caught his attention.

Chaz Bohen was the first to respond with a coffee cup held up in the air. "If it wasn't for you, Joe, I wouldn't be here." Everyone at the table knew well of the time when Joe and Chaz, then just young street cops on patrol, chased a holdup suspect into a pitch-black alley. As the story goes, Joe rushed between his partner and the drug-crazed junkie who started throwing lead all over the place. Chaz was pushed to the ground and only saw the motion of bodies during the strobe light of gunfire. Seconds later, as he scrambled to his feet, Chaz had found Joe kneeling on the back of the suspect, who was facedown and cuffed. Each time the story was told, Chaz seemed to recall that there were more shots fired and the suspect was crazier and bigger.

With appreciation, Joe gazed at each of the men. At the table was the nerve-wracked Lieutenant of the Burglary Squad, Chaz Bohen, who had retired eight years earlier due to a heart attack and hypertension. Then, seated next to Joe was his right-hand man when he headed the Homicide Bureau, Detective Sergeant Harry Doyle, now a Private Investigator. Next was Staff Sergeant Vern Chosky, the first cop that took Joe under his wing and taught him the true basics of working the streets. Vern retired five years before Joe, and still teaches Martial Arts. Last, but far from least, was the six-foot-five giant of a man who had replaced Joe as Commander of the Homicide Bureau, Willie "Big Will" Williams. The nickname "Big Will" was coined by those who knew him best, not because of his first name or his size, but because of his relentless drive, dedication, and willpower. Literally, he had a "big will." When you needed something done, it was Big Will who got it done.

It was a menagerie of characters that had once formed a tight knit group that unofficially solved departmental problems, with the specialized help of a few others. It was a trust of kindred spirits. And so, the afternoon passed with a good meal, glasses of wine, and remembered feats of old. Old cops telling the same old tales. Although the company of old friends distracted Joe for a while, reality and anxiety soon returned when his trusted friends departed.

CHAPTER 4

Introspection and Guilt

Joe wrestled with the note through the next couple days. He tried to think of all the possible enemies he had made throughout his career. There were too many hurt feelings to recall, as he attempted to sort through the endless number of arrests. There were hundreds that he'd sent to prison, and of course some had to be taken down hard. The perps were almost always able to walk into court to claim their innocence. And in his whole career there were only two lives that he took, and that was in self-defense, the two holdup men that killed Junior Taylor. That was eleven years ago. He'd now been retired for six of those years. But he recalled that day vividly. It was a nightmare that would surface in his conscience with only the slightest triggering.

Joe also recalled the days after. As was the tradition in the Police Department, when an officer was killed in the line of duty, he'd be posthumously promoted and buried with the higher rank. Lieutenant Alfred Taylor Jr. was laid to rest on March 20, 2008 at Forest Lawn Cemetery. His father, Lt. Alfred "Freddie" Taylor Sr., couldn't have been prouder, or sadder, or angrier.

Joe now knew that feeling. His days were filled with self-doubt and guilt, that he possibly could have been the cause of Sean's death. Nothing made sense. He could not fathom why someone would think that he'd intentionally make someone's family suffer. Whoever was trying to rattle his cage had succeeded. Joe could only rationalize that the note was a sick prank from a twisted mind. Perhaps someone just wanted Joe to second-guess himself and his whole career. But that all changed when Joe checked with Mike on the progress of the Hit-and-Run investigation.

Joe had made a habit of checking in with his son every night – partly to see what was happening with the family and partly to reassure Mike that the "old man was still kickin." If Joe didn't call by 9 p.m., then Mike would be calling him by 9:05.

"Hey, Son," was the familiar greeting. How's everything going?"

"Fine. And how are you doing, Dad?" would be Mike's usual response.

But for the past week there was nothing *usual* about their evening calls, except that Joe's first question would now be, "Anything new on the investigation?" And during this week the answer was routinely unsatisfying. But this night, Mike's voice crackled with some enthusiasm, "There are some new developments. The Sheriff's Department found the car out in the woods near the southern county line. It was reported as stolen the night before Sean's accident."

"Did they get any prints or anything from it?" Joe asked.

"No. It was torched. Totally destroyed. No evidence at all. You could barely recognize the make and model. It was a gray 2000 Ford sedan that they had to ID by VIN numbers on the engine block."

"And the owner? What does he have to say?" Joe asked.

"A couple Sheriff's Deputies questioned him, and they were satisfied that he had nothing to do with it. The owner's wife actually reported the car missing from the Uptown Super Market while she was shopping. Like I said, the car was taken more than 24 hours before the accident."

"The Sheriffs, huh? Did anyone from our Department talk with them? Joe persisted.

"Of course, Dad. And we checked the security video of the Uptown Super Market parking lot. You could see a figure trying the driver's side door, which apparently was unlocked, because it opened, he jumped in, and ten seconds later the car was speeding away. But the video had no detail from that distance. Couldn't tell if the person was black or white. Hell, we couldn't even tell if it was a male or female."

"Well how do you know that it was the same car that hit Sean?" Joe questioned.

"From all the video we reviewed, from the security cameras in a five-block area of the accident, there was only one car, similar to that one, that kept driving past your building."

Joe could tell by the hesitation in Mike's voice that there was something more that he wasn't saying. "Yeah? And what else, Mike? What else did you find?"

"There was one camera at the deli on your street, Parkside at the corner of Hertel."

"Yeah, I know the place. Ahmed Al-Afif owns it. A good guy!"

"Dad. That video showed the car heading up Parkside toward your place, and they were able to make out the plate. It parked about 100 feet before your building. The lights were turned off. But nobody got out of the car. Whoever it was just waited there until Sean parked and started to cross the street."

"So, you think it has to be someone who lives, or was visiting someone, right where I live?" Joe asked.

"That's what we thought initially. So, we had detectives and uniforms out canvassing the neighbors." Mike's voice dropped to a whisper. "About 9 o'clock, a lady was walking her dog on Parkside up to Washington Park. She recalled seeing a young guy sitting in the car with the engine running. She didn't think much of it until she was walking back to her house ten minutes later. He was still sitting in the car with the engine running. She thought it looked a bit suspicious, but couldn't get a good look at him without being obvious, so she just walked by."

"Well how did she know it was a young guy if she didn't get a look at him?" Joe asked sarcastically.

"She said that she could tell it was a young kid by the music. She said he was playing the radio too loud. Even with the windows closed it was obnoxious. She said it sounded like Rap music."

"So that's all we have? Some kid, sitting in a car drunk or stoned, listening to Rap music?"

"No, there were a couple other neighbors who heard the squeal of tires just seconds before the impact. That was, by all accounts, about 9:35 p.m. And that pretty much coincides with the time stamp on the video from the security camera at the deli on Parkside, 9:37. No. We don't think it was a neighbor."

Joe let a faint groan slip before he erupted. "Son-of-a-bitch. A DWI with a stolen car."

Mike countered, "No Dad. The woman who saw the car parked, idling, said the car was parked just one building south of yours. The Accident Investigation Unit found tire marks that went directly from the curb to the opposite side of the street where Sean was hit. Whoever it was… it was not accidental. He waited for your car to park and burned rubber to get up speed." Then Mike's voice cracked as he stated, "Sean didn't have a chance. It might be that someone was out to get you."

The salty retired Captain choked out, "Intentional? You mean Sean was murdered by someone thinking it was me?" Tears welled up in the old man's eyes as he pieced together the content of the note and paired it with the thought that Sean was killed because he let his grandson drive his car. Joe was unable to talk at that point and could only compose himself long enough to force out a low whisper, "Later, Mike. We'll talk later." And the phone went silent.

Joe was dismayed that the whole of local law enforcement couldn't make a quick arrest on this case. The rest of the evening was spent mulling over the known details, looking for options, comparing everything to the words in that damned note. It was another sleepless night.

CHAPTER 5

Old Hands Being Helping Hands

Joe Morgan found it difficult to not doze off during the afternoon, since he could not get a solid hour of sleep at night. It reminded him of those few cases through the years that held him captive until they were solved. Those were cases that sometimes required the combined effort of the Coterie, the group that he proudly belonged to from its inception. But it was also this group of friends that Joe allowed himself to drift away from since he retired.

Joe was totally frustrated with the lack of progress in the investigation. He knew that his son would keep him in the loop if there were any new developments. But as days passed with nothing to report, he began to think that the Department's investigation was going cold. Joe knew that his only recourse was to turn to the coterie of cops who used to deal with this type of dilemma.

It seemed like an exceptionally long number of rings before the phone was finally answered. "Hello?" came the familiar gravelly voice.

"Harry. This is Joe. Joe Morgan."

"Damn. This isn't an April Fool's call is it?" Harry joked. "I didn't think that you'd call, Joe. I take it that you're in need a cup of coffee and a friend to talk to." Harry Doyle was always direct.

"Yeah. I guess so, ol' buddy. Do you still see the rest of the guys?"

"Which other guys are you talking about? You mean…."

"Yeah. The Coterie."

"It's pretty much a breakfast club now. We get together a couple times a week. Usually Tuesdays and Fridays at the usual place."

"Still at 8 in the morning?"

"No Joe." Doyle laughed. "Most of us are retired, so there's no need to be there that early. We get there about 9:30, so we get there after the early breakfast crowd. You want to join us tomorrow? I won't say anything to the other guys. Boy will they be surprised!"

"Thanks, Harry. I really need to talk to you all, but especially you, Harry. How about you and I get there a bit early… say, at 9 o'clock?"

"Absolutely Joe. See you there." As Harry hung up, he was filled with mixed feelings. He was happy that Joe reached out to him but knew that Joe must be dealing with some turmoil, and suspected that it had to do with Sean.

IT was 8:50 a.m. when Joe strode into the Towne Restaurant and positioned himself at a back table where he had a commanding view of the entire restaurant.

The waitress, an older woman with grey hair, thin but spry, approached the table. "I haven't seen you in so long, I thought you'd probably died."

"I may as well have, Lavon. I retired. And can't say that I've missed you either." Joe shot back.

"So, if I recall correctly… coffee black and a double order of rye toast, crispy, lightly buttered," she rattled off.

"Heavy on the butter." Joe countered.

"How could I forget? Same table, same order every morning for a decade. Of course, I remember, Captain. You're meeting with the rest of the gang?"

"Yep. Why? Do you mind taking an additional order?"

And as the waitress began walking away, she hesitated a moment, as if she wanted to say something else, but then continued toward the kitchen.

Joe wondered if he was doing the right thing, meeting with the old coffee klatch. He reminisced of stopping at the Towne Restaurant at the beginning of his day shift and meeting with the guys who had just finished their night shift. Eight o'clock every morning, exchanging information and conducting "unofficial" business. He recalled how they selected their tables and stood guard over their meeting place, which they affectionately called the "Round Table" - although it was usually only three small square tables pushed together to accommodate whoever was able to show up. Before he could delve further into the wisdom of meeting with the group, he caught view of Harry Doyle as he ambled into the restaurant.

As soon as Harry's eyes locked onto Joe, a smile spread across his face and his pace picked up. He extended his arm to shake Joe's hand. "Thanks for reaching out, Joe. We are here for you."

Then Joe wrapped an arm around Harry's neck. "I know. I know." And the two men slid three tables together and sat at the backside of the tables with a full view of the entrance across the room.

Joe was a bit hesitant to open the conversation, so Harry took the lead. "So how are you dealing with Sean's passing, Joe?" Harry inquired.

That was just enough to allow Joe's honest reply. "I'm mad at the world, Harry. Now I know how Freddie felt. Not only were they in the wrong place at the wrong time, but I'm the one who should've been through that door first. And I'm the one who should've gone home to feed my damned dog. It should've been me."

"Joe, we've had this talk before. Like in Nam when our buddies didn't make it home and we did. It's survivor's guilt. We question why? Why them? Why not me? There are no answers. Junior is the one who wanted to stop at that store. And it's Sean that wanted to drive over to your apartment. You were not responsible for what happened to either of these people. We can only deal with what we have and promise ourselves to bring their killers to justice."

Joe listened and nodded affirmatively. "What you said is true. I know it, but it doesn't make me feel any better. What difference am I making?

I promised Freddie that as a friend, and the Chief of Homicide, I would get the last of the crew that killed his son. Now Big Will is the Chief of Homicide, and he is making the same promise to Mike and me. I doubt that Junior's killer will ever be caught, and I fear that Sean's murder will go unsolved."

Harry lowered the readers to the tip of his nose and looked over the frames at Joe. "You can take this to the bank. We will find the person behind Sean's death. I swear that to you, Joe."

It was quarter after nine when the rest of the group began arriving. The first was Vern Chosky. The eighty-year-old appeared more like a man in his mid-sixties. He always wore a Vietnam Veteran cap, as typically a proud Marine would. With a muscular build and square jaw, Vern presented a formidable presence on his five-foot-seven frame. He nearly stopped in his tracks when he spotted Joe and Harry at the Round Table. He quickly joined the pair.

A few minutes later, Chaz Bohen arrived. Oblivious to the persons seated at the Round Table, Chaz headed directly for the men's room with short quick steps, which was his routine.

Before Chaz could return to the dining area, the main entrance was filled with a massive figure. Captain Willie Williams was usually the last to arrive, as he had to report for the day shift. And if there were no fresh bodies waiting for him in the morning, he'd manage to slip away from Headquarters for an hour or so on Tuesdays and Fridays. That was one of the main benefits of being the Commander of the Homicide Bureau. As he approached the Round Table his grin dominated the dark complexion of his face. Joe was quick to notice, by the bulges in his oversized corduroy sport coat, that the Captain was still carrying two .45s in a cross-draw shoulder holster.

"Big Will, it's good to see that you haven't changed a bit. You still taking care of my Bureau?" Joe asked while the two shook hands.

"Doin' the best I can, Joe. But things ain't the same as when you were there. There's a lot more phone and computer work and less face-to-face." Big Will knew that face-to-face was Joe's forte. "Look man, I'm so sorry 'bout your grandson, Sean. I can hardly talk to Mike when I see him in HQ. I mean, what can I say?"

"I know," Joe responded. "It's an awkward conversation from both ends." Then Joe noticed that Chaz was walking across the dining room.

"Hey guys" greeted Chaz' smiling face. Each rank came with a nod. "Captain, Captain, Lieutenant, and Sarge. Looks like roll call is done," Chaz announced as if Captain Joe had never missed a breakfast at the Round Table.

Although most of the group were retired, had been close friends for decades, and were otherwise on a first name or nickname basis, Chaz always followed department protocol and addressed his friends by greeting them with their rank.

As he managed to take a seat at the end of the table he declared, "The doctor has me on water pills. They keep me pissing every twenty to thirty minutes. So.... "

"Of course, Chaz," Harry interrupted. "That's why we saved the aisle seat for you."

"As usual," Vern added, followed immediately by a round of laughter.

"So, anybody seen Lieutenant Freddie yet?" Chaz asked, referring to the Narcotics Squad night shift Commander, Lieutenant Alfred Taylor, Sr.

Big Will answered, "Freddie is where Freddie always is, fishing in Florida." He may as well retire like the rest of you pension pirates. With forty years on the books, he is losing money every day he comes to work."

"Yeah, but he's got so much vacation and comp time that he never works." Harry said. "He's been in Florida for the past month."

"That's the only reason he didn't show up at the funeral, Joe," Chaz offered. "You know he would've been there if he was in town."

The conversation then became more somber as the elephant in the room was addressed. Harry broke the awkward silence, "Again, on behalf of the entire Coterie, we are so sorry for your loss, Joe."

Then Chaz asked, "Is there any new development in the case?"

Joe looked toward Big Will. "Anything?" he asked.

Will Williams looked around the table. "I wish there was something to report fellas, but we came to a standstill after the burned-out car was found."

"No witnesses? Nothing?" Vern asked. "Back in the day we'd have the perp in cuffs and begging to make a deal by now. Your dicks should have…"

"Hold it right there," Big Will scowled. "We turned over every rock we could find, Vern. Don't you go spouting off about what my detectives should have done. Don't you think we were goin' the extra mile for one of our own? I really don't know what else we could've done. I think that it's just gonna come down to a point where someone in the future gets busted and will give up information for a deal."

"Maybe," Joe said. "But I, for one, am not satisfied with waiting for a snitch. There has to be something I can do. Maybe something WE can do!"

The individuals looked around the table to find agreement, and each of the assembled nodded their head.

"What the hell else do we have to do? Sit in a rocker, drool on our chest, and watch *The View*? God forgive us," Harry asserted. "We're in," he declared.

Then Chaz added, "We just have to figure out WHAT we're in for."

CHAPTER 6

REACTIVATE THE OL' COTERIE

The typical Wednesday morning would start at 7:45 a.m. with Captain Williams settling in at his desk to sort through a mound of paperwork from the previous night shift. It was a process that would require 45 minutes, a cup of black coffee, and a jelly filled donut to determine which reports needed a careful review and which just needed a signature. As the day shift began arriving at 8:30, he would meet with the shift supervisors, who in turn would brief the day detectives. But this was not a routine Wednesday.

As Big Will stepped from the elevator, he found Joe Morgan propped against the door to the Homicide Bureau. "How'd you get up to this floor?" Will asked.

"I hitched a ride from the janitor."

"So much for security."

"If it's any consolation, it wasn't any better when I ran the show." Joe declared. "I even had a detective kidnapped from this office."

Big Will started to laugh, "Yeah, I remember that one. The ex-wife, right?"

"Uh-huh. She marched him right out of here with his own gun stuck in his back. That's when we put in the buzzers and prohibited personal visits."

"So, is this business or a personal visit?" Big Will queried as he slid his card through the magnetic reader.

"Both, Will. I was hoping that you would let me peruse the case file."

With a slight hesitation he answered, "Of course. So, you want to double-check to make sure we're doing our job?"

"It's not that, Will. You know I have the highest confidence in you or I wouldn't have pushed to have you take over the Bureau," Joe explained. "I just have to do something myself. I just can't sit home and wait to hear..."

"I got it, Joe. Look, here's the complete file. Photos and all. They're pretty nasty." Will lifted the stack of several manila folders from the corner of his desk. "Here. Take this into Interview 1. Take as much time as you need. I'll be in my office if you need anything."

"Thanks," Joe replied appreciatively. He then sequestered himself in the interrogation room that had not changed a bit through the years, partly because it did make people feel uncomfortable.

It was near noon when Big Will stuck his head into the room. "How you doin'? Any questions?"

Joe motioned for Big Will to have a seat across the table. Then he spread out an array of photos and directed Will to a couple in particular. "Here you have tire tracks at the murder scene. And these pictures from the scene of the abandoned burned-out car. I see how you ID'd the stolen vehicle as the H&R car. The tires on the car are burned away but it is clearly a 2000 Ford Taurus. The tire marks you ID'd at Sean's murder scene are Goodyear P215/60R16s. That's a standard factory tire for Taurus. And they match the tread with the tire tracks leading up to the burn-out. But what are these other tire tracks. Dual truck tires. Were you able to ID that vehicle?" Joe pointed to a photo showing tire tracks on the shoulder of the road where the Taurus had been driven off the country road.

"No. It looks like someone came by and picked up the driver after he torched the vehicle. Unless a good Samaritan picked up the driver near the burning vehicle, there had to be an accomplice."

"Which means, this was a hit job. An organized hit." Joe concluded.

"Looks that way, Joe." We've already begun to go through the arrest blotter covering the last couple years before your retirement, to see if there was anyone who might have it in for you. When did you retire? Six years ago?" Big Will asked for verification.

"Yeah. It was two years before Amy passed. And in all those years since, I've never once heard from anyone that I busted. I can't think of a single reason why anyone would…"

Big Will interceded, "And there's nobody else you pissed off for any other reason? Joe, you know the drill. I have to ask. We're looking for a motive."

Joe's eyes locked onto Big Will's. "We've got to do better. We need to do some brainstorming."

The Homicide Commander sat back in his chair and his eyes rolled as if he were searching for an answer. "Are you insinuating that we…"

"Exactly." Joe exclaimed. "I'm asking that we pull all the stops and do whatever we must to get this investigation moving."

Reluctantly, Big Will agreed and acknowledged, "Well, we could use the extra manpower. My detectives have been swamped lately with new cases. Just last week we got some old homeless guy who OD'd, and we got a gang-banger who caught a lethal dose of lead poisoning… if you get my drift. It ain't that we're not working Sean's case. It's just that it ain't the only case we got."

A half hour after Morgan left Police Headquarters, Captain Williams began putting the suggestion into action. His first call was to Boca Raton, Florida.

"Another day in paradise," the cheerful voice answered the phone.

"Hey Freddie. It's Will Williams."

"I figured that when I saw the caller ID. What's up, BW? The only time you call me down here is when there is a problem or bad news. Which is it?"

"We need you back up here. It looks like we have to reactivate the Coterie."

"I thought that was a dead issue", Freddie announced. "We promised that we weren't going to do things like that anymore. Hell, I'm too close to retirement."

"Yeah, but this is an extreme situation. Remember a couple weeks ago when I called to let you know about Mike's son being killed?"

"Of course. And I'm sorry that I couldn't make the funeral."

"Joe and Mike understood. But we've come to a standstill with the investigation. We thought we'd get the Coterie up and running again, solely for brainstorming. Nothing physical!" Big Will explained. "So, what do you think?"

"Count me in." Freddie agreed. "Although I have some appointments down here over the next few days that I can't miss, there's a six o'clock flight from here on Saturday. It's the best I can do. Is that okay with you?"

"Oh yeah. Sure." Will was happy with Freddie's response. "That would be great Freddie."

Before hanging up, the Narcotics Lieutenant asked, "BW, could you have one of my night platoon detectives pick me up at the airport, say about 9:30 Saturday night?"

"Better yet," Will countered, "I'll pick you up myself."

CHAPTER 7

Business is Business, So Cut the Shit!

Bax Brown was an east side entrepreneur, or as he liked to refer to himself, an "undocumented pharmacist." A very successful drug dealer. He had an established supply chain and a loyal workforce of several dozen junkies. He kept them dependent with their daily personal needs and provided them with sufficient pocket money to maintain a degree of flash and respect on the street. When business got to the point where violence was required, he had no qualms with dispatching such force. But his most valuable asset was inside information, for that he paid dearly.

Bax ran his operation from the Evelyn Tower of the inner city's Freedom Housing Projects. Appropriately, he thought, he named his organization The Freedom Boyz, which he commanded from a third-floor apartment. After the Freedom Boyz infiltrated the high-rise, he persuaded some of the tenants to abandon their apartments on the third floor. The building's tenants who remained did so with the understanding that it was not their building…it belonged to The Freedom Boyz. Once he had secured his base, Bax had secret passages constructed between apartments throughout the third floor and even a private staircase up to the fourth floor, where another part of his operation was situated. Bax had lookouts positioned on the second and fifth floors, which provided expansive views of the perimeter and parking lots. Nobody came or left without his knowledge. The Municipal Housing Authority had no knowledge of the structural alterations that were made, and likely they did not want to know.

"Yo. Ya got the man!" Bax declared after he picked up the phone.

Roz, his main girl was reclining on the sofa in front of the 80-inch TV that took up a large portion of the wall. Dutifully she turned down the volume as he spoke.

"Yeah, I got you covered. No sweat, man," he continued. "Ok, ok. I'll meet you at the spot. You got what we talked about?" he asked, followed by an animated punch into the air. "Of course. I got your cash ready. Seventy-five large. Fifty for the delivery and twenty-five for your other services. Right? Have I ever let you down?" Bax boasted. While he spoke, he strode around the apartment, with gold chains draped around his neck - each worn as a General would wear medals on his chest. "We take care of business tonight at 8 and then, as I always do… I'll drop you off wherever you want. Cool."

As soon as the call ended Bax hurriedly began dialing. "Yo. It's me. Get the crew up on the fourth floor tonight. We got business to take care of. Yeah Bro. It's payday. When I get back here you better be ready to cut."

It was exactly 9:30 p.m. when Big Will drove up to the Arrival lane of the terminal. Freddie was already standing at the curb with two suitcases and a duffle bag. He leaned into the open passenger window. "We must have caught quite a tailwind, because we landed twenty minutes ago."

"Welcome home, Freddie," Will greeted as he opened the trunk for the bags.

As the two settled into the front seat of the Captain's SUV, the police radio crackled, "12-North. Shots fired. Genesee and Moselle. Units covering?" Several patrol units quickly responded, and Will asked, "Did you miss any of this?"

"Not a bit. As a matter of fact, it was so good to be away from anything blue, or crime related." Then Freddie asked, "So what's going on BW?

What's happening with Joe and Mike?"

"Well, what we know for sure is that Mike's boy was intentionally run down and killed. There's a possibility that the suspect was a young black male, but that's just a hunch. The vehicle that was used was a stolen 2000 Ford sedan. It was found burned-out twenty-two miles south of the city. And unfortunately, that's all we've got," Big Will bluntly conceded.

"So, if the driver was from the city…" Freddie supposed, "how did he get back to the city?"

"There were truck tire tracks, dual wheel tracks, found near where we recovered the stolen car," Will explained. "Tread design is too popular to narrow it down much. If we find a suspect's truck with those dual wheels though, the tire tracks are good enough to make a positive ID."

"Not much to go on," Freddie agreed, staring thoughtfully out the windshield. After a moment he pressed on, "And what about the Coterie?"

"All the guys are willing to help with whatever we can do. Granted, we're not the same group that we were a couple decades ago. I mean, not physically. But there is a wealth of experience and knowledge we can offer to solve this for Mike. Or at least we can help to get it moving forward."

"Alright, BW. Let's see what the old timers can do. When are we meeting?" Freddie asked.

"Tomorrow morning at the Towne," Will said. "10 a.m. Sunday brunch."

"Okay BW. I'll be there. Now can you get me home without chasing any calls?"

Two SUVs and a pickup pulled around to the front of the Evelyn Tower, totally closing off the entrance. Two heavily armed men positioned themselves inside the lobby and summoned the elevators. Several others hauled a number of heavily loaded backpacks from the open hatch of a white Escalade to the elevators. Bax's soldiers piled through the first open door carrying their cargo, while Bax remained in the Cadillac observing the operation. Suddenly a hand banged on the driver's window, startling Bax.

"We're all clear," announced Tyrell, one of his most trusted workers.

"Okay, my man. Good job. Get the wheels out of here and meet me upstairs," Bax calmly directed. "Nobody comes near the building tonight. Got it?"

"Yessir!" answered his Number Two.

Moments later Bax stepped from the elevator to the fourth floor where a guard was posted. He took measure of the guard, standing alert with an AK-47 held at the ready. Bax gave him a nonchalant nod of approval then looked toward the sentinel positioned at the end of the corridor. "Tyrell in there?" Bax asked his sentry.

"Uh, he just checked in on the radio. He's on his way up." Almost as soon as he finished his report, the bell of the elevator rang and the doors opened. Instantly, all weapons were raised in the direction of the opening doors.

"Whoa," Tyrell shouted. "It's me. Chill."

"You don't tell them to chill, Tyrell." Bax's voice was calm but filled with icy menace. As he spoke, his 9mm stayed aimed at Tyrell's chest. "I want them to be ready for anything. And not just when I'm here. All night they gotta be on point, because if anyone steps on this floor that ain't supposed to be here. They dead. All of 'em. Is that clear?"

"Bax, Bax…" Tyrell scrambled to explain. "I called and told them I was comin' up. And I wasn't tellin' you to chill."

"All of you sons-a-bitches can be replaced." Bax announced, waving his arm to cover everyone in his view. "So, don't think because we're tight that you gonna get over on me." Bax emphasized with the muzzle of his pistol jabbing into Tyrell's chest. An instant later his voice changed completely as he slid his weapon into the waistband of his pants. "Now my man, let's take care of 'The' business," he said, accentuating "The" with a broad smile.

Halfway down the hallway Bax stopped and looked to his guards in both directions. After each nodded to him, he knocked on the door with a specific series of taps. A voice from inside asked more of a pass phrase than an actual question. "Who's knocking on my door?"

"It's me. The big bad wolf," Bax responded. With the sound of several locks being undone, the door swung open to reveal a maze of plastic sheets hanging from ceiling to floor. The sound of thick plastic sheeting crunched beneath their feet as Bax and Tyrell moved toward the adjoining rooms. The space was filled with groups of people covered with hospital gowns, masks, and caps. Each group was consumed with performing their specific tasks. As they moved about, the open back gowns exposed the fact that nobody was wearing undergarments.

Even as the first few backpacks were being emptied and separated into stacks, the kilo packages of heroin, fentanyl, cocaine, and marijuana were carried to their proper stations. Each of the adjoining apartments had a workstation for specific tasks. Sections of the rooms were partitioned with the plastic sheeting to prevent drafts or breezes. Bax walked through the first station, where a group of people was cutting the heroin with fentanyl, which they referred to as "Dog Food." They finished the product by further cutting it with a triple portion of baby laxative. The final mix was then divided into proportions for distribution to subordinate dealers who would inevitably step on the "Food" a few more times for their own profit. A sizeable portion of the product would be cut by an 8 to 1 ratio, and packaged in small glassine bags. Thousands of them. These would be supplied directly to the dozen or so street dealers working under the direction of Bax Brown.

Continuing through to the next apartment Bax looked over the shoulders of his people as they divided the cocaine into two prep stations. One would cut the cocaine to make what they called a "Soft" product. This was the powder for people of moderate financial means to sniff. The other product line was the cocaine they called "Hard," the crack cocaine, which required more work and cooking in the microwave, but was much more profitable when marketed to people of lesser means, to smoke in their pipes.

Bax walked through the rooms, inspecting the operations, his eyes missing nothing. He stopped at one of the armed guards and quickly sized up the man and his weapons. "You got this?"

"100 percent!" snapped the man.

Bax reminded the guard, "Nobody comes or goes until we're done. No phone calls. Nobody leaves the room for any reason." Then as he headed toward the door, he snapped his fingers and pointed to Tyrell. "You make it happen. You got this job."

CHAPTER 8

Sunday, March 31, 2019

Special Meeting

The small banquet room at the Towne Restaurant was usually reserved for gatherings such as birthdays, baby showers, and other family events. There was an association of retired cops that held their annual reunion there, usually in July when the days were longer, the weather warmer, and the snowbirds came home to roost. But this was a special Sunday meeting of the Coterie.

Joe Morgan was the first to arrive, knowing that he was central to the abrupt calling of the meeting. For a moment he was able to lay aside the day's agenda to reflect on when it all started…thirty-some years earlier at Bloody Eight. The Eighth Precinct was an old brownstone station house that was built on the doorstep of the twentieth century. The interior was as dark and foreboding as the stark exterior. Through the years there were renovations that tried to brighten the mood of the building to make it more welcoming to the community, but the reputation of its inhabitants remained. Each community had its own force of protectors and they varied with the needs of that community. The old Polish neighborhoods of the city's east side called for a police presence that would walk the beat and visit with the shopkeepers, chat with families as they sat on their stoops, assist in the search of a lost pet, and instill fear in the hearts of those who would prey upon those good folks. It was an expectation that carried well into the 1980s when young Officer Joseph Morgan was assigned to Bloody Eight.

It was a time when families were fleeing the city for the relative safety of the suburbs. Landlords looking to make a buck picked up cheap properties and filled them with low income renters, who also contributed to the deterioration of the precinct's neighborhoods. The only things going up in these areas were the crime rate and the number of victims. The longtime residents that couldn't afford to move out learned to protect themselves.

On his first midnight shift, Morgan was assigned to work with Officer Vern Chosky, a second-generation Police Officer of Russian-Polish ancestry. The cruiser was only called out of service to back up other units and to answer several minor disturbance calls. It was a relatively quiet night with a list of 20 calls on the run sheet. The last turned out to be the best.

The dispatcher assigned the call to Chosky and the rookie, Morgan. "Eight-West. Prowler reported at rear of 277 Paderewski Street."

Chosky accelerated as he jerked the steering wheel hard to the left. "Answer the dispatcher, damnit!"

"Eight-West. Responding." Morgan announced excitedly. He then heard Eight-South and Eight-Lincoln chime in as backing up Eight-West.

The 8-L call sign was the Lieutenant's car. The senior officer knew what to expect. "The Loot will show up, so you'd better put your hat on. He's a stickler for hats."

Familiar with the streets and the hoodlums, Chosky turned the headlights off and cruised up to an alley at the end of the block, which separated the rear fences of houses on Paderewski and the ones on Peck. "The other cars will go to the exact address. We're going to wait right here. If there is anyone doing anything, the other car crews will flush them out."

"Why not go halfway up the alley and wait?" Morgan asked. "Wouldn't we be closer?"

"Several of the yards have dogs. We don't want to rile them up. It will give away our position," Chosky explained with a whispered voice. So, each officer stood in the shadows on either side of the alley and waited.

Sure enough, Chosky had been right. Morgan saw a flicker of flashlights coming from between houses halfway up the alley. Then he heard voices yelling, "Stop or I'll shoot." Amid the clanking of metal garbage cans, the rattle of chain-link fences, and several dogs barking, two silhouettes popped out from the yards, into the alley, and started running straight toward the end of the block. The first of the two bodies approaching the opening to Smith Street never even saw Chosky as he jumped out from the shadows, not to mention Chosky's nightstick before it caught the running man under his chin. The perp's feet kept a forward motion while his head and shoulders momentarily remained stationary. As soon as he dropped to the ground, the second culprit stopped cold in his tracks. He looked ahead at Chosky, then back toward the flashlights that were drawing closer. Officer Chosky shouted, "Don't jump over that fence. I'm not chasing you over that fence!" It almost sounded like a dare.

As anticipated, the suspect hurled himself over the chain-link fence. A moment later there was a violent cacophony of cries for help amid the vicious wrenching growls of a watch dog feasting on fresh burglar. "Help me! Help me!" pleaded the man.

"Okay, sir," Chosky yelled back over the fence. "I'll go around to the house on Paderewski and have the owner call his dog in. Okay? Now you just hang in there." Of course, he had his younger partner walk around the block to notify the owner.

The remainder of the shift was spent standing guard for three hours while the prisoners were treated at the County Medical Center, followed by another hour and a half of paperwork at the station house.

The midnight to eight shift was followed by what is called a "double back" for the four to midnight shift. Granted, there was a shortage of sleep in between shifts, especially if an officer was scheduled for 9 a.m. court, but the days between the double backs were a full 24 hours off duty. However, many officers worked a second part-time job. Considering that there were also more than a few hours consumed by officers unwinding at the copper's watering hole just a half block from the station, police life was nearly all day, every day. Many of the cops, coming off the four to twelve, made a stop for "just one beer" on the way home. Of course, this "one beer" sometimes lasted well into the morning hours. Each precinct had its own cop bar and Bloody Eight had Porky's Pink Flamingo.

It was there that Joe Morgan began socializing regularly after his afternoon shifts. He became part of the regular group that consisted of Vern Chosky, Harry Doyle, Howie Smyth, and Freddie Taylor. The guys would recount stories and laugh at each other's misgivings. It was purely an unwinding social thing. But as time went on, and the complaints with the system became more frequent, the group agreed that they had to take a slightly more proactive stance to protect the people of their precinct. Somewhere through the following months and years, the collection of cops on a mission began referring to themselves as the "Coterie." Actually, it was Howie that proposed the name to describe what they were all about. He was the only one with a master's degree and an extensive vocabulary. Nobody had even heard the word before. They thought it was a cool word that nobody else would understand. Like a code word. And its definition fit perfectly: a small group of people with shared interests or tastes, especially one that is exclusive of other people.

Through the years, the officers supported each other as members moved up through the ranks and attained choice positions and assignments. It was an evolution of the Coterie that grew from a handful of precinct cops dealing out street justice, to an organization that could shape and influence the criminal justice system ever so slightly to ensure some degree of societal recompense. Simply put, the group found ways to prevent the rule of law from favoring the criminals.

Joe was startled back into the moment by Vern Chosky entering the room. "Oh, Vern. I was just thinking of you."

"Hey, Joe. How are you doing, my friend?"

"I'm alright. Well, as well as anyone could be under these circumstances," Joe uttered. "Lord knows, I've had better days."

Big Will, carrying a banker's box, entered next and greeted Joe. "And I thought that I was goin' to be the last one in. How you doin' Joe?"

Before Morgan could respond, two more familiar faces appeared. "Harry Doyle and Chaz Bohen," Joe announced. "I love you guys. All of you."

A voice raised up from behind the clustered group, "And what about me? No love for me after I came all this way?"

"Sorry, Freddie," Joe offered, trying to keep a straight face. "I didn't see you there in the back of the crowd. Besides, no one likes you anyway." Everyone chuckled a little at that, but seriousness crept back onto all of their faces. Joe then addressed the gathering in its entirety. "Thank you all so much for being here. Please take a seat. And I see that the only one absent is the Chief of Ds, Howie Smyth."

Although Captain Smyth was quite beholden to the group for their support in his appointment to Chief of Detectives, over the years he became a strict proponent of departmental policy and rules. He sometimes attended the social get-togethers of the Coterie, but in no way would he sanction this meeting. They all still considered him a friend, but Howie had long since been dropped from their agenda.

Joe looked to Big Will. "Do you want to get this thing started or shall I?"

While the attendants claimed seats at various tables, Big Will suggested, "Go ahead, Joe. You got this. I think you know better than anyone else why we're all here."

Suddenly Chaz Bohen jumped to his feet and started to head toward the door, "Excuse me, Captain Will." Chaz hesitated a moment, but with an apologetic look stated, "I didn't mean to interrupt you, but these damned water pills." Chaz stepped quickly out of the room.

Joe smiled briefly but then acknowledged that he would proceed with a nod and a clearing of his throat. "Oh-kay... First, let me say that I am so proud to have worked with such a great bunch of cops for as many years as we have. When the chips are down, there is nobody I'd rather have in my corner than you guys. So here is where I need your help. Big Will and his Bureau, though not for a lack of effort, and the whole damned Department have hit a brick wall with the investigation of Sean's murder. If any of you are not already aware…we now know without a doubt that this 'accident' was intentional. I'm hoping that we can put our heads together and find something that they may have missed, hopefully the straw that will break this camel's back."

Voices from the group affirmed their support. "Where do we start?" rasped the gritty voice of Harry Doyle.

"You're a P.I. With your history as one of the most experienced homicide investigators that I've ever known, I figured that you might think of something outside the box. Like the Randolf case. Remember that one, Harry? You broke that one open all by yourself."

"But Joe, that was a long time ago." Harry answered.

"Don't sell yourself short, Harry," Joe rebutted. "I've heard how you do these insurance investigations. You do a great job and you get results." Perusing the room, Joe's eyes settled on Freddie Taylor. "Aside from the Chief of Ds, you and Big Will are the only two that are still on the job. We need you to be our official liaison with the department and sources for computer files."

Freddie winced as he questioned, "Joe, you do know what you're asking of us? We'd be putting our jobs and pensions on the line. I have over 38 years invested here!"

"Freddie, I'm not asking you, or anyone, to do anything you are not comfortable with. If you want to step away, I will completely understand. All I can say is that I would lay it all on the line for any one of you guys. And a couple of you know personally, that I have."

Freddie grumbled something and then spoke louder, "I told BW that I was on board. And I am. We always have each other's back. But I just wanted to make sure that everyone is aware of how much you are asking of BW and me."

"Point taken, Freddie." Joe acknowledged. "And I thank you for having my back." Then to fortify their support, Joe passed out photocopies of the note he received at the cemetery. "Here is the main reason that I need your help. It appears that someone was out to get me. Or it could be that after Sean's death they sent a note just to torment me. Or to make me and Mike wonder if this was something either of us did wrong." Then Joe's voice sunk to a solemn tone. "I have to say that the probability that I was the jackpot, that my grandson paid for with his life, sickens me."

Silence smothered the gathering as they read the incredible threat.

Chaz returned to the room as distracted as ever. "Did I miss anything?"

The attention of the group shifted to Big Will as he opened the banker's box on the table in front of him. "No, Chaz. Your timing is perfect," Will said as he handed Chaz a copy of Joe's threatening note. When the snickering settled, Big Will continued, "These files contain everything from field interviews to photos. You can examine whatever you want. But nothing, and I mean nothing, can leave this room. I want to get some of your ideas on how to proceed. Just maybe, there's something the Department may have overlooked. Make notes. Don't hesitate to list anything you think might possibly help to solve this murder."

After the coffee, tea, and pastries were delivered the group began picking through the reports and documents that filled the stack of manila folders. As the review process appeared to slow down and guys had paired off to compare thoughts, Joe clinked his spoon against the side of his coffee cup. "It's about noon, gentlemen. We're going to order lunch. Help yourself to whatever's on the menu. It's my way of saying thank you to everyone. As we wait for the food, why not jot down any ideas or suggestions you may have so that we can all have a discussion after lunch?"

By 1:30 the tables were cleared of all signs of lunch and the gentlemen were ready to begin the debate. Joe had already made the rounds of the tables and collected scribbled notes. Joe returned to the front table with Big Will, while the others claimed tables of their own where they could spread out copies of news articles, records, standard department reports, bulletins, computer printouts, investigative memoranda, and other documents. As he started to read the notes, the men interjected their individual thoughts causing more questions to be raised.

"So, there is no physical evidence except for tire tracks?" asked Chaz.

"That's right," Big Will confirmed. "We have no witnesses except for a woman who didn't get a good look at the driver and can't even describe the vehicle. Although we determined from security videos in the area that it was a silver or light colored four-door Ford Taurus, the cameras couldn't provide any images of the driver. However, the Sheriff's Department found a car matching the BOLO we put out. Although it was totally destroyed, the tire prints found at the Hit-and-Run scene matched perfectly to the tracks of the Taurus where it was driven off the road. When the Deputies examined the spot where the car left the road, they found tire tracks of the Taurus and of a truck with dual wheels. Both were freshly imbedded in the shoulder of the road and we took casts. The dual tire tracks crossed over those of the car, so it had to arrive on scene after the Taurus left the road. There is nothing else in the area or any good reason why that truck might stop there. It had to be an accomplice. That covers the physical evidence."

Freddie followed up with a related question, "So BW, you think that if we can find the truck with those specific dual tires, we can make a positive ID of a suspect?"

"Those tracks can place the truck there. Positively! But it would be up to us to interview the owner to find out who was driving it. But it's our best lead up to this point," Big Will answered.

"What about M.O.?" Vern asked. "Any other hit-and-runs with burned-out cars? Or any other murders where a stolen car was used as the weapon?"

"Nothing even close," Big Will replied, shaking his head. "We've checked the Local, State, and Federal databases and found nothing."

In frustration Harry added, "Of the basic elements we can only prove intent and method of the crime. We've got nothing for a motive… except that this was a possible hit meant for Joe."

"Who said it was a hit on him?" Chosky challenged pointing at Joe. "Maybe someone was out to get the kid?" Vern turned to Joe, "Sorry. I didn't mean to imply…"

"No." Joe concurred. "It could have been me, or Mike, or Sean who was the target, or even someone we don't even know. We do know that it happened after Sean parked MY car in front of MY building, but it just wasn't me driving. My car had just left Mike's house six minutes earlier. Until we can figure out definitively who the target was, we won't know what the motive is, which would lead us to one or more suspects."

Everyone nodded and agreed. Joe turned to the Captain, "So, Big Will, what do you suggest?"

"If we're going to proceed in search of a motive, then we'll have to do some profiling of the possible targets." Big Will stared directly toward Joe. "What do you think?"

"If the victim was anyone else, I would have suggested that as a starting point. I've got nothing to hide, and maybe someone else here could see things more clearly than I. Maybe I'm just too close to the crime to see things objectively."

Big Will charged the men with a timeline for preliminary information. "Today is Sunday. Do you think we can scratch the surface by Friday?"

Multiple brief discussions settled with agreement. "Good," Big Will stated purposefully, "then at least we know how to start. I suggest that we pair up to profile one possible target each. "Harry and Vern," Big Will suggested, "you got Mike."

"Sure, Big Will", Vern answered.

"I'm good with that," Harry agreed.

"Then we have Freddie and Chaz. You two want to look into Joe's last few years on the job and the time he's been retired? Freddie, you'll be able to access the court records. Chaz, you know most of the guys that Joe has worked with."

The two nodded and answered almost simultaneously. "Absolutely."

Then Freddie added, "As long as those damned water pills don't slow us down!"

Big Will rested his huge hand on Joe's shoulder. "I'll handle Sean's background myself. I've already started it. You know the drill, Joe. It's part of doing the investigation." In a more serious tone he directed, "What I need you to do is spend some time with Mike and Chrissy. Make sure they're okay. You don't want to intrude too much, but see what you can find out about a couple kids named Robert Ralston, Greg Brooks, and Raynero Vazquez. I had Sean's cellphone dumped and he was on the phone with them quite a bit every day. I'd like to know who they are before I go to interview them."

"I've never heard Sean talk about them," Joe said. "But I'll have a talk with Mike and Chrissy to find out if they know these kids."

CHAPTER 9

BACK TO SHOE LEATHER

Joe called his son on Monday night to check in and see how he was doing. "Hey Mike. How would you and Chrissy like to go out for Chinese tomorrow?"

"Sounds good to me," Mike answered. "But let me check with her. Hold on." Before returning to the phone Mike wondered why his father would suggest Chinese when he knew that he was not particularly partial to that cuisine. He picked up the phone and reported, "She'll be glad to get out of the house. Besides, Chinese is her favorite food. So, when and where?"

"The Shining Star Buffet on Broadway," Joe suggested. "6:30 okay with you?"

"Sure, Dad," Mike said. "That will give me plenty of time to get home, shed the uniform, shower, and dress for dinner."

Tuesday morning had Vern Chosky and Harry Doyle meeting at the Krispy Kreme bright and early.

"Just like old times, huh Vern?"

"I'm just here for a cup of green tea," Vern answered. "I never could understand why you guys would stuff that crap down your throats and gulp down cup after cup of all that caffeine. Didn't you realize what that stuff was doing to your bodies? I'm surprised that any of you survived the donut shops."

"Well excuse me, Mr. Atlas. We all couldn't be holed up in the gym during our lunch hour. But we were glad that you did," Harry chuckled. "We needed a door-kicker."

"So, how do you want to go about this?" Vern asked as the two men picked up their order of green tea, a double-double coffee, and two dozen donuts. "You want to hit Three or Fifteen first?"

By 8:30 the day platoon had already had orders read, and received their assignments. Harry and Vern arrived at Precinct Fifteen shortly thereafter. Harry dropped a box of donuts on the front desk as he addressed the Desk Sergeant. "You're still working, Mullins? I thought that you'd be gone with the rest of us dinosaurs."

"No way, Harry. You know that when you retire the odds are that you'll die within five years," Billy Mullins declared as he ambled up to the long counter. "Now, that's a fact."

"That's bullshit," Harry grumbled. "Hell, I've been out for six years and Vern has been gone for over a decade. We're still here."

"You two are a couple of the lucky ones. And what brings you here to-day? Don't tell me you guys deliver donuts for Krispy Kreme?"

"Not exactly," Vern answered. "We stopped in to see you, Billy."

The Desk Sergeant directed one of the uniformed officers, "Keep an eye on the desk while I take care of business with these gentlemen." Mullins scooped up the box of donuts and led them to the break room.

"How long you been here at the Fifteenth?" Harry asked.

"I was transferred here in 2008," Mullins replied.

"Wasn't that when you were injured on duty?" Harry queried. "As I re-call, that was the shootout at that little deli in Riverside, Precinct Thirteen. Was that the one where a couple coppers were shot, and one died?"

"Joe Morgan and I were the lucky ones," the Desk Sergeant exclaimed. "I was IOD for the better part of a year. When I returned to work, I made Ser-geant and landed up here…on the desk. I think that's about the same time when Morgan was promoted to Captain. Junior Taylor wasn't so lucky,"

Mullins recalled. "So, it's been eleven years that I've been riding this desk. But I'm not ready to give it up yet."

"You've been here longer than most of the coppers assigned here. Do you remember when Mike Morgan was here? I think Mike might have been a Sergeant back then," Vern clarified.

"Of course. Sgt. Mike Morgan, he was a good boss. A bit easy on the men, but the job got done, you know. We all took good care of each other," Billy stated.

"What do you mean? You all had each other's back? That should go without saying," Harry concluded.

"Yeah. That and more." Added Billy.

"More what?" Harry persisted.

"You know…he'd cut the guys some slack with early quits. Sometimes he would even cover them for a whole shift. You know…."

"And what did the guys do for him?" Vern asked.

"Once in a while on the midnight shift, Sergeant Morgan would post the men and then he would disappear until the end of the shift. You know…" Billy repeated.

"So, what? He had a dolly on the side?" Harry asked.

"That's what the rumor was. But what the heck," Billy declared, spreading his hands to show it was none of his business. "That was his own personal life. It didn't affect anyone on the job. A lot of guys have some side action. The main thing is that everyone looked out for each other."

"And that's all? Was Mike a drinker or doing anything else that you were aware of, Billy?"

"No. He was as straight as they come. Why? What's with all the questions about Mike?" Mullins asked suspiciously.

"You heard that a few weeks back, Mike's boy died in a car accident?" Vern started to explain.

Mullins nodded. "Yeah. And I also heard that it probably wasn't an accident."

Vern continued in a confidential tone, "Harry and I are pitching in to do some of the leg work, trying to find out if maybe someone had some problem with Mike. And maybe…"

"There is nobody here that would do anything to hurt Mike or his family. Especially family. You NEVER mess with another copper's family!" Mullins' gaze hardened as he continued, "If that's what you guys are looking for, you can stop right now. Because there is nobody here who had any bad feelings toward Mike. Not another copper. Not even anyone he locked up, as far as I can remember. And I booked them all at this desk."

About an hour later Doyle and Chosky arrived at the Third Precinct. Here, they had to be more delicate as it was Mike's last assignment before he moved to HQ.

When Vern and Harry approached the Desk Officer, they looked at each other and shrugged. Neither one recognized the young officer.

"Is the Captain in?" Asked Vern.

"Who are you, and why do you need to see Captain Kilburn?"

Harry plopped a box of donuts on the desk and Vern stated, "We have a gift for the Captain. Just say that Vernon Chosky and Harold Doyle are here."

A few minutes later the officer announced, "The Captain has time for you." As the officer gestured for the pair to proceed around the end of the desk, he began to escort them down of the hall. Harry barked, "We know the way. Third door on the right."

The young officer stepped aside as Vern and Harry proceeded down the corridor and stopped at the open door. "Come in, gentlemen," commanded a female voice.

"Captain Claire Kilburn," Harry exclaimed. "Congratulations Cap! When I retired Claire, you were just a Sergeant working for me in the Robbery Squad. Now you're a Captain? Pretty good advancement. But then you were always a hard charger."

Captain Kilburn stood behind her desk with a wall full of plaques and diplomas as a backdrop. She smiled. "A lot has happened since you retired Harry. And Staff Sergeant Chosky, I hear that you are doing quite well for yourself."

Vern was impressed by the tall, millennial woman's presence. She was pretty, with a milk chocolate complexion, but her expression was all business. "Yes, Ma'am. I have my own studio. A Dojo in Amherst."

"What's with the donuts, Harry? That supposed to be a bribe?" the Captain asked with a more pronounced smile.

"Nothing like that, Claire. You know that when you go to someone's house, you never go empty-handed. I thought your day crew might appreciate a dozen for lunch."

In response Captain Kilburn rolled her eyes and took her seat. "But this is not a social call, is it? Of course not," proclaimed the Captain. Then purposely not using his first name she asked, "Please, close the door, Mr. Chosky."

The sudden attitude change took Vern by surprise as he followed the directive. "No Ma'am. We are here…"

"To inquire about Mike Morgan," Captain Kilburn finished Chosky's sentence. "Okay, quit the tap dancing. What is this all about?"

Harry was surprised with the speed that their business had been conveyed from one precinct to the next, and he feared that all commanders had been alerted. "I suppose that you spoke with Billy Mullins recently?"

"I have a lot of sources," she stated. "The Desk Sergeant assumed that you'd be stopping here sooner or later. He gave me a heads-up. He's a good man. But then you already know that Harry, or you wouldn't have stopped in to see him."

"So, you know why we're looking into Mike's background," Vern said. "We're just looking to see if anyone might have a motive to hurt Mike, or his family."

"And by digging up dirt on him, you're not going to hurt his family?" Captain Kilburn questioned. "I can tell you that when Mike Morgan was promoted to Lieutenant he was assigned to my command. He performed his duties well and was nothing short of professional."

Harry barked back, "Claire, you know me. I would never hurt another copper. Certainly not the son of a good friend. Mike is not the only potential target here. We need your help to protect Mike and find who killed his son. So, for Christ's sake, Claire, can you help us?"

The Captain motioned for the men to be seated. As she sat in the swivel chair behind her desk she asked, "Alright Harry… what do you need to know?"

CHAZ fumbled through the cushions of his sofa to find his buzzing phone. Locating it at last, he answered, "Hello?"

Freddie began without a return greeting, "Chaz, you remember that we were going to work together, right?"

"Yeah. I was just about to call you. Where do you think we should start?"

"When I got back to the office yesterday afternoon, I started filtering through Morgan's arrests. Not so many during the couple years before he retired. Not like when he was patrolling the Eighth. But we have a couple hundred to check out. You feel up to it?" Freddie asked.

"Hell, yeah. Where do you want to meet?" Chaz replied.

"Since we have to go to the courthouse, there's no sense in taking two cars. As long as I have the city car, you shouldn't have to pay for parking downtown. I'll pick you up in ten minutes, okay? Or make it fifteen," He offered. "That'll give you enough time to go to the bathroom."

Ten minutes later the black Chevy Impala with dark tinted windows and two spotlights pulled up to the front of the Bohen residence. Five minutes later Chaz came out, limping as he walked to the passenger side of the unmarked police car. He backed his butt into the seat, plopped down, and then swiveled his legs into the vehicle.

"What happened to you?" Freddie asked. "You fall or something?"

"Oh, nothing's wrong, Lieutenant Fred. It's just the arthritis in my knees. The knees, sometimes one, sometimes both, are stiff in the morning. But they loosen up during the day. So, there's nothing wrong." Chaz reiterated. "And, how are you?"

Freddie just shook his head and pulled away from the curb.

The pair fingered through arrest reports all morning and into the afternoon. They cross-referenced what they found with the Sentencing Reports and searched for statements made by the convicted before being transported to their new "public housing." It was near 4:30 p.m. when the Chief Clerk politely asked the officers to wrap it up.

"If you have more files to rifle through, you can use the conference room tomorrow." With a glance over the top of her glasses, she reminded them, "We open at 8 a.m."

Chaz began putting the folders back in order while Freddie made a list of convicts who had expressed anger or threatened some misfortune to their arresting officer, Joe Morgan. He also integrated a list of inmates who would have been released from prison in the past several months. There were only four names that apparently had a beef with Joe Morgan and had recently been released from custody. This was their short list of potential suspects. "Tomorrow we're going to have to do a deep dive on these four, Chaz. And follow up with face-to-face interviews."

"Before we leave, you think I could hit the head one more time?" Chaz asked.

"What's it been Chaz," Freddie inquired, "four or five times since we've been here?" Before Chaz could respond, Freddie answered, "I know. Those damned water pills!" In Chaz' absence Freddie gathered together the several sheets of paper that comprised the short list of suspects and the background files for each. This represented their full day of work with yet more to do.

"Thanks, Lieutenant Fred," Chaz offered as he returned.

"Tomorrow I'll be following up on these dirtbags," Freddie stated as he waved the several sheets of paper. "Do you think you can work the phone and contact some of Joe's old comrades? See what they have to say about him. Off the record, of course. Pick their brains for the good and the bad. Understand?"

"Uh-huh. I can start making calls tonight and finish up in the morning. What time do you want me to call you tomorrow?"

"Tell you what… I'll give you a call about noon. We'll take it from there."

It was quarter after six when Joe arrived at the Shining Star and selected the most secluded table. A couple minutes later, Mike and Chrissy entered. Joe stood and slid a chair away from the table for his daughter-in-law. "Well at least you won't have to cook tonight," he laughed.

"And you won't have to help with the dishes," she countered.

As they would usually sit at the dinner table, Mike was at the head of the table, Joe at the opposite end, and Chrissy sat to the right of Mike. The empty side of the table was still uncomfortable for them to look at.

"So, anything exciting happen at work?" Joe asked, more as a routine opening.

"Not really, Dad. Although I did hear some talk about a bunch of retired cops meeting in the Homicide Office this morning. I wasn't invited, but…"

Joe interrupted, "Yeah, that's an outreach program. I can tell you about that later. But right now," Joe reached his hand across the table and patted the back of Chrissy's hand, "I just want to know how you are doing, my dear?"

Chrissy managed a smile. "We're doing okay, Dad. It's hard when everything I do, I notice that there's a vacant spot, I feel the void. Every day I see that someone is missing. Now I worry every day when Mike leaves for work. I never felt this way before. I'm afraid to answer the door before Mike gets home from work. Afraid that it will be two other officers accompanied by the Police Chaplain."

Joe squeezed Chrissy's hand gently. "It's going to take a while. But things will get better. And you don't have to worry about Mike. He'll always be there." Joe glanced at his son and noticed that Mike had dropped his head as Chrissy was comforted.

Mike looked up to catch his father's stare. "Shall we get in line, folks?" Mike asked before he specifically addressed his father, "I know how you love Chinese."

After dinner, as they walked to their vehicles, Joe asked, "How about stopping by my place for a drink? We can talk."

Mike agreed, speculating that the offer was to discuss that "Outreach Program." "That would be fine, Dad." Then he looked for Chrissy's approval, "Okay Honey?"

The three sat around the coffee table in Joe's living room. After turning on the TV, Joe walked to the kitchen to pour several glasses of wine. As expected, Mike followed.

"So, tell me what's going on? What is Captain Williams doing with Sean's case? How come nobody will tell me anything? I have a right to know, Dad."

Taking several glasses from the cabinet, Joe addressed his son without looking at him, "Will reached out to me and a few other guys to see if fresh eyes might see something his detectives missed. That's all that's happening."

"Well why didn't someone tell me? I'm Sean's father."

"And that's exactly why you were kept out of the loop."

"So, what am I supposed to do? Sit around with my thumb up my ass?" Mike complained. "I have to do something. I have to be involved."

"You can be a big help, Mike. I need to talk to you and Chrissy about Sean's friends. I need to get names, addresses, and phone numbers. Who are his closest friends, schoolmates, any girlfriends?"

Just then Chrissy walked into the kitchen. "Why do you have to know all about Sean's friends?"

Mike answered, "It's part of the investigation. It's routine. The Homicide

Detectives are going to talk with anyone Sean spoke with during the week before he died. They're trying to develop a lead. Right Dad?"

Joe nodded. "And there are a couple names that have already come up that are of interest. Do you know who Robert Ralston, Greg Brooks, and Raynero Vazquez are?"

Chrissy thought for a brief moment. "I know that Rob Ralston and Greg Brooks were on the Track team with Sean. And I heard Sean talk about Ray a few times. He's a kid in his homeroom. But I don't know Ray's last name. I never met him. You think one of those boys were involved in Sean's death?"

"No," Joe replied. "Captain Williams just needs to talk to them to see if Sean had any problems with anyone else at school. That's all."

Mike added, "We'll write down all the names that we can think of, Dad. We'll check his computer to see if there's anything unusual there."

"Really, Mike?" Chrissy questioned with a surprised look on her face. "We never did anything like that before. We always trusted Sean. He never gave us a reason not to trust him."

"It's not that we don't trust Sean, Chrissy," Mike suggested. "But maybe someone sent something to him. Something he didn't think was a problem, but with what happened… Maybe there's something that we should know about."

"Alright," she conceded. "But you're going to check his computer. I don't want to see what's there."

CHAPTER 10

BIG WILL'S BACK IN SCHOOL

Captain Williams had barely settled in at his desk when he was swamped with a series of calls. The first was from Captain Danielle Redmond, commander of Precinct Fifteen, inquiring why two retired detectives were interfering in an official investigation and bothering her Desk Sergeant. The second call was from Captain Kilburn who had pretty much the same complaint as her counterpart at Fifteen. The last complaint that surfaced was from the Police Union President, Jamal Tyson. When it was explained to them that there were extraordinary circumstances, and that there was an urgency from higher up to clear the Morgan murder case, the Precinct Commanders supported Captain Williams' decision to utilize the experience of the retired officers. Even the PBA President conceded. Although, he suggested, that more manpower from the Detective Division should be used with authorized overtime. The Homicide Chief agreed to recommend that possibility to Commissioner Howes.

Joe Morgan thought he would wait to give Big Will a chance to have his first cup of coffee before checking in with him, giving the Captain a little time to get settled. Little did he know that there were several calls before him, and that Big Will had spent the morning trying to defend himself from awkward questions about utilizing retired investigators. To top it off, Will was an hour overdue for his coffee and jelly donut.

"Good morning, Joe," Big Will groaned.

"What's up, Will? Problems?" Joe asked sensing his disturbed tone of voice.

"You wouldn't believe. I got an army of people crawling up my ass because our guys are already ruffling feathers."

"Isn't that what they're supposed to be doing? You know any bunch of dicks that do it better?" Joe asked.

Big Will raised his eyebrows resignedly. "You're right, but I didn't expect them to get people so upset so quickly. The only ones that I haven't heard from yet are Commissioner Howes and Mike himself, who undoubtedly has received a few calls."

"Look, I'll handle Mike," Joe offered. "I can keep him from calling you. I'll keep talking to him. It should help."

"As soon as I get my coffee, I think I'll call the PC and let him know what's going on. Of course, the tricky part is letting him know what's going on in such a way that he won't want to know what's *really* going on."

"Plausible deniability?" Joe suggested.

"Enough to keep him off my back too, if I can help it. But we have to keep this investigation moving. Did you get anything from Mike and Chrissy?" Big Will prodded hopefully.

"Yeah. Mike is going to check Sean's computer for contacts. I'll email you any new names of the kids Sean associated with. I also have some background on the boys you were asking about. You want me to go with you to interview these kids?"

"No. That's my job. We can get together later. Touch base with the other guys and see if they're having any luck. Remind them that we'll be meeting for lunch on Friday."

CAPTAIN Williams pulled his SUV up on the sidewalk in front of John F. Kennedy High School. He had already made contact with the Principal and was scheduled to meet with the Guidance Counselor, Betty Hopkins. Hopkins had arranged for several students to come to her office.

The first student summoned was Gregory Brooks. He was the Captain of the Track team, held the State Track record for the 100 Meter Sprint, and was also an Honor student. Williams thought that he'd be the most solid starting point to set a baseline of facts. Will knew that although kids instinctively cover for each other and have an inherent distrust of adults, he figured he could win Gregory over by playing to the young man's accomplishments.

Captain Williams was standing when Brooks was ushered into the Guidance Office by Ms. Hopkins. The counselor then excused herself and to ensure privacy, closed the door when she left.

"Please, take a seat Gregory," Williams offered.

The young man looked around the room and noted that there was a swivel chair behind Ms. Hopkins' desk, two wingback chairs positioned in front of the desk, and a leather sofa and loveseat set in the corner of the office. He chose to be seated on the loveseat.

Williams then situated himself on the sofa and introduced himself, "My name is Will Williams. I am the Chief of the Homicide Bureau, and I am working on the investigation of Sean Morgan's death. He was a friend of yours, wasn't he?"

The young man showed no emotion. He was not impressed by Williams' title, his size, or his obvious effort of compassion. "Uh-huh. Sean was a friend."

"Were you two close friends?" Williams asked.

"Yeah. He was like one of my best friends. We worked out a lot together. We ran together."

"When you say, 'you ran together,' you mean you actually ran together?" Williams looked for clarification. "You both were on the Track team? Both seniors?"

"Uh-huh. Yeah."

"I understand that you hold the State Track and Field record for the 100 Meters. 10.4 seconds?"

"Uh-huh."

Concession of abilities is one approach that often worked for Williams. "Man, that is really flying. From the block to the tape, the best I could ever do is 10.8."

The expressionless face raised up. "I don't think you ever could have run that fast. Like, you're too tall, and way too heavy. You don't have a sprinter's body."

Williams smiled. "Well, it was a long time and many pounds ago, kid. And I wasn't on the Honor Roll either, as you are. I was always kind of a mediocre student. But we're not here to talk about me. How well did you know Sean? Aside from track. What else was he into?"

"Uh-huh," repeated the young man. "We were the best of friends. We hung out together. Did everything together. He also enjoyed playing chess and cards. I really miss not having him around."

"What kind of cards do you guys play?"

"Mostly poker and blackjack. Just for quarters."

Williams slouched back into the sofa. "You know why I'm talking to you today?"

"Uh-huh. You're investigating Sean's accident."

Williams leaned forward to explain, "I am the Chief of Homicide, not an Accident Investigator. There was nothing accidental about Sean's death. Now, do you know of anyone who would want to kill or hurt Sean?"

The cold fatal fact finally struck Gregory as his face drained of color. Hesitantly he answered, "I'm sorry officer. I don't know of anyone who would want to hurt Sean. He was a great friend, and he wouldn't do anything to anyone to, like, piss them off that much."

"Who did else did Sean hang out with?"

Greg Brooks gazed at the ceiling for a moment to consider his response. "Sean played cards with a regular group - me, Ray Vazquez, Don Wayland, Robby Ralston, and John Jacobs. We would get together and play cards maybe once a week at each other's houses. When we played at my house, we'd have a card table set up in the basement and my mother would bring down snacks for us. But we spent most of our time, him and me, running in Delaware Park."

"So, the other guys, Ray, Don, Robby and John were not on the Track team?"

Greg paused a moment before answering again, "Robby is a Junior. He ran with us, but he's still on the JV team. The other guys were just good friends from school. Like, we all just hung out on weekends."

The few following questions were also responded to with extremely guarded thought, so Chief Williams decided to move on to the next student on his list, Robert Ralston.

This time Chief Williams stood between the two chairs in front of the desk. As young Ralston entered, the officer pointed to one of the chairs. "You can sit here." He then asked, "Robert Ralston?"

"Yes, sir," replied the young man.

"Your friends call you Robert, Rob or Robby?"

"Mostly Rob. My closest friends call me Robby," he answered respectfully. "What can I do for you?"

"Rob, my name is Captain Will Williams. I am Chief of the Homicide Bureau. I am investigating the death of Sean Morgan."

Young Ralston's eyes were wide open as he concentrated on the officer's words. "I had nothing to do with that. It was hard enough to see Sean in the funeral home. I wouldn't do nothing to hurt Sean. Honest!"

Chief Williams noted the kid's trembling hands. "I'm not here to point fingers, Rob. I'm here to elicit your help. I know that you were on the Track team with Sean, that you would run with him in Delaware Park, and that you guys would play cards for quarters. What I want you to tell me is what I don't know."

The kid stared at the officer. "What don't you know?"

Chief Williams sensed that the high school Junior was not prepared for a barrage of questions. He dropped his voice slightly, adding just a touch of accusation to his tone. "I don't know what else Sean was involved in. I don't know who would want him dead. And I don't know why you're holding back…unless you are somehow involved."

Rob's eyes began to fill with tears as he fought the urge to run out of the room. "I swear that I don't know anything about how he was killed or who would do that. All I know is that Sean would smoke with us when we played cards."

"You mean weed?" Williams asked.

"Yes sir. He was the one who got it for us because we were friends. The other kids at school had to pay for their weed."

"Sean was selling dope to other students?"

"Yeah. But he didn't charge us because we were all friends. It was only marijuana. Not dope like cocaine or heroin."

"Do you know where Sean got his supply from?"

Rob thought carefully. "No sir. He never said who he got it from. He was just a good guy who shared his pot. Nobody would kill him for that."

Williams maintained his tone and asked, "Do you know who else Sean associated with? In school, or outside of school?"

"It was just the guys on track, us guys who played cards once a week, and a couple kids from homeroom. I don't know of anyone in his neighborhood."

"Do those kids have names?" Williams inquired.

"Sure," Rob answered. "The ones that I know are Ray Vazquez and Donnie Wayland – they're in Sean's homeroom. Me and Greg Brooks ran track with Sean."

The Chief of Homicide fingered through his notes. "Is that all? Anyone else?"

"No sir. Not that I know of."

"How about John Jacobs?" Chief Williams added.

"Jacobs?" Rob repeated with curiosity. "He's in Sean's homeroom too, but he didn't hang out with us that much. Hardly ever," Rob declared.

Williams slowly perused his notes again, allowing the young man to worry in silence. Then he handed Rob his business card and stated, "Call me if you think of anything else, Rob. And don't worry about the weed, but for your own good you should cut that shit out." The huge officer stood in front of Rob and looked down. "It's nothing to worry about, but it certainly isn't any good for you. Go on, you better get to the rest of your classes now."

"Thank you, Sir." Rob heaved a sigh of relief. "I hope I helped a little."

"You did good, and thanks for being honest with me," Williams assured.

Raynero Vazquez had been sitting on the bench outside the Guidance Office for the better part of an hour. Periodically he would stand and walk back and forth in front of the bench.

After Chief Williams updated his notes, he stuck his head outside Ms. Hopkins' office. He startled the young man who had his back to the door. "Excuse me. Are you Raynero Vazquez?"

"Yeah, I am," came the nervous response. "Are you the cop that I'm supposed to talk to? Ms. Hopkins said that there was a cop who wanted to talk to a bunch of us."

The Chief waved to the young man, "Come right in. I've been looking forward to having a chat with you. Would you like to have a seat?"

Vazquez stepped into the room, plopped himself into one of the wing-back chairs, and draped his leg over one of the chair's arms. "So, did you have to talk to two white boys first so that it doesn't look like you're hassling the Puerto Rican kid? You know that I ain't done nothing, man!"

The Chief moved around the chair until he was squarely planted in front of Vazquez. Will had always found that when you are as big as he was, encroaching even slightly into someone's personal space often produced results. He towered over the slouching youth with a stern expression of disapproval aimed at Vasquez's leg. Sinking back into the chair, Vasquez removed his leg from the arm of the chair. "That's better," Will approved quietly but with unspoken menace. "Is this the way you want to be treated?

Or can we discuss things like men?" Williams inched forward and squared his broad shoulders.

With a second thought and an attempt at an ingratiating smile, Raynero suggested, "Uh, maybe we got off to a bad start. Okay, I'm checking my attitude."

The Chief backed away from Raynero and propped himself against the Guidance Counselor's desk. "I suppose most people call you Ray. You mind if I call you Ray?"

"Everybody calls me Ray. Go ahead."

"Well let me explain where I'm coming from, Ray. My name is Captain Will Williams. I'm Chief of the Homicide Bureau. I, and a lot of other officers and detectives, are trying to piece together what happened to Sean Morgan. Since you, like Rob and Greg, were friends of Sean's, I need your help to find out who would want him dead. Is there anyone who hated him or his family that much?"

"Fair enough," Ray conceded. "And just so you know where I'm coming from…I am not a rat. Not a snitch."

"Okay," Williams accepted the statement benignly. "I'm not looking for anyone to rat on anyone. What I expect is that his friends would have his back and if they knew anything about how or why Sean was killed – they would step up like a man, like a friend, to get justice for him. That's not ratting anyone out."

"Alright officer, I can respect that. But since I don't know anyone who had a hard-on for Sean, especially to do him like that, I can't tell you nothing. I couldn't even take a guess. Everyone liked Sean."

"Why, because he supplied the pot when you were playing blackjack? You weren't selling that shit along with Sean, were you?"

"No, Man!" Ray denied vehemently. "We all blew a little smoke, sure, but selling? No way! I can't say what Sean was doing when we weren't with him. And like I say, I don't rat on people."

"And you certainly don't have your friend's back. Do you?" Will countered.

"Now I suppose you're going to ask me where I was on the night Sean was killed. Huh?"

"No. That would be an interrogation. And then I'd have to inform you of your Miranda Rights, and I would have to notify your parents. So, no. I'm only talking to you to get some help in our investigation. I'm not going to mention your pot habit to anyone. I just thought that we could talk." Williams took one of his business cards and spun it through the air toward Vazquez. It struck him in his chest and fell onto his lap. "If you're really a friend of Sean's, I would expect a call from you with any helpful info."

Ray picked up the card and stuck it in his shirt pocket. "Can I go now?"

"Absolutely, Ray. You could've left any time. Hope to hear from you."

The Chief of Homicide utilized the Guidance Office for the next two hours to question both specific and random students. Captain Williams' interviews of the other students provided cover for the few students that did provide useful information, while others simply confirmed some facts with their passive agreement and body language. And more often, what kids didn't say was the most revealing of all.

CHAPTER 11

The Blessing from Above

The southeast corner of the second floor of Police Headquarters was the domain of the Police Commissioner. From the suite of three connecting rooms he had a clear view of Church and Franklin Streets, and a less clear view of the entire department. Also, on the second floor at the north end of the corridor, was an auditorium that could accommodate a hundred people in the audience plus a dozen people on the raised stage. The auditorium was normally used for in-service training, press briefings, and the monthly Admin Staff Meeting held by the PC. Despite the fact that it was two weeks before the next scheduled Staff Meeting, the Commissioner called together all his Precinct Commanders, all Supervisors within the Detective Division, and staff Support Managers.

As the administrators settled into their seats, the PC, the two Deputy PCs, and the Chief of Detectives positioned themselves on the stage, seated behind a vacant podium. Once the mumbling and chatter of the crowd had subsided, the PC rose and stepped up to the podium. The room went quiet within seconds.

"Thank you," Commissioner Howes acknowledged the assembled officers. "That only shows me that you all can keep your mouths shut when you're in the view of others." Then he raised the morning edition of *The Daily News* as he pointed to an article on the lower half of the front page. The article was titled "Police Suspect Murder." "As far as I am aware, our Public Relations Office has not put any of this information out for public consumption. At least, not that I authorized." He paused, looked around the room and stared at a couple of individuals, but made no accusations. "My intention for this meeting was to address a few complaints I received regarding several retired detectives making inquiries about an officer who is still on the job. I'm sure you are aware of whom I speak. That was my intention, until this came across my desk!" he fumed, throwing the news-paper down on the podium. "Now I have a different thorn stuck in my paw! I want a full-court press on this case. Reach out to anyone who lives, works, or walks on our streets. We don't stop until we have the suspect or suspects in custody. And I don't want to read about it in the paper!" the Commissioner demanded.

A hand raised in the middle of the crowd. The PC acknowledged the raised hand, "Question, Captain Kilburn?"

"It's regarding the retired officers, are they allowed to conduct a separate investigation?"

Another hand raised from the rear of the gathering. Captain Joe Mor-gan stood up to be recognized.

Commissioner Howes responded, "Captain Morgan, you are retired. As you are aware, the Admin Meeting is for on-the-job administrators. But, given the unique circumstance…what is it you would like to say?"

"Thank you, Commissioner, from the bottom of my heart. Many of you have worked with my son, Mike. Hell, I have worked with almost every one of you. Whether at Precinct 8, 12, 13, 15 or in Homicide, over the years I have backed up each of you no matter what the call. Now I'm asking you to back me up. So far, retired Detective Sergeant Harry Doyle, retired Staff Sergeant Vern Chosky, and retired Lieutenant Chaz Bohen have stepped up. Not because they were asked to. Not for overtime pay or any other com-pensation, but because they are my friends and they are some of the best damn cops I have ever known. So, I apologize if they stepped on some toes. I'm sorry that they were not introduced in a more formal manner. But they will be continuing their efforts and will work in conjunction with the Department." Morgan looked to Chief of Detectives, Howard Smyth, "Chief, we will provide an activity report to you through the Chief of Homicide, daily if you wish. If there is anything you want us to do, individually or as a group, you can direct your request to us through Captain Williams. Is that alright with you?"

Chief Howard Smyth stood and moved up to the podium. He looked to the Commissioner for guidance. The PC nodded back. "Okay, Joe. But you gotta keep those guys under control. It's not the Wild West anymore. We understand how you and your friends feel and we appreciate any help you can give. But remember, first and foremost, this is the Department's Homicide investigation. Not yours." He let the words sink in for emphasis before conceding, "But we appreciate your help."

Another hand shot up. The Chief of Detectives recognized the Commander of the Narcotics Bureau, Captain Riccardo Amico.

"Then are we to understand that the Morgan case IS the priority for all units?"

Again, Chief Smyth looked toward the Commissioner. Again, came the nod. "You have it right from the top, Ric," Chief Smyth announced. "Business for all units will continue as usual, but there will be an emphasis to collect whatever information, from whatever sources you may have, concerning the Morgan case. Everything will be channeled through my office and directed to the PC," Smyth explained. "And there will be no leaks to the press." Smyth's disgusted expression emphasized his point. "Understood?" After a short pause, "Any other questions?"

By the end of the day all Bureau Chiefs and Precinct Commanders had briefed the supervisors in their command. Major Case, Robbery, Narcotics, Juvenile, Sex Crimes, and Auto Theft Bureaus as well as all Precincts had received the call for "all hands, on deck." Of particular interest was any information regarding a truck with dual rear wheels.

AT 10 p.m. the night squad began arriving at the Narcotics Bureau's third floor office. By 10:20 p.m. Lieutenant Freddie Taylor began the tour with the routine nightly squad briefing. It usually consisted of an update of current operations and was augmented by any new orders.

"Ziemecki and Appleford, Team One," the Lieutenant announced. "Nice job on that hand-to-hand buy last night. Felony weight. A couple more and we will have enough for search warrants. Maybe we'll have some new confidential informants in the making."

"We should have two more buys by next week and we are still trying to flip the mutt from the Jackson Street raid," Ziemecki added.

"Ransford and Ulewski, Team Two. How are you doing with your source on the Freedom Boyz operation? Do you think it's doable?" the Lieutenant asked.

Ulewski guarded his response, "Our guy, 337, has been spot-on in the past. But for obvious reasons, he doesn't want to give up his supplier."

"Or doesn't want to be killed," Ransford suggested.

"In either case, 337 has been shying away from giving up any of the Freedom Boyz. So far, he has given us several names of Freedom Boyz players, and they checked out to be accurate. But he hasn't given us anything actionable. I think that we're going to have to motivate him better," Ulewski declared.

"And what do you recommend?" Appleford questioned. "More money or a felony and two misdemeanors hanging over his head?"

Ulewski shrugged as if to say he wasn't sure which would work better. After the chuckling and chatter subsided the Lieutenant returned to the briefing. "Santucci and Stafford, Team Three. I need you to check the Chippewa strip for any new faces that might be dealing, get some plate numbers at the usual places, and hang loose to backup One and Two. But most of all, work your CI's."

"Is that all Boss?" Appleford asked.

"Oh yeah," Lieutenant Taylor added. "This comes right from the Commissioner himself. All units in the Department have been instructed to be on alert for some kind of truck, probably a pickup truck, with dual wheels. It's believed that this truck was involved in the Hit-and-Run murder of Lieutenant Mike Morgan's kid. We look after our own. All units are to consider this a priority investigation!"

"Sure, Lieutenant." Santucci agreed. "Make, model, color?"

"Tooch, you have every bit of information I was given," Taylor replied, his voice tinged with frustration. "I know there is nothing to go on, but who knows what could develop if we put enough eyes on alert?"

"You're right, Boss," Santucci admitted. "Who knows, that truck might run a red light and smash into a cop car."

The Lieutenant ended the briefing with his signature blessing, "Okay, guys. Hit the street and may the Good Lord be looking out for us."

As most midnight tours would go, there was a lot of surveillance and scouting for individuals to talk to. Most of the time there were tidbits of information that may be interesting, but did not warrant any more than a brief notation in a team's Activity Report. At the close of the tour, each team submitted a synopsis of what they accomplished, or attempted to accomplish, during the midnight shift. Lieutenant Taylor would review the teams' Activity Reports after the crews were dismissed, so that he would be able to brief the Narcotics Chief when he arrived at 8:00 a.m. Most of the reports were routine and often inflated with old info. But what caught Taylor's attention was the notation in Team Two's report.

"Detectives Ulewski and Ransford met with 337, who provided three more names of Freedom Boyz members: 1 - African American male is Jerome Corn (or Korn) drives an older Caddy – no plate number; 2 - African American male is 'T-Bone' (real name unknown but will find out) who sells various drugs near the Main Street college campus and several City High Schools. No known vehicle; 3 - African American male is Tyrone or

Tyrrell (last name unknown) who might be one of the shot callers for Freedom Boyz. He drives a tricked out black F350 crew cab dually with a long bed and cap - no plate number."

CHAPTER 12
Friday, April 5, 2019

WHO'S GOT THE MOTIVE?

J OE THOUGHT LONG and hard about attending the Friday breakfast at the Towne, even though it had been his idea. In a way, it felt like he was betraying Mike by working behind his back. But Joe was enticed by the possible results his investigative cohorts might develop. He didn't expect any of them to have already found a motive for Sean's death, but the possibilities were intriguing. This group was the best bunch of investigators he had ever personally known. Joe Morgan had resigned himself to the inevitability that their digging may turn up some uncomfortable history for himself and other people that this investigation put under the microscope. Mike was one of the subjects to be examined, and the parent of the victim. As such, Joe felt justified in extending an invitation for Mike to meet with the Coterie… at least for breakfast. Besides, it would be more efficient if Mike could respond directly to·any findings that may lead to a motive, rather than have to relay it through Joe.

Entering the Towne Restaurant with Mike, Joe expected to be the first at the Round Table. He was surprised to find Big Will waiting with a cup of black coffee in front of him.

Big Will stood as the two approached. "Morning Joe. And Mike, how are you doing today?"

As Joe and Mike scooted around the tables to be seated in the back, Joe asked, "I hope nobody would mind if I invited Mike."

"No. I can't see anyone objecting, Joe. Especially under these circumstances. Mike's presence can only help further our work. I wished that I would have thought of bringing Mike in sooner." Big Will turned his attention to Mike. "I, for one, am happy you could be here. I suspect that you need to have your boots on the ground."

"Thanks, Captain," Mike responded. With a quizzical look he stated, "I didn't know that you were with this retired group. I mean, years ago I heard of the Coterie, but I didn't think it was a real thing. I, ah…"

Big Will just heaved up a belly laugh. "That's okay, Mike. You can call me Will, Big Will, BW, or whatever the heck you want. You'll find that we're all friends here. And that's why we are here." Then he leaned in toward Joe, "That was quite impressive how you crashed the Commissioner's Admin Meeting. Now I'm responsible for you guys."

As usual, Chaz Bohen strolled in and made a beeline for the restroom.

A moment later Vern Chosky entered the restaurant.

By the time Chaz was able to join the Coterie, all but two chairs were filled - the one on the aisle reserved for Chaz, and the one where Freddie Taylor normally sat.

Joe was the first to question Freddie's absence, and Big Will supplied the answer, "Lieutenant Taylor, unlike the rest of you guys, was up all night… working. Freddie called me this morning when I got in to let me know that he had a meeting scheduled with his Chief and he was then going straight home to bed."

Chosky suggested with a snicker, "Or he was too cheap to spring for a breakfast tip."

The group laughed, as Freddie always counted his tip money to the penny.

"You'd think that he was claiming Lavon as a dependent," a second wave of laughter rolled over the table.

"At any rate… I'll contact Freddie later to bring him up to speed on our meeting." Big Will added.

The waitress appeared at the table. "Did I hear someone calling my name? Why are my ears ringing?"

"You don't miss anything, do you Lavon?" Harry asked.

"You'd be surprised what I hear in this restaurant, Harry." Then Lavon turned to all the attendees. "Are we going with the regular orders all the way around?" Then her eyes fell on Mike. "You look like a waffle, short stack of pancakes, two eggs, and bacon," she guessed.

"You are good. Definitely good at this job," Mike stated.

"And you are definitely a Morgan!" she quipped before making a notation of the order and heading toward the kitchen.

"How did she know I was related to you?" Mike asked his father, as he sat in full uniform with his nameplate clearly visible.

Again, there was a roll of laughter. "It must be a Lieutenant thing," Harry suggested.

"Okay, before Lavon starts bringing the food," Big Will redirected the conversation, "would you guys like to give a summary of what, if anything you've found? Anything that could be a motive for Sean's murder?"

Harry looked at Vern, who turned to Chaz, and they all looked toward Joe. Finally, their eyes locked onto Mike.

"What?" Mike asked. "Am I supposed to say something here?"

"No," Big Will asserted. "I think that they all feel a bit uncomfortable with you here. Your being here was not expected, and some of this discussion may be difficult."

"Will, do you want me to leave?" Mike asked. "If that's what you want… but I really should be a part of this discussion. Don't you think?"

Harry leaned as far across the table as possible toward Mike before answering in his gravelly rasp. "I've known you since you were born. You and Chrissy are like my own kids. Your Dad was my best man when Ellie and I got married. So, believe me when I say, you're like family. Pretty much every one of us feels the same way. So, it's not that we want you to leave the table. It's just that it might get awkward and honest here, and nobody wants to hurt your feelings."

Mike's head bobbed appreciatively. "Harry, you've been like an uncle to me through the years. I've known you, Vern, Chaz, and Captain Williams…, ah, Will, almost all my life. Open any can of worms you want. I understand what we're doing here, and I can take it. You're not going to hurt my feelings. This is for Sean."

And with that, everyone was put at ease. "Okay, I'll start," Big Will pronounced. "Since Sean is the victim here, we have to profile him first. I started with his friends and classmates."

"So, you already interviewed his friends?" Mike questioned.

"Of course. And that led me to a few outsiders, and here's what we found."

"What do you mean we?" Joe asked.

"We, Joe," Big Will explained. "My bureau detectives and myself."

"Oh. Sorry Will. I was thinking that this was our investigation. I forgot that it was… first and foremost a Homicide Bureau investigation."

"Well as I was going to say," Big Will continued, "Sean was a smart, friendly, athletic kid, and well-liked by his teachers and other students."

Mike started to smile with pride. But that soon faded as the Homicide Chief proceeded. "He was also a very enterprising kid," Will gave a side glance to Mike. "He, and a small band of buddies, had a regular business going at the school. It seems like they would buy at least a pound of grass every month and had regular customers. It was also implied that a couple teachers were also buying from Sean's group."

Mike's jaw dropped. "Are you absolutely positive, Will? Sean would never even smoke cigarettes because he was a runner. And to sell that stuff to other kids?"

"My information came from several sources, Mike. We know a few of the kids he was involved with, and even though this wasn't exactly life-changing money, to some it could be a motive for murder. These kids came up with three grand a month to buy a pound. Selling gram bags, that's 450 baggies at $15 each? That would double their money easily every month. Yeah. It sounds like there could be a motive here."

"Did the school find anything in his locker?" Mike asked. "Because there was no sign in our home that he was smoking or selling pot!"

"Like I said. Sean was quite an enterprising kid. We think that one night a week he 'played cards' with a few of his buddies. That's when they'd meet. They may have played cards – but they definitely did more than blackjack. I think they kept their supply in the basement of one kid's house, probably Greg Brooks, where they did the bagging and split their profits. That would also be the money that they played cards with. Then they used an empty school locker as a stash location."

Mike dropped his head, then turned to see the disappointment on his father's face. "So, what happens now? I mean, with these other kids?"

"I was going to turn over all this information to Freddie today. But, as you see, he couldn't be here. So, it will remain in the Homicide files until I can hand it off to him. These kids aren't going anywhere."

Harry then asked, "You know how long this has been going on and where the money and marijuana is?"

"As soon as word hit the school that Sean was killed in a car accident, someone cleaned out their secret locker and all the weed was undoubtedly moved out of that basement. They are just kids, but they aren't stupid," Big Will stated. "But that's not what we were looking for. We were looking for a definitive motive. The weed, the money, the whole operation, may be something that someone would want to take over. But my gut says I really don't think it's the motive we're looking for. Everything was going smooth for them until this happened. Everyone was making a little money, and nobody was talking." Will looked down the table, not feeling comfortable meeting Joe or Mike's gaze, "Sorry, Mike."

Joe let out a long breath, rolled his head and shrugged his shoulders as if recovering from a punch to the chin. But he prodded the next team to proceed, "Vern and Harry, or Chaz and Freddie?"

Harry spoke up next. His eyes lifted to Mike as he pulled a wad of papers from his jacket pocket. "We may as well get this over with. Vern and I did some digging into your past, Mike. And I want you to know that everything that surfaced stays here, within the Coterie."

Mike cautiously agreed, "Sure. Whatever."

Harry unfolded the several sheets of paper. "You remember Rob Swanson?"

"Of course. He works the second platoon at Precinct Five," Mike answered.

"It appears that he still has a belief that you cheated on the Sergeant's exam, which cost him his promotion," Harry grumbled. "And he never scored high enough on the next couple exams to get promoted. The list you got promoted from was the best rating that he achieved. And he says that you stole that chance from him."

Mike rolled his eyes and exclaimed, "With Rob, its always someone else's fault."

Then Harry hesitantly continued, "A friend over in Personnel gave me a rundown on your complaint file. Three excessive force accusations, falsifying time sheets, an uncharged misconduct, and a couple verbal reprimands were noted. It looks like you where doctoring the sign-in sheets at Precinct 15 and had a bullying problem at 3, Mike. Do any of these problems end up with violence?" Harry asked.

"Naw," Mike shrugged. "When you run a platoon there is always somebody who will disagree with the way you do things. Sure, I cut a few guys breaks. Let a couple men slide out on quiet nights, but we always got the job done," Mike seemed confident defending his actions.

"Then there were a couple guys who worked for you a few years back who claimed that you were leaving work for full shifts," Harry added with a probing look.

Mike attempted to explain away that accusation with a poker face, "There were a couple times I had to leave work on short notice. You know, emergencies at home."

Vern folded his arms across his chest and signaled to Mike by shaking his head left to right like a bobblehead doll. "Does the name Molly McCoy ring a bell, Mike."

Mike's face turned red, as his jaws flexed. "Why is this becoming an inquisition?" Mike struggled to contain his anger.

Joe placed his hand on Mike's forearm. "Simmer down. We aren't here to judge. Don't think that you're the only cop that's had a paramour."

"Paramour?" Mike questioned. "Molly was just a friend. That's all."

Vern was not the most artful inquisitor. "Look, Mike. I don't give a flying fart if you were bopping Ms. McCoy or you just felt you had to have a TV companion for the late show. But when you've been seeing this gal for several years, and she ends up getting divorced... Well, that's gotta cause some hard feelings for someone. Right? Like her husband? That's the kind of thing that can become a motive."

"Along our careers a lot of guys get sidetracked with their relationships. It happens," Harry afforded. "But how did her ex take it? He knew about you and her, didn't he?"

"No," Mike replied. "He was screwing around for years. She finally left him. That was what, five, six, years ago? I don't think that Sam even batted an eye at our friendship. He didn't have a jealous bone in his body. Besides, I haven't seen Molly in a year or more."

"Samuel McCoy?" Vern asked innocently. "That's funny, because he's got quite the rap sheet. Several assaults and harassment charges. Then there's a DUI, larceny, and an attempted rape. The guy's a real charmer. And to top it off he was just released from County Holding last month. That would have been a week before Sean was killed."

Mike shook his head. "No. That's just a coincidence. He wouldn't..."

Vern interjected, "Or maybe you don't want to believe that you might have been the intended target? That maybe Sean paid for someone else's mistaken identity?"

"No Vern," Mike insisted. "Sam wouldn't do that. And as far as my personnel file goes, you all know that if a guy was a do-nothing during his whole career, he won't have a single complaint in his jacket. But if you're out there kicking ass and taking names… Yeah, your file will have a few complaints." Then as Mike looked around the table he concluded, "I don't see anyone here who has an unblemished personnel file!"

Big Will interceded, "Alright Mike. I think you made your point. And you would know what this Sam is capable of. But for the sake of our investigation, I want Vern and Harry to dig a little deeper on his alibi and motive." Then Big Will diverted the conversation, "Okay, Joe. Your turn in the barrel."

"Fine with me," Joe offered. "Chaz, what did you and Freddie come up with? Undoubtedly there is someone who wants me in the ground. Who are we looking at?"

All heads turned toward Chaz Bohen. "We dug deep through court records, sentencing reports, reached out to DOC for certain parole hearing transcripts, and reviewed parole and probation officers' follow-ups. Joe, you kicked some ass in your day." Chaz announced. "You managed to get some people really pissed off at you, as you put some away for long stretches. But everyone we talked to brought us to one conclusion, you were tough but fair."

Big Will wondered if there was anyone that Joe would consider an enemy, "Is there any one person that you arrested unfairly, Joe? Is there even one person that you would fear running across in a dark alley?"

Stoically, Joe reflected for a moment and replied, "Honestly, I can't think of one." With a slightly sinister tone he added, "But there are a couple miscreants that I'd love to run across again."

Vern barked out a laugh, "If you were twenty years younger, maybe!"

The focus came back to Chaz. "We also went through your personnel file and found a fairly clean record, except for a couple wrist slaps. But then there were those two times that you were brought up on departmental charges. I remember what that was about," Chaz said dismissively.

Mike objected, "Hold it. You check out my personnel file and drag my name through the mud on a few rumors and allegations. I was never brought up on charges, not once. And yet, you don't even want to discuss Dad's incidents that ended up with formal charges?" Mike quickly turned toward his father. "I know you're my father, but Jesus, this is not fair."

Joe smiled at his son. "That was nothing but politics. That's all."

"Departmental charges? Just politics?" Mike scoffed.

Harry began to explain to Mike, "It was about twenty years ago when the Gossett brothers were knocking off corner stores and gas stations on the west side. Everyone knew who was doing the stickups, but they wore gloves, masks, and scared the hell out of witnesses. The only way to stop those guys was to catch them in the act. And that's exactly what happened. One night your Dad was on the way home and spotted two guys with stocking masks get out of a car and enter the deli on Niagara Street, where the Community Center is now. Anyway, it was before we had cellphones, so he couldn't call for backup. He parked his car behind the vehicle the holdup guys got out of, only leaving them about two inches of space. Then he stands to the hinged side of the entrance door. When the two Gossetts started to leave the store, he let the first one through the door heading toward the car. As the second brother started through the doorway, Joe threw his body into the swinging door, stopping the guy in his tracks. The guy was dazed, but he managed to get to his feet, staggering toward Joe with a pistol in his hand. Joe slams him a second time with the frame of the door, knocking the pistol clear and causing him to fall backward into the store. So when Joe turns his attention to the other Gossett, who was standing next to the getaway car looking for the driver who had blocked him in, Joe hears this horrendous cracking sound from behind him. Seems that the guy Joe had door-checked had been knocked cold and slammed his head on the store's concrete floor. Even the brother near the car was distracted by the sound. The younger Gossett pulls a revolver out of his waistband, but not before Joe tackled the man. They rolled on the ground exchanging punches until a passing squad car pulled in. As it turned out, the Gossetts were some half-assed relatives of the DA. Go figure."

"So, you should've gotten a commendation," Mike mused.

"No, Mike. I told you this was twenty years ago. The political stars didn't line up that way. It was under Mayor Giavetti's administration. The DA was Italian, the Commissioner was Italian, and they all were staunch party line Democrats. Your father was an Irish Republican. So, guess what? No commendation. Instead he gets charged with Excessive Force and Rights Violations. Even the shop owner testified for the scumbags at the civil trial."

"What?" Mike decried. "So, what happened?"

"It all worked out. The departmental charges relating to the holdup arrests were dropped. Jerrod Gossett took a plea and received 7 to 15 years. The older brother, well he was awarded 500 grand by a bleeding-heart jury. He hit the floor so hard, he was paralyzed from the waist down until he died a few years ago. He got to enjoy that money from the waist up and he never went to prison."

"And that's what you call fair?" Mike challenged.

"No. I said it was politics," Harry declared flatly.

"And the second departmental charge you mentioned?"

A look of satisfaction washed over Joe's face as he recalled, "Conduct Unbecoming an Officer and Official Misconduct. Those were the official charges."

"For what, Dad?"

Chaz, Vern, and Harry started to chuckle. "Here's where your father may have crossed the line," Harry suggested. "Go ahead, tell him, Joe."

"Well as soon as I heard that there was a conflict of interest between the DA and the scumbags, not realizing that they all were scumbags, I went to talk to the DA about recusing himself. In fact, I demanded that he call HQ in my presence to have the charges against me dropped. One thing led to another, and I may have threatened to throw him out of his fourth-floor window. I was suspended and brought up on the second round of charges before I could get back to headquarters."

Rather pridefully, Big Will went on to explain, "The Coterie stepped in at that point. We reached out to a few influential people, called in a couple favors, and made a couple…uh, promises, of our own. That's how the charges were dropped, and the deals were made."

"Oh, by the way, Mike," Vern uttered, "you reminded us that all the charges against you in your jacket were dropped. They should have been dropped, because they were bullshit. But, how do you think that happened? The system rarely gets it right without a bit of a push. You can thank the Coterie for that one."

Chaz resumed his report, "That was politics then and now. But as far as your father is concerned… Freddie and I researched all of Joe's arrests going back to when he was a rookie. We found four people that Joe arrested that harbored any meaningful hatred, served some heavy time, and were released within the last six months. But three of them have solid alibis: one's in a hospice unit waiting to die; another has been arrested on other charges and for the last three months had been confined to his house with an ankle monitor; and a third person has been living in Cleveland since his release and can prove that he's been there throughout this whole time period."

"And the fourth guy?" Joe asked.

"Not a guy at all, Joe. Do you remember Bouncing Betty Johnson?" Chaz offered.

"Yeah." Joe acknowledged. "They called her Bouncing Betty because of her explosive personality. She sliced off her husband's gonads, stuffed them down his throat and choked him to death. Yeah, she was crazy! So, you say that she was recently released?"

"Uh-huh." Chaz confirmed. "She was paroled back on the 10th of February, and by the end of the month she was arrested in Atlantic City for pocketing some chips at a casino. She spent two weeks in jail before being released. That would account for her up to the beginning of March. Nobody's seen her since. She's a possible suspect but unlikely because of the time and distance. But it doesn't rule her out completely."

Then Joe reconsidered his earlier response. "Okay. Maybe I wouldn't want to run into her in a dark alley. But I don't think she's up to this level of planning."

Big Will then reclaimed the lead of the investigation, "So, to recap, we found no evidence that there was a direct threat to Joe, although it was his car driven back to his apartment from Mike's house. It was probably too dark for the perp to positively identify who was driving. And with no other known motive, we assume that the target was Joe." Big Will looked around the table to note the assessment before continuing. "With Chaz and Freddie, we found that Mike had a few dustups with other coppers, and," looking toward Mike for his reaction, "some sort of extramarital relationship. None of which would provide a certain motive." Williams paused for a thought, "Harry, on second thought, I will have my Homicide detectives visit Mr. Sam McCoy, just to be sure."

Harry agreed, "We didn't have a chance to talk to him yet, Will. We wanted to get Mike's input first. But maybe active gold shields will carry more weight with their questions."

Then Big Will continued, "My findings with Sean's activities at school indicate that he was definitely involved with drugs. And where there are drugs, there's drug money. And where there's drug money, there's a motive. I know that we're not talking tens of thousands of dollars. But in time it could've headed in that direction. It's a possible motive for someone to stalk and kill young Sean. I think that what we'll do is turn all that info over to Freddie and let his narcotics detectives connect the dots. They can refer it back to my Bureau if they find some connection between drugs and his death."

"Ah…" Harry started to speak but waited to be recognized by Big Will.

"Did I forget something, Harry?"

"No Big Will. But it's what we haven't thought of that concerns me."

The entire table looked toward Harry, confused. Then he continued. "I don't wish to have this sound callous, but I'm hoping that we find a definite connection between Sean and the reason he, specifically, was killed."

Mike recoiled. "What are you talking about, Harry? You actually want there to be someone out to kill my son?"

Harry cleared his throat before clarifying his intention. "I was just thinking… If it wasn't young Sean that was supposed to be the victim, that means that there is someone who might still be looking to kill the intended target. Maybe you? Maybe Joe?" Harry posed the question.

Big Will then replied. "We're handing this info on Sean to the Narco Squad for them to work. We'll deal with whatever they come up with. Freddie can keep us informed. Let's not jump to conclusions."

Everyone at the Round Table nodded with agreement as Lavon was delivering the first of the orders.

"Uh-oh," Chaz grunted as he jumped from his chair. "Excuse me. I'll be right back," he apologized before scurrying across the floor to the restroom.

Almost unanimously the group harmonized, "Damned water pills!"

IT was late morning when Chief Will Williams returned to Headquarters. When he stepped from the elevator on the third floor he hesitated. Instead of walking down the hall to the left to return to the Homicide office, he turned right. He entered the section where the Narcotics Bureau was located and knocked lightly on the door lettered with gold stencil: Captain Riccardo Amico, Chief of Narcotics Bureau.

"Come in," sounded a cheerful voice.

Entering the expanse of corner office windows, Williams spread a wide smile across his face. "Morning Ric. Hope I'm not interrupting anything."

"Heck no. At least nothing that can't wait. What can I do for you Will?"

"That's just the thing. It's what I can do for you. As you know, all units are beating the bushes for any leads on this Morgan investigation. I appreciate all the help we can get on this one. But while we were doing a few interviews at JFK High School, where Sean attended, we came across a bunch of kids selling marijuana. Sean was one of them. Thought you might be interested."

Chief Amico lowered his head slightly so that his eyes peered over the top of his glasses. "I appreciate your help, Will. But we're really not interested in a few kids selling a couple nickel and dime bags of pot. We've got bigger fish to fry."

"These kids are moving about a pound a month, that I know of. What's that, three, four thousand dollars a month?"

Amico's interest perked up. "They're selling that much a month at JFK?"

"As best as I can determine. I was going to drop off this information with Freddie when I came in this morning, but I guess he got tied up in a meeting with you before finishing his night shift. So, figured I'd deliver this info directly to you."

"No. We didn't have a meeting this morning. As a matter of fact, he and the whole night crew were gone before the day shift arrived. But I really appreciate you dropping off this intel. I'll get my day shift on this, and maybe we can follow the food chain upstream."

"If you get any information that remotely relates to Sean Morgan's…"

Ric cut short Will's request, "You'll be the very first person I call. Thanks again, Will."

Big Will returned to his own office and wondered why Freddie would mislead him about having to meet with the Chief, and why he didn't have time to meet with the Coterie? When Big Will's curiosity was raised, answers would follow. It was just a matter of persistence.

Then his curiosity about Freddie was interrupted by a phone call. "Chief Williams, Homicide Bureau," he announced.

The voice on the other end was definitely Hispanic and very young.

"Chief Williams. I was thinking about helping Sean. He really was a friend. So I just want to help you get even with who killed him."

"I understand," Williams agreed.

"Well, you should be lookin' to talk to a black dude named T-Bone. He's around the school all the time, but he ain't been around since Sean was killed. Maybe he's laying low? I don't know. That's all."

The Chief was about to say *Thanks Ray*, when the caller hung up.

By 1 p.m. the question of Freddie's absence still gnawed at Williams, and even more than before, he wanted answers. Will thought of calling Freddie but felt that it was a matter better handled face to face. An hour later Will was pulling into Freddie's driveway. He thought that it was sufficient time for Freddie to catch a few hours of sleep after a long night shift. The sprawling ranch style house had a three-car attached garage. Even before exiting his car, Will observed that the grounds were professionally groomed, and that there were several security cameras. There were no other vehicles parked in the driveway or on the street in the immediate area.

Williams approached the front entrance and rang the bell. He could hear the chimes as they sounded throughout the house. There was no response. Will, ever a dutiful investigator, went around to check the rear of the house. Making a complete circle around the house, he peered into the garage. There were two empty bays and a Corvette up on blocks in the spot closest to the house. Freddie was not home.

THE Desk Sergeant at Precinct Twelve laid a small stack of blank forms on the counter and pushed them across. There was a fair amount of paperwork to be filed when reporting a stolen vehicle. "Here are the required forms for a UUV."

"For a what?" the young man questioned.

"That's what we call it. A UUV, Unauthorized Use of Vehicle. So, let me see your license and registration, Sir," the officer requested.

"Why? You giving me a ticket? Man, I'm not speeding. Someone ripped off my damn truck. Why you hassling me? I need you to find my truck!" The young man, in his mid-twenties, began to get more frustrated as he threw his registration and license across the desk. "Sir, you realize that it probably took less time to steal my damn truck than it will take for me to fill out this damn paperwork!"

"I asked for your license and registration," the officer paused as he looked at the name on the documents the man had tossed at him, "Mr. Donalson, so that I could help you file the vehicle theft reports. But since you're so cooperative, I will need you to fill out the top of the Stolen or Missing Vehicle Report, and then you'll have to fill out the first three sections of the Incident Report." Then the officer slid his pen down to several more lines and placed checkmarks. "And fill out these lines, and then we only have one more report to file, the DMV Affidavit. You can use that table over there," the officer pointed across the room to a small table that was bolted to the wall. "Call me when you're done, and I'll check it over for you."

A half hour later, a more sedate victim walked up to the desk. The young man seemed to have changed his attitude completely. "Officer? I got that paperwork done. Officer?"

The Desk Sergeant smiled at the complainant as he took the reports from the young man. "Tyrell Donalson. You still live at 318 Evelyn Tower?"

"Yep," he answered.

The Desk Sergeant began comparing the information on the license and registration to the information written on the reports. "This is a 2018 Ford F350 pickup truck? Black?"

"Yep."

"And when did you last see the truck?"

"Last night when I parked it in the parking lot about 9:30... and before you ask, yes, it was locked. I really need that truck for my work. What are the chances you'll get it back for me?"

"Usually stolen cars are taken for joy rides. Trucks? Now that's a different matter. Those usually end up in chop shops or at the bottom of the Niagara River."

"Niagara River?" Tyrell balked. "What do you mean?"

"Oh yeah. There have to be dozens of vehicles in there. Especially where the river runs into the lake. The current can carry cars a mile downstream before they get buried in the silt on the bottom. And the current is so strong that even police divers won't go down there. If that's where your truck ends up, forget about it. Just take the insurance money and get a new truck," the officer suggested.

"Thanks for your help officer." As soon as Tyrell departed the police station he called for a ride.

"Hey Bax. It's Tyrell. Uh-huh. Got it all under control. The truck is gonna disappear tonight. And I know a place where nobody will find it. Uh-huh. Oh, by the way. Can you get someone to pick me up at Genesee and Humboldt? Thanks, bro. See you tonight."

CHAPTER 13

IDENTIFICATION AND REVELATION

Two detectives stood at Big Will's half-opened office door. "Boss?" the one spoke to attract his attention.

Without raising his head from the paperwork spread out before him, the Chief answered, "Have something for me?"

"Yessir. On that homeless OD last week. We can confidently say it was not an accidental overdose."

"Oh no? How's that?" Williams asked as he lifted his hand to receive their report.

The first detective announced as he handed the file to Williams, "The homeless guy was identified as Gus Trumble. Last known address several years ago was Poughkeepsie, New York. DOB - oh nine, fourteen, thirty-eight. His rap sheet goes back to long before I was born. Mainly burglaries, stolen property, and a few assaults. No drug charges though. None."

Then the second detective added, "The M.E. found no track marks. There were numerous old tattoos, gang related. The old guy had scurvy, scoliosis, and advanced lung and throat cancer. He probably was going to check out by the end of the year anyway. There was no reason to kill this poor bastard."

The other detective suggested, "Maybe it was a mercy killing. The toxicology report shows that the heroin in his system was near pure and would have killed him instantly. Yet there were no works found."

Williams then asked, "So your determination is that he was murdered?"

"Looks that way Boss. Trumble was put down like a dog."

"Thanks Bob, John. Let me look over this file and I'll get it back to you," Williams stated. "Just what I needed. Number 32 for the year, and its only April."

As the one pair of detectives left the commander's office, another pair waited outside the door. Chief Williams waved, gesturing for them to come in. "And what do you have for me?"

Without hesitation one detective offered, "Chief. We think it's a drug deal gone bad. Looks like he got ripped off."

"What the hell are you talking about? Who got ripped off?" Williams asked.

"Sorry, Chief," the second detective interjected. "The victim was identified as Clarence 'T-Bone' Benson, 22 years old, low level drug dealer for the Freedom Boyz. He had no ID, no money, and no drugs when he was found on Dutton. But what is really interesting is, what you asked us to look for. We checked with the evidence unit and they did document dual tire tracks by the body. Just thought you should know."

"Thank you, guys. Give me the Benson file as soon as you have your work-up done."

"Sure thing, Chief." The first detective acknowledged.

FREDDIE Taylor was sitting at his oversized rolltop desk in the study of his home. He crossed his feet, resting his heels on the edge of the desk as he dialed his phone.

"Chief of Homicide, Williams," declared the answering voice.

"Hey BW, how are you doing?" Freddie asked in a chipper voice. "I heard that you were looking for me. Something I can do for you, BW?"

"Ah. Oh, yes. Yesterday I came across some information I thought you'd be interested in. Thought I'd give it to you this morning, but Amico said that you left early. So, I left it with him. It's probably something best for the day shift to work anyway."

Freddie lifted his feet off the desk and spun to the left where he replayed the video, which was recorded by his security cameras earlier in the day. He watched Big Will as he walked around the residence, looking into the house and garage windows. "Oh, so that's all it was? I thought it might be something really important. But while I got you on the phone – that meeting with Amico didn't materialize this morning, and it was just as well because I ended up helping a friend with a big problem. Did I miss anything important at the Round Table this morning?"

"It was informative, Freddie. I can tell you that. It got a bit testy for a few minutes there, but everything worked out in the end."

"There was some contention with what the guys dug up?" Freddie questioned.

"You could say that. As it turned out, Mike's boy was selling weed to other kids at school. He had a regular little business going."

"Really? That must've been a shocker for Joe and Mike," Freddie stated. And with a slight tone of sarcasm he added, "Bet Mike never seen that coming."

Big Will sensed a touch of cynicism in his response. "What do you mean by that, Freddie?"

"Oh nothing. Just that something like that is so unexpected. People always think that their kids can do no wrong. That's all," Freddie explained nonchalantly. "So, that's the info you left with Chief Amico?"

"Yeah. That's all it was. Now I suppose you're gonna catch a couple hours nap before coming in tonight, so I'll let you go."

"No. I'm taking off tonight. Lempke will be filling in on the midnight shift. But if you need anything, BW. Just give me a call. I'll be around."

"Okay, Freddie. Thanks."

After the call was concluded Big Will now had a few more questions that were gnawing at him. The conversation had produced an emotion that he just couldn't bring into focus.

IT was almost quitting time. The afternoon shift had begun to straggle in when another knock came to the Chief's door. The knock failed to break his trance-like concentration. The second knock was louder and startled Big Will.

"Day dreaming?" asked Joe Morgan.

"No. You ever get a feeling… like a memory that you just can't visual-ize?"

Joe shrugged his shoulders. "Uh-huh. Happens all the time."

"So, what brings you up here? We just spoke this morning. How is Mike doing?" Big Will asked.

With an air of distraction, Joe looked over the reports and files that were sorted and spread out in neat stacks on the Chief's desk. "Oh. It was quite a shock. A family of cops and the kid is dealing dope." Joe shook his head. "I was going to ask you if maybe you'd like to stop for a couple after work?"

"I'll have to take a rain check on that, Joe. Sharleen is making pot roast tonight. And if I didn't show up after she put so much effort into dinner… there just might be another homicide."

"So, how is Shar doing? I know you said that she was taking it hard with the last of the kids moving out-of-state." Joe continued to peruse the files.

"She's doing better. Now she is obsessed with cooking. Can't you tell? I've put on ten pounds."

Joe laughed as he looked at Big Will's waistline and then looked up to his face. "How would I notice just ten pounds?"

"Well, you just blew it, Joe. I was about to ask you to join us for dinner."

"Thanks, Big Will. I'm thinking I'll just grab a bite on the way home, or maybe stop at Mike's to see how he is doing. I'm sure he wouldn't have said anything to Chrissy."

"Okay my friend. If you need anything…"

Then Joe asked, "These are new cases?" He pointed to the several files.

"Yeah. Why?"

"What's with this old guy here?" Joe quizzed as he slid the photo out from the manila folder marked 19-032 TRUMBLE, Gus.

"Just a homeless guy. An overdose that we now think was a murder. Why?"

"I don't know... just a feeling. A hunch," he said as he examined the photo of a broken old man with a ratty mane of gray hair. "Could you make a copy of this photo for me, Will? I just want to check something out. I'll get it back to you Monday," Joe promised.

Big Will grabbed a fresh manila folder, slid the photo in, and told Joe, "Take this one. There are dupes. You can give it back when I see you Tuesday at the Round Table."

CHAPTER 14

WORD TRAVELS FAST...IN ALL DIRECTIONS

TEN OFFICERS ASSEMBLED in the briefing room at Precinct Thirteen to prepare for the 4 to 12 tour of duty. Lieutenant Kelsey Clark called the platoon to order.

"Sergeant Oliver will be the Field Training Officer for Recruit Officer Theo Radcliff, who has been detailed to us for two weeks," she said to introduce the new face. "Sarge, make sure we send him back the way we got him." The Lieutenant requested, before reading the standing orders, for all patrol units to be on the lookout for a truck with dual rear wheels. She added, "You all know what that's about."

One of the officers challenged the others, "Last night I pulled over three trucks with tandem wheels. I bet nobody can top that tonight."

Another officer asked, "What happens if we find the right truck? How do we know if we got lucky? Just because the truck has dual wheels?"

Another officer shouted, "You'll know if you get lucky. The driver will look like J.Lo and she'll give you her phone number."

As the group started to get rowdy Lieutenant Clark intervened, "Oliver, you take the L car with Radcliff. I'll use one of the unmarked cars. The rest of you know your call signs: 13-N, 13-S, 13-E, and 13-W, as usual. And no more than one car out of service at a time for lunch." As the group started to file out of the briefing room, the Lieutenant handed out the nightly "Hot Sheet"- a list of vehicles stolen within the past 48 hours.

THE days were starting to get longer, and with daylight savings time, Tyrell had to wait until almost 10 p.m. before he dared to pull his truck out of the abandoned garage where he had it stashed.

"He don't have to tell me again," Tyrell complained to himself before placing the phone back to his ear. "Yo, Bax. I got it covered. Yep. Yep. I got Frenchy with me. He gonna follow me to the foot of Ferry Street where I'll run that sons-a-bitch off the pier. An he's gonna bring me back." Tyrell lowered the phone again, rolled his eyes, and mouthed another profanity. He brought the phone back up to his ear again. "Okay, bro. Okay. I'll leave the plates on the truck. Uh-huh. I promise you, nobody will ever see that truck again!"

Frenchy was the nickname for Maurice, whom his friends thought sounded like a French name. Frenchy was one of the favorite drivers for the Freedom Boyz. When Bax wanted to be chauffeured, Frenchy was the man. Whenever the Boyz needed a car for short-time use, Frenchy would boost one. A few days later it would end up in a chop shop. There wasn't a car that he couldn't hotwire, and given a decent set of wheels, he could outrun any driver on the road. That included the police.

"This 911 moves like lightning," Frenchy bragged, as if the car was his. "We're gonna make some cash on this one. The paddle shift is sweet, but we can't mess around with it now," he cautioned. "Maybe later we'll have some fun."

"Just do what you're told Frenchy," Tyrell insisted. "Follow me over to the west side and keep the speed down. We don't need to have any cops stopping us for bullshit traffic tickets. We'll take the side streets over there, run the truck off the end of the pier, and I jump in your car and you bring me back. It's that simple."

"Got you covered, Tyrell," Frenchy assured.

And all went according to plan until Tyrell made the wrong turn onto Grant Street and headed north, when he needed to be traveling west. It wasn't entirely his fault since he was an east side kid who was totally out of his element on the upper west side. To compound the problem, Frenchy realized what happened but was unable to call Tyrell, as he was busy steering the powerful car while his phone was still in his pocket. Frenchy flashed his headlights as he attempted to pass Tyrell's pickup. The move failed to get Tyrrell's attention, but it did catch the attention of a police cruiser headed south on Grant.

Sergeant Oliver spun his car around and instructed the rookie, "Check the Hot Sheet to see if that Porsche is on it." Then he called out the letters and numbers. "Charlie, Adam, Edward, Eight, Six, Seven, Five."

The young officer answered, "It's on the list." And he repeated the plate numbers.

"Notify the dispatcher that 13-North is in pursuit of a white Porsche 911, northbound on Grant toward Forest." He then switched on the siren and overhead lights.

The 911 then darted into the oncoming lane and shot past the F350.

The young recruit then started yelling, "What the...look Sarge! It's the pickup with dual wheels. And that's on the Hot Sheet, too." Unfortunately, he was shouting into an open mic.

There was a T-intersection coming up at Forest Avenue. The Porsche made a hard right and accelerated as it slid around the corner. The Ford pickup made a left and headed westbound. Now that Tyrell was on one of the main streets of the city, he got his bearings and proceeded to make a left turn onto Niagara Street, which ran parallel with the river. Tyrell was determined to reach the Ferry Street pier and boat launch.

Sergeant Oliver grabbed the mic from the rookie and called out the chase as he drove. Multiple units were converging on Niagara Street at various points. Three cars blocked off Niagara just north of Ferry.

Meanwhile, Frenchy had shaken several patrol units that attempted to keep up with him. He continued to zigzag through the unfamiliar neighborhood looking for Tyrell.

"Damn!" Tyrell shouted. He attempted to swerve around the barrier of squad cars, sending the pickup careening across one lawn, smashing through a picket fence, taking out the corner of a garage, and fishtailing onto the adjoining side street. The next block allowed Tyrell to continue onto other side streets, until he found himself westbound on Ferry. He knew that if he floored it, he could blow through the intersection at Niagara and make it to the pier. "Fly Mother, Fly!" he screamed as he stomped the accelerator to the floor.

The officers who witnessed the event estimated that the pickup had to be going at least seventy miles an hour when it entered the intersection.

Some of the officers who were trying to keep up with the Porsche, northbound on Niagara, said that it was probably going close to a hundred, when the two vehicles collided in the intersection at Niagara and Ferry. It was a spectacular, legendary airborne crash. More amazing was the fact that neither driver was killed. Both ended up in critical condition, under guard at the County Medical Center.

WORD travels fast among police circles, from the officers on the scene, to those in other precincts, to the off-duty officers, and sometimes even to the retired ones. It was just before midnight that Joe was startled from his sleep. Usually, only bad news comes at that hour.

"Hello?" Joe answered the phone cautiously.

"Joe. Big Will. I'm at County Medical Center…"

"You okay, Will?" Joe asked with great concern.

"Yeah. Yeah. I just wanted to call you to let you know that I was called out on this MVA."

"What? Why were you called out on a motor vehicle accident? Was a copper involved?"

"No. Nothing like that. We got the truck with the dual wheels. Or what's left of it," Big Will confided. "It was reported stolen earlier today, and then it was involved in a crash with another stolen car. Look, the accident is not the point. The point is, I'm sure that this is the truck with the dual wheels that we've been looking for. The one that we think picked up Sean's killer after they torched that car."

"Did you get the driver?" Joe questioned.

"The driver's in custody here at the CMC. And get this, the truck that was reported stolen was being driven by the registered owner. So, it wasn't actually stolen."

"Did he say anything about Sean's case?" Joe pried.

"He's not saying anything to anyone. The dude's in a coma. It'll be a miracle if he pulls through. But we know who he is, and that is a big lead that we didn't have before. Tomorrow morning I'm going to have the lab guys compare the tire tread on this truck to the casts we made at that burn-out, and the tracks at the Dutton Street homicide."

"What homicide on Dutton?" Joe demanded.

"I'll fill you in on as much as I can tomorrow, after I get the report from the forensics team." Big Will was almost as excited giving the information, as Joe was to receive it.

"Thanks, Will. I can't wait to talk to you tomorrow."

Big Will had a smile spread all over his face. "I just wanted you to hear it from me, Joe, and for you to get it as soon as possible. Now get some sleep. I'll talk to you tomorrow."

"Thanks again Big Will. Like I'll be getting any sleep tonight."

Will laughed, "Neither will I. Look, I really have to go. The reporters are coming in."

BAX was pacing back and forth, looking at his Rolex, and ranting about incompetent low-lifes. His girlfriend tried to calm him. "Honey, you gotta settle down. You get like this, and then you blow up. Shit happens that you can't control, Bax," she pleaded. "Chill out, honey."

His rage exploded as he spun around with an open hand that caught Roz across the side of her head and sent her tumbling to the floor. "I told you, Roz, don't ever try to tell me what to do. I tell everyone else what to do, and when they don't… one way or another, people will die!"

Before Roz could lift herself up onto the sofa, the phone rang. Bax answered the call during the first ring. "Yo, it's me. Where the hell you been? I called you and texted you and heard nothing from you. Damn it. You answer when I call."

"Well excuse me," responded a cool, hushed voice. "I've been pretty busy trying to get information for you."

"So, you know what's happening? You know that damn Tyrell screwed up so bad that he's gonna get the cops breathing down my back. Ain't no way!" Bax vowed. "Now tell me, what do you know about the situation?"

"I can tell you that both your boys, Tyrell and Frenchy, are at CMC. They are both technically under arrest, but neither one will be talking for the near future. Tyrell is in a medically induced coma. Your other boy, Frenchy, is in surgery now. So, the police can't even question him."

"Jesus, these stupid-ass bastards. Can't do a simple thing right. All they had to do is dump that damn truck. Which is where?" Bax inquired. "Where's that truck now?" Bax demanded.

"Probably in the police impound by now. It'll be held in secure storage as evidence," the voice explained.

"So, what can you do?" Bax asked.

"About the truck? Nothing."

"What the hell am I paying you for?" Bax yelled into the phone. "Can you make sure that neither one of those punks get the opportunity to talk? You know what I mean."

"Perhaps. But taking a chance like that… it's going to cost you extra," the voice stated without emotion.

"I don't care what it costs!" Bax shouted into the phone. "You just make sure that they don't talk! Understand? Nobody's takin' me down!" he screamed as he threw the phone against the wall.

A few minutes later, after pacing until he had calmed himself, Bax reached into the metal box at the end of the coffee table and grabbed another of the cheap disposable phones. He dialed a number and on the second ring it was answered. "That's better. So, today's phone is out of commission. For the next 24 hours you can call me on this number. Okay?"

The calm voice agreed, "As soon as I have anything definite, or if one of them should stop breathing, I'll call you." The phone beeped twice and went silent.

"Damn you, you son-of-a-bitch. You don't hang up on me!" Bax ranted, although Roz was the only person who heard him.

IT had been two hours since the crash occurred, and the chaotic cluster of press reporters had staked out their positions at the entrance of the emergency room. Their cameramen had already picked the bones of the accident scene.

"Wonder what took them so long?" Lt. Lempke asked Chief Williams. "They listen to our radios and sometime get to a crime scene before we do. Weren't you off-duty, Chief?" Then he raised his head as if a thought registered. "Oh, sure. Now I remember. You were probably called in because this might be part of that murder case. Lt. Morgan's son."

Will Williams maintained eye contact with the Narcotics Lieutenant, absent of any emotion or verbal response.

The Lieutenant just continued jabbering, "I would've been off tonight too, but I took the overtime when Freddie Taylor booked off. But I called him to give him a heads-up on what he was missing." Then he looked around at the crowded waiting room filled with dark uniforms and many rumpled suits. "This is a pretty big thing, huh?" he asked the Chief.

At that moment, Big Will was distracted by the bright lights of cameras, the grind of reporters shouting questions, and a couple people pushing their way through the mob as the door to the ER opened.

"We heard that there was a car chase?" one reported asked.

"Was anyone shot?" another begged.

Yet another questioned, "Is this about the cop's kid that was killed?" The reporter turned to his cameraman, "Cops are like that when it comes to their own families. Shoot first and…"

The reporter was shoved aside by the Chief of Detectives and the Duty Officer as they pushed forward toward the ER entrance.

"Are they still alive?" was the last question yelled before Chief Smyth emerged into the relative sanity of the ER waiting room. He looked across the crowd until he found a familiar face that stood out in, and above, the crowd. Smyth quickly headed in that direction.

"The last time there were this many top cops gathered at a hospital ER was two years ago when an officer was ambushed while responding to a domestic call," Lempke rambled on.

Williams looked to the Chief of Detectives as if he was the cavalry arriving.

"What the hell are those vultures hanging around for?" the Chief of Detectives asked. "They don't think that we're going to tell them anything. Do they?"

Big Will responded, "Just the usual. This is an ongoing investigation that is developing. We'll know more tomorrow and will release whatever information we have then."

"Commissioner Howes should've offered you that PR job," Chief Smyth said.

"He did. But I'm just fine where I am," Williams rebutted.

"So, what do we have here, Will?" Chief Smyth asked, trying to edge close enough to Will to create some semblance of privacy.

Big Will summarized, "Two perps with stolen vehicles. That's all they're being charged with at this time. Just to keep them on ice. However, both have the same gang tats, FB4EVER."

"Freedom Boyz," Smyth declared. "Ric Amico has had his share of problems with them. Then you think this is drug related somehow?"

"You mean with Sean Morgan?" Big Will asked. "As you know, we only have a suspicion that the one vehicle, the pickup truck, may have been at the scene where the Sheriffs found the burned-out car, which we believe was the vehicle used to kill young Morgan. But," Will cautioned, "we don't have proof of that yet. We're waiting for forensics."

"And that would tie Sean Morgan into this drug ring, how?"

"I didn't say it would, Howie. I'm just saying the Freedom Boyz may somehow be linked to Sean's murder. Not that Sean Morgan was one of them. We got a long way to go yet. A lot of the puzzle pieces are still in the box."

"Well, what's the status of the prisoners?" Chief Smyth requested.

"The one driving the pickup truck is identified as Tyrell Donalson. He's one of the shot callers of the Freedom Boyz. He's in critical condition. Still unconscious, in a coma actually. The second perp is Maurice Montour. They call him Frenchy. He's a trusted gopher for the gang. He's been in surgery the past couple hours. He learned the hard way that, when it comes to collisions, a F350 will beat a 911 every time," Big Will smirked. "It looks like the Freedom Boyz are gonna be short a couple geniuses at the breakfast table."

"Excuse me," Lt. Lempke interrupted. "I couldn't help but hear you Chiefs mentioning the Freedom Boyz. Should I have notified Chief Amico? Do you want me to call him now?"

Chief Smyth answered, "I don't think that will be necessary, Lieutenant. It's two in the morning, the prisoners won't be going anywhere soon, and I will be talking to your Chief in the morning." Then as an afterthought, he directed Lt. Lempke, "I think it would be prudent to post an officer at each of the suspect's rooms. And," he emphasized, "keep those damned news jackals fifty feet from the ER entrance."

THE Saturday morning sun rose about an hour after Joe fell asleep. Shortly after that, the phone rang and destroyed any prospect of him getting two continuous hours of sleep. Joe rolled over and reached for the phone. "Hello? Big Will?" Joe asked.

"No, Dad. It's me. Mike."

"Oh. Sorry. What time is it, Mike?" Joe mumbled.

"Seven fifteen. Thought you'd be up already. I didn't mean to wake you."

No, that's alright. What's up?" Joe asked.

"I just got a call from a Sergeant friend at HQ who said that they found the pickup truck that was involved in Sean's death. I was going to go to HQ and see what's going on. He said that everything was hush-hush, and he didn't have any more details. I just wondered if you wanted to go with me?"

"Yeah, Mike. I'm already on it," Joe announced. "Just waiting for verification of the facts."

"It's Saturday morning. You were sleeping. How would you know anything about this? I just got the call myself!"

"The Coterie works in mysterious ways," Joe confided. "I'll call you later when I get all the right information. Okay? In the meantime, I'm going to try to get a few more hours of sleep." Without saying good-bye, Joe hung up the phone and rolled back to a comfortable spot.

CHAPTER 15

WORDS OF WISDOM AND SUPPORT

FORTY YEARS AGO, a very young police officer, his bride of two years, and a son only months old, moved into the house on Barclay Drive. It was a fixer-upper that was barely affordable in a solid neighborhood, with an excellent school district, and within walking distance to St. Catherine of Sienna Church. Joe, Amy, and Mike always attended St. Catherine's eleven o'clock mass on Sunday. Throughout the years the church played a major part of Joe's life where the Morgan family received all the sacraments, including the marriage of Mike and Chrissy, the Baptism, First Communion, and Confirmation of Sean, and the funeral of Joe's beloved Amy, four years ago. When the most recent crisis arose, Joe again turned to St Catherine's and Father Sullivan for strength.

It was after the service that Joe remained in the same pew where he had sat for decades, waiting for the church to empty. Sitting half on the seat, and half kneeling, Joe's forearms rested on the top of the pew ahead, while his hands were clasped in prayer. He was so entranced by the inner conversation he was having, that he did not notice Father Sullivan had knelt down next to him.

The soft voice asked, "Is there something troubling you, Joe?"

For an instant Joe thought it was the Lord speaking directly to him. He opened his eyes and looked to the priest. "Oh, it's you, Sully."

"I'm sorry to disappoint you, Joseph." Sully used his full name when he wanted to get Joe's attention. "Thinking about Sean?" he asked.

"Thinking about all of it, Sully," Joe acknowledged. "For the past month, it's all weighing me down. Amy's death. Now Sean. Maybe, somehow, I brought this on myself?"

"It's the business we're in, Joe. The people business. I sprinkle water on a newborn's head, and a few years later I give the same child his Last Rites. You, you do what you can to help people. Offer a helping hand. Try to do what is right. And sometimes it bites us in the ass. No, it is not fair. You'd think that God would make things fair. But perhaps it's one of the ways he tests our faith. That's all I can figure."

"Well, you're no help, Sully." Joe lamented. "But perhaps you can help," he said as he pulled a manila folder from inside his jacket. He then held the well-worn note that Father Sullivan delivered to him so many weeks earlier. "I know that you didn't read this back when it was given to you, but I thought maybe now you should." Joe handed the paper to Sully.

After a moment of reading and contemplation, the priest responded. "Oh, my dear. Who could have written such an awful note? Why would someone do this to you?" Sully probed.

"That's what I'm trying to find out, Sully." Joe handed the priest a photo. "Is this the man who handed you the note, to give to me?"

Father Sullivan did not have to study the picture long before answering. "Yes, it is. The hair is the same. Long, hanging over his ears. The sad face wrinkled with time. Like a worried man. But he was not as pale as in this picture. But it's definitely him. What did he have to say about this horrible note?"

"He's pale because he's dead, Sully. I never got a chance to talk to him."

"Now I know what's bothering you, Joe. Because someone wrote a nasty note, obviously meant to torture you during a low point in your life, you are going to trust a stranger's warped opinion over your own faith. I would bet he was a tortured soul himself."

Joe reflected for a moment. "What you say makes sense. I know it. Believe me, I've turned my memory inside out, looked in all the corners of my mind, and can't think of anyone that I have caused to hate me like this."

"We have very little control over hate, Joe. We can only control love. That which we give and, hopefully, receive in return. Love is not something you have a shortage of. So, please, trust in yourself. Trust in your friends. And most of all… keep the faith."

"Now that helped," Joe acknowledged. "Thank you, Sully."

CHAPTER 16
Tuesday, April 9, 2019

Good News and Bad News

With the phone calls that were flying back and forth over the weekend and the "Special Reports" that were broadcast on all the local news channels, the Tuesday morning assembly of the Coterie had everyone at the Round Table before 9:30 a.m., anxious for an up-to-the-minute update. Even Lavon felt the electricity in the air as she added another placemat to the normal setting of six.

"I won't bother to take up your time," Lavon stated. "I'll just fill the regular orders...unless anyone wants to make a change." Without a single response she hurried off to the kitchen, while Chaz hurried off to the restroom. When Chaz returned, he reported the roll call with his greeting: "Captain Big Will, Captain Joe, Sergeants Harry and Vern, and Lieutenant Freddie. All present and accounted for, plus one, Lieutenant Mike."

Joe cleared his throat to speak. "There have been definite advancements in the investigation since we last met. Some originating from our own efforts. But most importantly arising from the event involving the two vehicles and their drivers, which I'm sure you all are aware of. But the most revealing detail is that the two suspects were members of the Freedom Boyz gang, who assumed their name from the Freedom Housing Projects where they mainly operate. Freddie can give us more on that aspect of the investigation in a few minutes."

Harry asked, "Then there is a drug connection?"

Joe answered, looking at Mike, "Not that we know for sure." He began counting on his fingers as he ran down what they did know. "One - there is the fact that Sean and a couple classmates were selling grass. Two - he was killed intentionally, possibly by a Freedom Boyz member, but that is only linked by an ID on the driver and owner of the truck, which wasn't the murder vehicle. And, three - the tires on the pickup that was involved in last Friday's crash were a positive match for the tire tracks found near the recovered murder vehicle. It's a loose connection. We have to work on making that connection between Sean's death and the Freedom Boyz. Once that hurdle is cleared, maybe we'll find the specific motive."

"Then that is the direction we're going in?" Harry asked for clarification.

"No, Harry," Joe said. "I'm just saying it's possible. Is it a coincidence that my grandson was selling weed and was killed by a gang notorious for their drug trade? Or did that gangbanger accidentally kill Sean, when it was meant for Mike or me? Personally, I think that someone was after me, and Sean just happened to be in the wrong place at the wrong time. But I can't figure out what connection there would be between me and that drug gang. Unless there is an old homicide case that I worked years ago, I just can't think of a case that specifically involved them. And, if that's it, why now? I've been out of that game for six years."

Big Will interjected, "It's the evidence that will solve this case, Joe. Not your feelings, or your guilt. We still haven't found a specific motive tied to you. As soon as we can talk with these two guys, Donalson and Montour, the sooner we'll get the evidence we need."

Vern questioned Big Will, "You haven't interviewed those bastards yet? It's been three days."

"There's a problem there, Vern. They are both still in ICU. Donalson is in a coma. Montour is recovering from surgery and is heavily sedated. The doctors won't let us talk to them until they're out of ICU."

"You got guards on their rooms?"

"Of course," Big Will assured.

"Well why not put one of your own detectives in uniform in the room. That way they could talk to the scumbags when nobody was around," Harry suggested. "That's how we would've done it back in the day."

"That day's come and gone, Harry. Can't play loose and free like we used to. But I can tell you this - as soon as we get the doctor's approval, we will be questioning those two. I've been promised that as soon as they are able to be questioned, I'll be notified."

Not satisfied, Vern pressed, "When do you expect that to happen?"

"Maybe today. Maybe tomorrow. There isn't anybody more anxious to talk to them than me," Big Will declared.

"And Narcotics will also have detectives there to question them," Freddie assured. "I will make it a point of being there with you BW."

"So, what can we do while we wait?" Chaz asked.

"The Narc Bureau is clamping down on the Freedom Boyz operation," Freddie explained. "We're applying as much pressure as we can. My guys on nights are stopping anyone that moves in the Proj. The day shift is doubling their surveillance efforts. We even swapped our two surveillance vans with the State Police, just in case ours were getting seen too much." Looking around the table, Freddie proposed, "A few more eyes on the street couldn't hurt." He winked when his eyes reached Harry.

"It'll be good to be back on the street," Harry declared.

"Hold it right there," Big Will interrupted, holding his hands up defensively. "I agreed that we all could pitch in with fresh eyes and experience, but there is no way I'm gonna let you dinosaurs loose in a war zone. We aren't the Coterie of years gone by."

"Are you suggesting that we're too old to be productive, Captain Will?" Chaz asked. "You know that you and Freddie aren't much younger than the rest of us. As a matter of fact, if I'm not mistaken, I'm a year younger than Freddie, and you and I are exactly the same age."

"Yeah, but I don't have to run to a urinal every fifteen minutes," Williams quipped. "And the rest of you guys...be serious. You all ended your careers as supervisors, not street cops. It's a young man's job out there. Jeez, you don't know how much this job has changed in the past five, eight, ten years."

Harry lifted his jacket away from his waist to display a Colt Cobra .38 snub, holstered on his belt. "We can take care of ourselves."

With a derisive snort, Vern added, "I'm in better shape than most cops half my age. Got a black belt. Granted, perhaps I can't run fast enough to catch some young punk running away from me. But then, I won't be running from anyone either."

"So, what are you suggesting, Vern?

"Look around the table Will. You have almost 200 years of experience here. Detective Sergeant Doyle is one of the most decorated officers ever to wear the uniform. He was one of the best Homicide detectives to come down the pike. He taught most of the guys in your Bureau."

Big Will nodded a begrudging agreement.

Vern continued, "Lieutenant Chaz Bohen. Sure, he pisses a lot, but he is a great strategist and equipment manager. He has busted up more burglary and fencing operations than you can imagine. He worries about those small details. He makes sure that materials and people are in the right place at the right time. And he's the go-to guy for all the gadgets and gizmos."

"Sorry about that joke Chaz," Big Will apologized. "It was out of place. But all the electronics that we used to use back then are outdated. Everything is digital and wireless now. There's stuff now that we never even thought of."

"I still have a lot of that gear in my basement," Chaz admitted. "Most of it works great and, well, if it's outdated, then nobody will be looking for it."

Vern plowed ahead, "And then we have Captain Joe Morgan. One of the best Precinct bosses that I've ever known. Balls as big as melons and as loyal as the day is long. How many shootouts has he been in? Like that last holdup back in '08. Even after taking two slugs, he dragged two cops to safety and was able to take out two shooters." The faces around the table froze, as if Vern had just stepped on a landmine, but he continued obliviously, "Not to mention, Big Will, that it's partly because of Joe that you have the Chief of Homicide job."

"Yeah. I remember that night," Freddie blurted. "I remember that night all too well! I'll never forget it! But it wasn't Joe that took those two slugs, Vern. It was Junior" Freddie exclaimed.

Realizing his insensitivity, Vern begged forgiveness, "Oh shit, Freddie. I wasn't thinking. I'm sorry." He remembered that Officer Al "Junior" Taylor was one of the wounded officers that Morgan dragged out of the line of fire. And it was Freddie's son who didn't make it to the hospital that night.

Joe's chin dropped to his chest and he crossed his arms in reflection. "It was a holdup that we happened to stumble across. Junior was the first one into the store and walked in on a robbery. He was hit before he knew what happened. I did everything I…."

"I know what you did, Joe." Freddie cut him off. "If anyone could have saved Junior, it would have been you." He rested a hand reassuringly on Joe's shoulder. Freddie then turned his attention to Big Will, "That's why Joe, Harry, Chaz, Vern, you and me have to be out there. It's probably the last hoorah for the Coterie."

"Yeah, but Freddie," Big Will began apologetically, "It's not just us. There are other people to take into consideration. Other people who are concerned about us."

"Like who?" Harry asked. "My ex? She's in Arizona. Vern is a devout bachelor, not lucky enough to find a good woman. Chaz' wife, Kitty, is driving him to his grave. How often does she throw you out of the house?" Harry needled Chaz. "Twice a year? And Joe's wife, Amy, has passed. So, who are you talking about Will? Your wife? Freddie's wife?"

"Point taken." Big Will acquiesced.

As Lavon approached the tables with the huge tray with most of the orders, Chief Williams' phone rang. The chatter around the table was quieted as Big Will answered, arched his brows, and exclaimed, "I'll be right there!"

"The hospital?" Freddie asked.

"Uh-huh. I think I'll be grabbing breakfast at CMC." As he stood, Big Will dropped a ten-dollar bill on Lavon's tray.

Freddie also jumped to his feet. "I'm going, too. But I have to make a quick stop back to headquarters, BW. I'll be there as soon as I can."

LIEUTENANT Taylor arrived at the ER and flashed his badge to the Admissions Receptionist. "Have you seen another plainclothes officer come through here in the past fifteen minutes? A really tall black detective?"

"Yes. He stopped to get the room numbers for Mr. Donalson and Mr. Montour. I told him that they were both still in the ICU on the fourth floor. He could check with the nurse's station there."

When Freddie stepped from the elevator, he could see down the corridor that Chief Williams was conferring with a doctor wearing a long white lab coat with the expected stethoscope hung around his neck. When he was half the distance to where the men were standing, he saw the Chief turn and step into a room. Freddie stepped up his pace to almost a trot. "Did I miss anything?" Freddie asked, walking into the room.

"No Lieutenant," Big Will snapped into formal police protocol. "I was just about to introduce myself to Mr. Montour."

Williams turned his attention and directed his comments to the young man in the bed with IVs in both arms, bandages wrapped around his head and most of his left leg, and a full cast on his right leg. "My name is Chief Will Williams. This is Lieutenant Alfred Taylor. It looks like you got banged up pretty bad."

The patient pursed his lips and shrugged his shoulders. He then turned away from the officers.

"We're here because we need to find out what happened? How that accident happened?" Taylor urged. "And where did you get that pickup truck and the Porsche?"

"I don't know what you're talkin' 'bout," Montour groaned as he rattled the cuff on his arm that was secured to the bed rail.

Freddie stepped forward as he reeled off a few facts. "We know that your full name is Maurice Montour. Nickname is Frenchy. You belong to the Freedom Boyz. And Baxter Brown is probably not too happy with you right now. I hear that he has quite the temper," Freddie pronounced as he slammed his portable radio on the metal tray next to the bed, trying to startle the young man.

"So, you know I got a name, and I got a record. So what?" Frenchy challenged Freddie. "I don't belong to nobody. And I don't know anybody named Baxter Brown."

Will stared at the injured man for a moment, then turned to Freddie as he posed a question, "When it comes to saving one man and letting the other one go, who do you think Bax will keep? Frenchy or Tyrell?"

Frenchy moaned and rolled onto his side, turning his back to the officers. "Go away, man. Leave me alone. Can't you see I'm hurtin'?"

"Not as much as your gonna be hurting when Tyrell walks out of here," Williams suggested. "You know what I'm talkin' about."

Freddie piled on, "Right now you're looking at Grand Theft Auto, Reckless Endangerment, and a handful of traffic charges. Whether it's you or Tyrell who wants to talk first, that's the one who gets the deal. You know how that goes down."

Though dispirited, Frenchy crowed defiantly, "I'm not afraid of catching some time. And I ain't afraid that Tyrell will talk on me. We don't do that!" Then he grumbled and pulled the covers over his head, trying to shelter himself from any more questions.

"C'mon, Lieutenant. We'll let him rest and think about his future," Williams said as the two left the room.

From under the sheets Freddie heard Montour say, "You not gonna get me or Tyrell to talk. You got nothin' on us. We actually got you by the balls!"

Frustrated, Freddie followed BW out of the room. No more than ten feet from the door, Freddie stopped, "Oh shit, BW. I left my radio in the room on the tray. Why don't you check with the doctor to see if we can talk to the other one? I'll be right there."

Montour was still sheltered under the sheets as Freddie picked up his radio and had to get in the last word. "Don't be so smart, asshole. Maybe you'll never talk. But we'll find someone who will." A few seconds later Freddie left the room with his portable in hand, a smirk on his face, and instructed the officer who was sitting outside the door, "Make sure only medical staff enter the room. No friends, and no relatives without getting clearance from Chief Williams." He then joined Big Will at the nurse's station and waited for the doctor to return from his rounds.

"Doctor, what is the extent of Montour's injuries?" Freddie asked.

"A closed head injury, compound fractures of his right femur, two fractured ribs, and some internal bleeding which is the most significant problem at the moment. He'll probably be in ICU another couple of days before he's moved down to a recovery room. You can probably talk to him again tomorrow if you'd like. Just keep it short."

"And the other one, Tyrell Donalson?" Chief Williams asked.

"He's still in a medically induced coma until the swelling of the brain is resolved. He also has cervical and spinal injuries. It's a miracle that that young man survived the crash. I don't think that he will be in any condition to talk to anyone for quite a while. At least not today or tomorrow."

"Okay. Thank you, Doctor," Big Will acknowledged. "Please give us a call if there is any substantial change."

ABOUT an hour later, that call did come in. Williams and Taylor were just walking into Headquarters when Big Will's phone rang. "Chief Williams," he answered.

"This is Doctor Nguyen at CMC ICU. You asked that I notify you of any drastic change in either patient."

"Yes. I'm hoping that this is good news, Doctor?" Williams guessed.

"No. I'm sorry to inform you that the patient, Maurice Montour, is deceased. He expired approximately a half hour after you left. We tried everything but could not revive him."

"What?" Williams asked in disbelief. "He was in his early 20's. What did he die from?"

"What happened BW? One of our prisoners died?" Freddie questioned, as Williams motioned for him to wait.

Apologetically the doctor suggested, "It's premature to list COD, but it looks like probable myocardial infarction."

"A heart attack?" Williams asked. "You've gotta be kidding me."

Dr. Nguyen went on to explain, "In a case like this, where a patient is in our care, has had recent surgery, is such a young age, and otherwise in apparent good health, we will submit a request to the M.E. for an autopsy. His postmortem examination will provide us with an exact cause of death. I expect that you will be conducting your own investigation, too, as he was also in your custody?"

"Damn right, Doc," Chief Williams responded. "Is Montour's body still in ICU room 412?"

"Montour is dead?" Freddie interrupted. "What happened?"

Again, Big Will motioned for Freddie not to interrupt.

"Yes, he is." Dr. Nguyen confirmed.

Chief Williams then informed the doctor. "This is being handled as a suspicious death and possible criminal act, and that room is to be considered a crime scene. There was an officer stationed outside that room. Instruct him to wait for me and to not let anyone into the room. I'll be there as soon as I can."

"Whatever I can do to help, Chief Williams," the doctor replied.

As soon as Will finished his call Freddie urged, "So what happened, BW? Did Montour die of his wounds? You want me to go with you BW?"

"I have no idea what he died of, Freddie. But we're sure as hell going to find out. Stay here at headquarters in case I need you. Okay? I'll call you as soon as I have some information."

WHENEVER a prisoner dies in police custody, the ensuing investigation is conducted as if foul play was involved and can be ruled out. This was further complicated with the fact that the death occurred in a hospital immediately after surgery. And naturally there were the obvious concerns about liability.

By the time Chief Williams arrived, his day crew detectives, the Evidence Unit, and Medical Examiner had all been notified and were in route. Williams greeted Dr. Nguyen at the entrance to Montour's room.

"Thank you, Doctor. You said that it was about a half hour after I left that the patient went into this medical emergency?"

"Yes," the doctor verified. "There was a cardiac monitor alarm at the nurse's station. Nurse Philips had just checked on the patient and took his vitals. Everything was within normal parameters. Then the ECG alarm sounded and he straight lined. Before she got to the next room, he coded."

"And the officer. Was he still outside the room? Did he go into the room at all?" the Chief inquired.

"As far as I know, the only time he was in the room was when we responded with the crash cart. He stepped in to see what was going on. Then he went right back out and sat on the chair outside the room."

"Thanks, Doc," Williams said as he jotted notes on his pad. "Oh. A couple other things, if you will. Could I have the names of all your staff who were in this room between the time I left and the time I got back here?"

"Absolutely," Dr. Nguyen agreed. "I'll prepare that for you now."

"And everything in that room - all the equipment, the furniture, and bedding needs to be examined by our forensics team, so nobody is to touch a thing until they say it's clear. Consider this room off limits to all personnel."

"Of course, Chief. Do you have any idea how long that could take?"

"After the M.E. takes the body, we should need only a couple hours," Williams estimated.

IT was later than Chief Williams had intended to stay at HQ. The call to Joe Morgan was the last thing he did before leaving his office.

"So, what happened at the hospital this morning? We haven't heard anything," Joe queried.

"Have you had dinner yet?" Big Will asked.

"I was about to make some mac and cheese, have a bowl of salad, and a beer. Why do you ask?"

"Well since I left the Towne this morning, I haven't had a bite to eat and I'm wondering if you'd like to have dinner? On me," Big Will added.

Joe sensed that there was a good reason for Will to ask him for dinner, especially if he was paying. "The mac and cheese can wait until tomorrow. Where do you want to go?"

"You tell me," Williams left the choice to Joe. "I'm just leaving HQ now. I already called Sharleen and told her I'd be working late." A place and time were agreed upon.

When Chief Williams' black Tahoe pulled into the parking lot at Chef's Restaurant, Joe was already out of his car, waiting. "Hope you're in the mood for Italian," Joe greeted Big Will as he exited the department's vehicle.

"That's funny," Will noted ironically. "Sharleen was making spaghetti tonight."

The current and past Homicide Chiefs were seated at a table where they had some privacy. "This investigation of Sean's murder is getting way out of control," Big Will confided. "Since we, and I mean mostly the Coterie, started to dig into this case, three people have been killed in as many weeks."

"What three, Big Will?"

The current Homicide Chief began to rattle off the victims. "There was that one guy, Trumble. You said that he was definitely the guy who passed the note to your priest. He's homicide number one that is directly tied to this case. His death was no mere overdose. It was a hot shot. He had enough heroin in him to kill five men. Where'd a bum like him get money for that much smack?"

The waiter approached the table and placed a menu in front of each of the gentlemen. "Take your time with your orders. In the meanwhile, would you like anything to drink?"

"You have Heineken on draft?" Joe asked.

"Yes, we do. One Heineken it is. And you, sir?" the waiter asked, turning his attention to Williams.

"Cutty Sark, on the rocks, please. Ah…," Big Will reconsidered, "it's been a long day. Make it a double."

"Very well, gentlemen. I'll be right back with your drinks."

"Where was I?" Big Will regained his train of thought. "Oh. Yeah. The second vic was T-Bone Benson. A definite member of Freedom Boyz. If you recall, he was the banger we found shot in the old warehouse on Dutton. Next to his body were truck tire tracks matching the imprints found by the burned-out car that we're certain was used to run down Sean. Chatter from the street says that the boss of the Freedom Boyz, Baxter Brown, had him whacked for killing a cop's kid."

"Tying up loose ends?" Joe wondered aloud.

"That's only rumor," Big Will continued, "but that would be murder number two. The third happened this morning at the Medical Center. Those two kids who piled up in the stolen vehicles – one being the driver of the truck that left the tracks at the Dutton murder scene, and also by the burned-out car. His name is Tyrell Donalson. His partner in crime is Frenchy Montour. He's another Freedom Boyz player. Freddie and I questioned Frenchy this morning about the truck."

"Did he give up anything?" Joe urged.

"You know these punks, Joe. They all think they're hard asses. He clammed up and stopped just short of demanding a lawyer. But I think he was really concerned that his partner might roll on him."

"You think that this Frenchy might have cracked?" Joe pressed.

"There's a chance. But we'll never know now. Somebody got to him between the time Freddie and I left the hospital, and the time we got back to headquarters. About 30 minutes."

"The killer was probably there when you and Freddie were there. How was he killed?" Joe questioned.

"The M.E.'s initial report indicates that he was poisoned. Someone closed the IV drip, injected a fentanyl-cyanide solution into the IV tube, and waited for someone to continue the drip. From the interviews I conducted this afternoon, it looks like the only people that came into the room were a nurse to check his vitals, and a doctor. The nurse recalls that the drip had not been started yet, although it was indicated on the chart. She opened the IV drip, and inadvertently killed him. And the doctor? We haven't been able to ID him yet."

"But who else could've spiked the IV?" Joe probed. "There was a guard at the door, right?'

"Yeah. He swears that the only people to enter that room after we left was a doctor, for just a few seconds who walked in and then came right out, and the nurse who we identified as Jan Phillips. I've already interviewed her. The officer was certain that the doctor just barely stepped into the room before turning around and leaving."

"And the officer didn't get the doctor's name?" Joe asked.

"No. The officer said that he was wearing a doctor's white coat and had a stethoscope around his neck. That's all he noticed. The officer said that he was reading a paper when the doctor went into the room. And before he could get up to check on what the doctor was doing, the doctor was on his way out. The detail officer said that he was only in there a couple seconds."

"Did he recall if the doctor went into the room before the nurse?"

Big Will shook his head, "No. I asked but he didn't recall."

"You believe him?" Joe questioned. "Or do you think the copper left his post? Or worse?" Joe hinted.

"I don't know what to think at this point, Joe. But what I do know is that it's getting really dangerous out there. I am afraid that one or more of our guys might get hurt. I don't want to risk that."

Morgan had fixed on Big Will's eyes. "Not because it was my grandson, or that my son has suffered such a great loss, but it's because we're all cops from the old school. That is why all of us are willing to take that risk. If it were any other of us that this happened to, we'd all still be here. It's not your call to make. You know that, Big Will. But if you want to tell them that you've lost your faith in them, go right ahead."

"C'mon, Joe. I love you guys like brothers. All of you. We've been through so much together through the years. I don't want to lose any friends to these ruthless bastards running the projects. As far as I'm concerned, they can all kill each other and it would only improve our world... even if it made a lot more work for the Homicide Bureau."

"Well," Joe consoled, "let's make sure that doesn't happen. You're not going to lose any friends. We'll just have to change our tactics a bit. Remember in the early days at Bloody Eight? We used to kick in the doors and drag the bastards out. Then when we got a bit older, and wiser, we learned how to smoke them out. So, let's put our heads together and figure out if this drug gang is behind Sean's murder, and if so how to deal with them."

"Damn you, Joe," Big Will exclaimed. "There you go again. You're the only man I know who can take the worst, most terrible idea in the world, and make it sound reasonable."

"Glad you see it my way, Big Will. You know we're going to have to arrange another Coterie meeting real soon. We have to start making plans."

"But we all have to agree on our course of action. Either we're all in, or nobody's in," Big Will demanded.

"I wouldn't have it any other way, my friend." Joe slapped Williams on the back and asked, "You ready to order?"

"Yeah. I think I'll go with the lasagna. I expect that I'll be having leftover spaghetti tomorrow," Big Will thought out loud.

"I'll start making calls tonight. When do you think we should meet? Keep it for Friday? Breakfast? The regular place? Joe asked.

"Something you said just gave me an idea," Big Will hinted. "Hold off on any calls until I can make a few arrangements."

WEDNESDAY morning Joe received a call from Big Will. "I have everything lined up for Friday morning, Joe. Notify everyone that instead of going to the Towne, we'll be meeting at the visitor's parking lot behind Headquarters at 9:30."

Joe listened attentively to the agenda. "Okay. I'll get right on it."

Vern, Harry, and Chaz were all notified of the change for Friday's meeting. All were available. Then Joe called Freddie.

"Hello," Freddie answered.

"Hey Freddie. Just called to let you know that the Friday morning meeting has been changed. Big Will wants everyone to meet in the lot behind HQ at 9:30. I think this should really be interesting for everyone. Well, at least the retired guys. You and Big Will are probably on top of this stuff, as you're still on the job. But we'll still need some guidance from you."

"For what Joe? What kind of guidance?"

"More along the lines of intel on that Freedom Boyz group. Big Will said that you were pretty much the expert on them. We're looking to go a little more proactive."

"Uh, okay," Freddie answered hesitantly.

"What? Is that a bad time for you? I know that you'll just be coming off the midnight tour…"

"No. Nothing like that, Joe. My wife, Angela, she spends the whole winter in Florida. You know, she hates the cold. She's still down in Boca. I was planning to string a couple vacation days onto the end of my long weekend, and head back to Florida for a week. Thought I might get an early start and leave on Friday."

"Gee, I'm sorry to interrupt your plans. You want me to contact the rest of the guys to move it back a week? I know Big Will already made some plans, but I'm sure we can postpone it for you," Joe offered.

"No. No. That's not necessary. I can adjust my plans. I can leave a little later on Friday. There's a later flight. I need to be at that meeting… ah, to give you guys all the information you need and whatever help I can. Unfortunately, I'll be gone a week after that. But I want you to keep in touch so that I know what's happening. Ok?"

"That is really generous of you, Freddie. Thanks."

CHAPTER 17
Friday, April 12, 2019

FIELD TRIP

THE GROUP HAD assembled as directed and filed into an unmarked police prisoner transport van that waited for them in the visitor's parking lot. Chief Williams and Lieutenant Taylor were the last to board.

"Welcome to the first 'field trip' of the Coterie, gentlemen. I believe that you will find this quite informative and interesting."

"Hey Big Will," Vern called out. "Is it true that we're going to the County Police Academy?"

"You got it, Vern. I'm hoping that you old dogs are able to learn some new tricks."

"How long of a ride is it?" Chaz asked.

Freddie looked over his shoulder to Chaz, "No more than twenty minutes. Why? You have to go?"

Again, in unison, the chorus sang out, "Those damned water pills!"

"No Lieutenant," Chaz replied, "I was just wondering, that's all. But I'll hold it!"

A half hour later the group was being escorted from the van to the south wing of the building that housed the Criminal Justice Department at the County Community College.

As they walked the corridor, their escort, Professor Jamie Simonian, Dean of the CJ Department, commented on the building. "To many of you, this may seem new, but the County built this wing twenty years ago specifically for this training center. After the City ceased training their own officers, they transferred their Academy to the County, where it was incorporated into the Criminal Justice Department at the CCC. We train and certify all officers for the Sheriff's Department and every Police agency in the county. On occasion, providing there is room, we'll train officers for adjoining counties."

While listening to Dean Simonian, the group failed to notice that they lost Chaz when they passed a men's room. The rest of them were guided into a huge lecture hall that had stadium seating for a couple hundred. While the handful of "old timers" found seats clustered in the first couple rows, Dean Simonian addressed the small gathering from a podium positioned to the left of a large projection screen.

"Chief Will Williams called me yesterday and asked if I could give a presentation on contemporary police equipment, tactics, and support services. He stated that you gentleman may have been out of the service for a number of years, and this was intended as a refresher course." He looked to Chief Williams for validation.

Big Will joined Dean Simonian at the podium. "Jamie, we are all friends here, so I'd like to introduce some of the best officers the City has ever been blessed with." He pointed to and announced, "Alfred Taylor, Lieutenant, Narcotics. We call him Freddie." Then he pointed to the next row, "Vernon Chosky, Staff Sergeant retired. He was one of the instructors at our old Academy. Then we have Lieutenant Chaz Bohen...," Big Will looked across the near empty hall. "Where's Chaz?"

Just at that moment he wandered into the room and declared, "Damned water pills!" Then asked, "I didn't miss anything, did I?"

"As I was saying," Williams chuckled, "this is our water boy, Lieutenant Chaz Bohen." As the laughter died down, Big Will announced, "Actually, he is one of the best tactical engineers we've ever had." Nodding to the man seated alone in the fourth row, "Detective Sergeant retired, Harry Doyle. He also instructed at the City's Police Academy. And finally, there's Captain, retired, Joe Morgan. Joe has been a dear friend and a leader in our Department for decades."

Big Will turned to the Dean of the Department. "He may look like he's only 30 or so, but I have known Jamie for over twenty years." Will explained. "He put a few years in with the Sheriff's Department and was the youngest Captain there, until he was appointed to this gig. He's been a good friend of mine, and a loyal supporter of Law Enforcement. So when Joe and I spoke yesterday, I realized we might need some help. Jamie was the first person I thought of. So, now that we are all introduced and friends, we can dispense with the ranks and titles."

"Gentlemen," Jamie rubbed his hands together with enthusiasm, "I am used to trying to inspire young people who have no idea what they are getting themselves into… other than what they see on TV. I am excited to have the opportunity to work with men who have done the job and are interested in seeing how it can be done better. I have some stuff here that will blow your socks off."

Harry raised his hand, "Excuse me, uh, Jamie. I don't mean to offend or anything like that, but have you actually worked the streets?"

"Harry, is it? Yes. I have some experience there. I worked the road for two years as a Deputy. Was promoted to Patrol Sergeant. A year later promoted to Lieutenant in command of the Marine Division, while serving as Second in Command on the SWAT team. After attending the FBI National Academy and earning my master's in political science and business, I was promoted to Captain of Patrol. I think it was a rather active six years."

"And you prefer teaching, rather than doing?" Vern asked.

"That's the thing. I am doing," Jamie explained. "When I was on the street, I was the best deputy I could be. It was one-on-one and I was in control of what I did. But only of what I could do. Now I am still in control but it's not just one-on-one. Now I do my best to train future officers. Out of a class of 150, there might be 50 really great cops and investigators. And of those, maybe 15 will have the qualities of being great leaders. Men and women who will make a definite difference on the street and move up through the ranks like I did. That is what I'm doing, and I enjoy it!"

"Thank you, sir," Vern offered, a little apologetically.

"So, to get back to our original program. Let me say that Law Enforcement of today is no longer carbon paper, teletype machines, and two-man cars. That is all history. Today's officer has a minimum of two years college, twenty-six weeks of the Academy, and has to be an expert on the range and on the computer. Today you will see exactly what a current police officer is capable of."

The lights dimmed and a video began to play on the large white screen. Sixteen minutes later the video ended, and the lights came up again. "That gentlemen, was the indoctrination video we play to welcome all police recruits and CJ freshmen. I beg your pardon for wasting the past quarter hour, but now I can honestly report to my superiors that I did present the introduction of Law Enforcement, which we do for all new and future officers. It's a prerequisite I have to follow. Now I can address your needs."

"You had me going there, Jamie," Williams smiled. "I was starting to question where you were taking us with that. I thought we were all going back to square one."

Jamie laughed. "Will has explained the situation and what you officers will be working on. I told him that I would give you an overview of what equipment is available and how it works, along with other services available through the County Sheriff's Department. But it has to be routed directly from the City PD to the Dean's Office, and then we can forward the request to the Sheriff's Office with our recommendation."

"I expect that you're going to tell us that the computer has become more important than the police radio," Chaz asserted.

"When it comes to dispatching calls, all unit broadcasts such as 'Officer in Trouble,' or 'in pursuit of a fleeing suspect or vehicle' – those are still absolutely essential. Nothing surpasses the efficacy of the portable or car radio. But other than that, nothing compares with the computers in each vehicle. You no longer have to wait for the dispatcher to get plate checks or warrants. You run them yourself. There is nobody with a home scanner who will intercept car-to-car communications on the computer, like they do with scanners. And with the Law Enforcement apps that are available today, there is so much more that can be done."

"Like what?" Harry asked.

"Well, how would you like to monitor the movement of a suspect's vehicle? A magnetic bug can be affixed to the vehicle in a matter of ten seconds. Once that is activated the computer will give you a printout of all addresses and coordinates that the suspect visited, how long the vehicle was there, who owns the property, and with a little more installation time you can plant an interior bug which will record audio and video inside the vehicle. For real time tracking, there are units with radio frequency transmitters. And if you are concerned that someone might be sweeping for an electronic bug, then you use the USB data recorder. There are no frequency transmissions with the recorder. It's undetectable. Although with that device, you have to physically retrieve the thumb drive and download the data to a computer, it sometimes has its advantages. And, of course, such installations can only be done with a court order."

"Is this the latest technology?" Joe asked.

"Oh, no. These have been around a long time. What the heavy-duty spies use now is infrared and laser technology that can penetrate buildings, lock onto vehicles, and track someone from halfway around the world."

"Like drones," Vern mused.

"Well, that's one platform they use. That's mostly domestic low-tech stuff though. A lot of surveillance can be done by spysats and military satellites, at more than 600 to 1200 miles altitude, intercepting all communications and with infrared photography. They can activate devices that have been turned off and reverse speakers to become microphones, such as TVs, radios, and cellphones. A laser beam focused on a pane of glass essentially makes the glass a sheet-like microphone. When people talk in a room, their voices vibrate on the glass, ever so slightly. But that is enough for a laser beam to detect, send back, and reconstruct the vibration into sound. And there you have it, a full recording of conversations from a room 500 feet away on an upper level of a building. And you never have to step one foot on the property. So, bugs no longer have to be planted, they're already where they have to be. It's the wonderful world of the NSA, DIA, Homeland Security, and a host of others. However, that is the super spy government stuff that we don't have access to. Down at our level, we do have the bionic hearing devices, like the parabolic dish devices that the TV networks use at NFL games. We also have the RF phone interceptor, which looks like a little TV antenna, but will intercept cellphone calls and give you the phone numbers of the caller and the person called. Again, older technology, but quite effective."

"And, of course those need court orders, too," Harry interjected gruffly.

"Yes," Jamie confirmed, but added, "the newer gear, like the body cams and audio recorders need no court approval. I thought you'd like to hear that, Harry."

"Digital cameras have extremely low light photo and video capabilities, near total darkness. And the digital telephoto lenses today have a 25-power magnification. Even the clarity of smartphone cameras is tremendous. These are just scratching the surface of the tools for investigators today. And weaponry… don't get me started."

Jamie then clicked the controller in his hand to begin a montage of images on the screen. "Here are some other things we can help you with. After the Sheriff's deputies found that burned-out Ford, they took GPS measurements of the entire area, and with the crime scene photos, our Forensic Technology class was able to make a diorama, an exact model, of the crime scene, to include the blow up of the tire track imprints." The images on the screen showed the construction of the crime scene model.

"You do that with all crime scenes?" Vern asked.

"No. This was a training assignment, because it was evidence recovered by the Sheriff's Department. But now that I am aware that it is connected to a murder investigation, the diorama will be set aside and preserved for the county prosecutor, should the case go to court. Since Will read me in on this investigation, the Forensic Technology students will also be recreating the crime scene where Joe's grandson was killed. We also make blown up maps, diagrams and charts. All the items that a prosecutor would present to a jury and enter into evidence. These are just some of the services we can provide through the CJ Department."

Rolling his eyes up toward his high forehead, Harry suggested, "So it's like getting a haircut at a barber school? What you get is just alright?"

"Trust me, it's better than that," Jamie argued. "Only our seniors can work on projects such as this one, and they produce professional level products."

Big Will then interrupted, "They also teach evidence collection, documentation, and chain of evidence control. Some of the PD Lab Techs instruct here on a part-time basis. There is a lot they have to offer here that most PDs don't realize."

"On this case, Joe, I will do whatever I can. If you need some equipment, I can loan it to the Chief of Homicide for 'field training' purposes," Jamie explained.

"Would our Narcotics Bureau be able to try out some of that gear?" Freddie requested.

"Don't see why not." Jamie answered, figuring it was a request made for the same purpose of this group's use. "The only caveat is, you break it, you buy it."

"Then I'll make sure any request goes through me," Will accepted the offer.

"The other things that I wanted to address are the issues of legality, and admissibility," Jamie added. "I know that police practice and policy was a lot different in years past. Currently there is a greater emphasis on public relations and criminal rights and safety. The law has gone so far beyond Miranda and Escobedo, that you wouldn't believe it."

Harry looked to Vern and they both rolled their eyes. "I'm sorry Prof, but I don't have velvet gloves. I never did," Harry rasped.

Jamie threw his hands up in the air, surrendering to the sentiment. "I know gentlemen. I agree. It seems like the pendulum has swung way too far in the other direction. Criminals seem to have more rights than the victims and the police do. But that's how things are now. We have to work with and through these circumstances. Especially on a case this serious. We don't want to lose a conviction because an officer, or an agent of the police, which you are, have violated the individual constitutional rights of one or more suspects."

Vern shook his head. "Nabbing someone nowadays is not as easy as it used to be. Now, not only do you have to be an investigator to find the crime and evidence, you gotta be a cop to make the arrest, a social worker to make sure the suspect is comfortable, a doctor to treat the suspect if he bumps his head getting into the squad car, a priest who can hear a confession but can't testify to it, and a lawyer who can sue the City if an "I" is not dotted or "T" is not crossed. Oh yeah. Now I remember why I retired."

"I get it, gentlemen," Jamie conceded. "I'm here to help. I don't write the laws, and these are the rules that we have to follow."

"But the bad guys don't have to follow the rules," Vern declared in frustration.

Joe spoke up, "They never did, Vern. That's why they're called criminals. But especially these days… especially on this case, we have to play it straight. Each one of us has to make sure that no court will dismiss this case because of one person, especially one of us, taking a shortcut."

Big Will addressed the group. "It looks like we can still catch the lunch menu at the Towne if anyone is interested. Jamie, would you like to join us for lunch?"

"That's very thoughtful Will, but I have a class to prepare for."

"Are you sure? It's on me," Joe offered.

"No. Really," Jamie declined. "But I appreciate it."

Then Freddie looked at his watch and reported, "I have a few things to pack before I leave for the airport."

"I'll take a rain check, too, Joe," Chaz said with a slightly embarrassed look. "Kitty has a half dozen things on her Honey-Do list."

The group again piled into the van and headed back to HQ. The discussion on how to proceed with their investigation consumed the twenty-minute ride.

"I think that it would probably be wise to do some reconnaissance around the projects, just to get the lay of the land," Vern suggested. "It looks like all the evidence points back to that Freedom Boyz gang, so at least we know where to start."

Big Will frowned. "I don't know if that's such a wise idea."

"The Precinct has stepped up patrols in that area, and all three shifts of the Narcotics Bureau are doubling their efforts there," Freddie added.

"I agree with Vern," Harry declared, undeterred. "If there is a stepped-up police presence there, then nobody would be looking at a couple senior citizens passing through. We're only going to do a few drive-throughs. You know, to get an understanding of the geography. Hell, except for Freddie and maybe Big Will, I bet none of us has been through the projects in ten years."

"Okay," Big Will relented. "But nobody goes in there alone, AND you have to notify the precinct that you'll be in the area."

"That's an excellent idea, BW," Freddie seconded. "I'll be in touch with my crew while I'm out of town. I will forward any information to you, BW."

"And what about Joe and me?" Chaz asked, looking like he felt a bit left out.

"Just sit tight," Big Will urged. "Joe, would you let Mike know what's going on? Chaz, you said that you have some old equipment from the job. Check it out. See if we can use any of it."

Harry then spoke up as if he had just remembered, "I also have some personal equipment I've accumulated for my PI business. Some of it I haven't had a need for in the past couple years, so we might as well use it. I'll drop it off to Chaz, and he can fiddle with it."

The van pulled back into the lot behind headquarters. Freddie was the first to get off and disappear. When Big Will disembarked, he addressed the rest of the group, "Sorry about missing today's breakfast, but I'll see you guys next Tuesday. Have a good weekend. And be safe." He emphasized his last statement with a stern expression and pointed at Vern and Harry.

CHAPTER 18

Chaz' Workshop

Vern pulled into the driveway of the Bohen residence. It had been years since he'd been there. Vern and Harry walked to the rear of the car where Vern opened the trunk.

"I can't recall the last time I used most of this stuff," Harry announced as he struggled to get the box out of the trunk.

"Need some help, Harry?" Vern offered.

"No. I can manage." Harry grunted as he lifted the box.

The two stood at the side door, with Harry leaning the box against the wall. Vern rang the doorbell. A moment later they could see the curtains move at a nearby window. Then a singular voice could be heard from inside the house. It was a high-pitched screech. "Chaaaaaz. Your cop buddies are here. Chaaaaz, did you hear me?"

A couple long minutes later, Chaz opened the door. "Sorry fellas. I didn't hear the bell. Harry, I see you brought something for me. Here, let me grab that box."

"Okay." Harry panted as he relinquished the box to Chaz. "It's all good equipment. I bought items here and there when I needed something for a specific job. But then, you know how it goes, as soon as I had it, I didn't get any more cases that required a night scope, or an infrared camera, or lapel mic. You know, stuff like that."

Chaz nodded his head, "C'mon in. Let me show you my workshop."

Chaz led them through the kitchen, down the hallway to a rear bedroom, or what once was intended as a bedroom. "I'll be in my room, Kitty," Chaz called to his wife.

From some distant part of the house the screech returned, "Yeah, yeah, yeah. I know."

Chaz stopped near the doorway as Harry and Vern entered the workshop. The two were amazed at the amount of electronic equipment that filled an entire wall of shelves. On the opposite side of the room was a long metal work bench, replete with three computers, inverters, several monitors, amp meters, and a pegboard above the work bench holding dozens of tools. There were also several types of lamps, a tabletop vice, magnifying glasses, spools of wire, and a soldering gun. Two stools indicated where most of the work was performed. At the end of the bench was a pile of green circuit boards on top of a filing cabinet. Several manuals on the bench lay open to pages of schematics and diagrams. "I've got all the necessities to check and repair just about any electronic component!" Chaz announced proudly, as he set the box on the bench.

At the far end of the workshop were four wooden chairs strategically placed around an old kitchen table, circa 1960, that hugged the wall and was laden with papers, notebooks, and a glass jar full of pencils and pens. Not far from the table was a dorm-sized refrigerator. Chaz gestured toward the table, "Here, have a seat. What do you think of the workshop?"

Harry looked around the room. There were charts and graphs taped to the wall. "I got to hand it to you Chaz, I am impressed. How'd you steal so much stuff from the Department?"

Chaz' face turned crimson as he started to stammer. "Wh-what do you mean s-s-steal, Harry? I've never s-stolen anything," Chaz replied indignantly, his back stiffening.

"Don't get your panties in a bunch, Chaz. I was just kidding. Just bustin' your balls, Buddy!"

Chaz relaxed a bit and accepted the apology. "Okay. I just don't like it when anyone even suggests that I took property from work. I never took nothing that was functional. Whenever there was busted equipment, the department replaced it with new and improved electronics. Instead of scrapping the old gear, I brought it home for parts, and in some cases, tinkered with it and got it working again."

"It is certainly impressive, Chaz." Vern agreed. "I have no idea what half this stuff is. So, you think you can fix up Harry's equipment?"

"I'll have a look at it. See what he has, and what we can use. In the meanwhile, I wanted to talk with you guys about what we're going to do."

"Okay. Let's get down to brass tacks," Harry growled. "More than the equipment, this is what I was hoping we could talk about. What's the game plan, Chaz?"

"Yeah, Chaz," Vern urged. "You have some ideas?"

"Of course, or I wouldn't have asked you fellas to come here this afternoon. You two are the most experienced in actual field work. You know, surveillance and those skills. Well…," and before he could finish the sentence he stopped abruptly. "Excuse me. Before we get into details. I have to go to the bathroom."

Harry smiled, "I know. Those damned water pills."

Chaz was headed toward the door when he paused just a moment to say, "No. It's a nervous digestive tract. Diarrhea." He then quickened his pace down the hall.

THE table had been set for the weekly Saturday dinner. While Chrissy was letting the sauce simmer, she added the ground beef and sausage, then drained the pasta. The garlic bread had already been sliced and placed on the dining room table. The men were still in the living room with college basketball on the TV, more for sound than entertainment.

"And what can I do, Dad? At the last meeting I attended, it seemed like everyone was stoning me. Since then, I haven't heard anything."

Joe listened patiently to Mike's complaint. "It was just a phase of our investigation. That's how things are done. It's always harder the closer you are to it, and no one is closer to this than you. Nobody was nailing you to a cross."

Mike seemed a bit mollified, "Well it sure felt like it. So, what's happening now?"

"At this point Chaz, Harry, and Vern are putting together a course of action. Freddie is out of town and Big Will is trying to keep on top of his caseload. That leaves you and me."

"And what are we supposed to do?" Mike asked.

"We wait a day or two to see what Chaz has planned. From everything that we've gathered so far, it looks like the Freedom Boyz are likely responsible for Sean's murder. They are definitely involved, but we still don't have a motive. We'll be working closely with Chief Amico and Narcotics. Whatever equipment we need will be available," Joe explained.

"So, there's no doubt that Sean was dealing drugs and Williams thinks that he was getting the drugs from this gang. And that's why Sean was killed?"

"Will, nor any one of us, can make that connection." Joe calmly explained in a hushed tone. "Not at this time anyways. It does appear that a person who was a member of the Freedom Boyz was the driver of the stolen car that intentionally struck Sean and fled the scene. We don't know if he was Sean's supplier, or if there was any personal connection at all. That's what we have to find out."

"But what can I do, Dad? I might work in Communications, but I'm still a cop."

"That's a unique and useful position to be in. As the supervisor, you have access to all dispatch logs and records. We need you to review all calls in the Freedom Housing Projects for the week prior to Sean's death."

"What am I supposed to be looking for?" Mike questioned - his interest piqued.

"It could be anything. We'll have to reinvestigate each call to see if anything leads to the Freedom Boyz," Joe said. "Investigations seldom lead to a suspect with the first few clues. Back in '95, the Murrah Federal Building was bombed in Oklahoma City. Over 160 people were killed, including children in a day care, and the blast damaged buildings in a 16-block radius. You know how they caught McVeigh? A city cop stopped him for not having a license plate, which led to a charge of Weapons Possession. Turns out there was a parking ticket in the vehicle that placed him at the crime scene with a time and date on the ticket. The same thing with David Berkowitz, the Son of Sam killer in New York City, 1976. He was also caught because of a parking ticket. It's those small things that can turn a case. So, review the dispatch logs for parking complaints at the Freedom Towers, or any other call that officers were dispatched to in that area."

"Okay, Dad. Point taken."

Then Chrissy's voice dominated the room as she entered, "Are you two going to watch that basketball game or would you rather eat while the food is hot? Dinner is ready."

VERN and Harry wandered around the workshop waiting for Chaz to return. "Chaz always said that the stress of the job wrecked his health. What do you think, Harry?" Vern asked. "You think he's a hypochondriac, or is he really as bad off as he seems?"

Harry considered the question for a moment before offering, "No. Chaz did have a heart attack, six bypasses and a pacemaker. That's not in his head. The constant pissing is due to the diuretic meds after his heart surgery. But I remember before he retired, he was always popping pills, his hands would shake, he'd complain of dizziness, and he had constant flatulence. Oh my God, it was unrelenting. I suppose the job did take a toll on him. Since he retired it seems like most of those symptoms have gone away."

"Well, except for him blowing mud today," Vern pointed out. "You know what they say, when you get to be our age."

"Yeah," Harry answered. "Never ever trust a fart!"

Just then the sound of footsteps drew closer in the hallway. "Amen, Harry," Chaz agreed as he entered the room. "I heard that. But let's get over to the table where I have something to show you."

Curiously Harry looked at Chaz and inquired, "Is that where you keep all the super-secret stuff?" He pointed to what appeared to be a closet door with three hasps and combination locks.

"Oh, that's nothing," Chaz insisted as they settled on the wooden chairs around the chrome-legged kitchen table. Chaz sorted out an array of photos. "I downloaded these from the computer. Aerial views of the Freedom Projects." He used a pencil to point to the positions on the various photos. "You probably recall that the housing project consists of eight high-rise towers and four rows of ground level apartments. The row houses surround the towers and there are three main parking areas - one on the outside of the east row of apartments; another outside the west row of apartments; and the main parking area situated in the center of the towers."

Vern studied the layout. "Just as I remember them," he stated, tapping the photo.

"Yeah," Harry recalled, "sure does bring back some memories of during the nineties when we had the riots and protests downtown, and at the college. I remember pulling into these lots and getting pelted with all kinds of shit from the towers. Good times." Harry's expression just hinted at his sarcasm.

"Strategically, I don't think anything has changed," Chaz announced. "The Andrea and Barbara Towers are the on the north end, and most distant from the center parking area. The Grace and Henrietta Towers are the most distant on the south end. The four Towers that would pose the most problems would be the Catherine, Deborah, Evelyn, and the Florence. I think that is where we should concentrate our efforts."

Harry lowered the readers from the top of his head to the tip of his nose to examine the photos. "What exactly do you mean, concentrate our efforts? What kind of efforts?"

"First of all," Chaz began his plan, "we need intel gathering by whatever means necessary. Surveillance. Electronic monitoring. Whatever we have to do to get actionable intel. Secondly, we channel the info through Big Will to Chief Amico in Narcotics. Let them handle the heavy work, since it's all driven by drugs."

Vern looked puzzled. "And what do we get out of that? You're saying that we do Narco's job for them? They get the bust and the credit. And what, hope that they throw us a bone?"

"No Vern." Harry interjected, following Chaz' plan. "We want them to make arrests. The more the better. Then in return for all our hard work, which allows them to make the busts... we get a crack at questioning the suspects for any ties between Freedom Boyz and our victim, Sean." Harry's explanation brought a dawning look of understanding to Vern's face. "Right, Chaz?"

Chaz confirmed, "Yeah. And who knows, we might possibly solve a couple other homicides for Big Will."

"Okay. Okay. I get it," Vern said. "But where do we begin?"

"I have some gear here that I wanted to show you guys. The best way to explain it is to show you. You know, to demonstrate. But...we can't do it here because it's meant for outdoor use. Basically, we'll be video recording, monitoring phone conversations, and some other talk."

Vern's eyes opened wide. "Isn't all that the kind of stuff we were told the police need a warrant or court order for?"

"Technically, yes. But the Department is not directing or telling us what to do. If we are in an open public space, we have every right to observe and listen to whoever else is also in that public space."

Harry scratched his head. He wasn't totally convinced. "As a PI, there are quite stringent rules to follow when it comes to surveillance, Chaz."

Chaz smiled. "If you are good at what you do, then nobody knows when you do it. And what would happen if you, as a PI, get tripped up by one of those surveillance rules?"

"I could lose my license."

"Then as plain old citizens, we have no license to lose. Right? And if we do what we're going to do and do it well…nobody will ever know. We'll just be passing information along to the proper authorities for THEM to investigate," Chaz reasoned. "To the force, it's just information received from confidential informants."

"And what about Big Will? Shouldn't we tell him what we're doing?" Vern asked, still looking a bit uncomfortable.

Harry peered over the top of his readers. "Vern, it's always better to apologize and ask for forgiveness than to ask for permission and be denied. And to be honest, what BW doesn't know can't hurt him. Besides, we can run it by Joe."

Chaz beamed at both men, "Good then. We're all on the same page."

"So, where are we going to try out this equipment?" Vern asked.

"Chaaaaz!" Came the shrill whine. "Dinner is ready. And I don't have enough for company," she added with an extra touch of annoyance. "Chaaaz, you hear me?"

"Yes, Kitty," Chaz yelled back. "The whole neighborhood can hear you. I'll be right there."

"Sorry, Vern. Harry."

"Nah," Vern cut him short. "We have to be leaving anyway. But when do you want to test out that equipment?"

"How about tomorrow. It's Sunday. A nice quiet day when there's little traffic on the streets," Chaz suggested.

Harry agreed. "Sounds like a plan."

"Want to meet at the Towne for breakfast, say 9 a.m.?" Vern suggested.

The three friends agreed and shook hands, before Chaz led them back down the hallway, and through the kitchen where Kitty was waiting near the table eyeing daggers at Chaz. She quickly replaced her scowl with an attempt at a smile, and in a sweet, demure voice, as if nobody had heard her previously said, "Have a good day, gentlemen. It's been nice seeing you again."

CHAPTER 19

COLORING OUTSIDE THE LINES

IT WAS UNUSUAL for the Coterie to meet on a Sunday morning, but then it was not an official meeting - just four old friends getting together for breakfast.

Joe asked Chaz, "You think this is necessary?"

"Breakfast is the most important meal of the day," Chaz answered with a wry smile.

"You know what I mean," Joe insisted.

Harry broke a moody silence and joined in, "Joe, as Chaz explained yesterday, we're only going to try out some equipment to see how it works. That's all."

Vern added his support. "What can it hurt? Big Will and Freddie probably use this type of equipment all the time and are quite familiar with it. What's the harm in us getting a little education so we don't look stupid?"

"Alright. I'm interested in how these thing-a-ma-jigs work," Joe admitted. "Yeah, we can discuss that after breakfast."

During ham and eggs, the conversation drifted back to the agenda. Harry asked where they were going to try out the equipment.

"Since I have my van here," Chaz answered, "it only stands to reason that we all should go in one vehicle. That way we all can be part of one conversation. I can show you, as a group, how to operate the trail cam, nanny cam, GPS tracker, parabolic mic, and the Radio Frequency detector."

"Yeah, I've used several of those things as a PI," Harry said. "I can help you demonstrate. Remember that I also have a van, Chaz, and it's more than just a family van. It's set up for doing mobile surveillance for insurance comp cases."

"Why don't we keep Harry's van in reserve," Joe suggested, "and use Chaz' van just for wherever he's taking us today."

When the waitress had picked up the last plate, the last sip of coffee had been taken, and the last tip had been placed on the table, the group got to their feet and began to leave.

"We can all meet out at my van," Chaz suggested. "I'm parked in the side lot. I'll meet you out there." As he strayed from the group to head toward the restroom, Chaz turned and warned, "Don't even say it."

JOE sat in the front with Chaz, while Harry and Vern sat in the middle row as the van slowly made its way into the Twelfth Precinct.

"Where we going, Chaz?" Harry asked.

"You know those aerial photos I showed you yesterday?" Chaz reminded.

"You mean of the Freedom Project?" Harry answered.

"Yeah. I thought that while we're all together we should take a ride through there. You know, just to check out the area. See what's changed. Get a feel for the place."

"Are you frigging crazy, Chaz?" Joe asked. "Four old white guys driving through there. Like we wouldn't stand out? You don't even have tinted windows."

"Jeez, Captain Joe, don't worry," Chaz replied. "The bad guys probably don't even get up here until after noon. And the folks that are up, you don't have to worry about. They're the ones that are going to church. We're just going to make a couple passes through and then we'll leave."

"Look who's saying don't worry," Harry scoffed. "You do know that there are no restrooms around here?"

The van turned onto Towers Road and the men quickly noticed that the surroundings had indeed changed. There were poor parts of any town, but this area was really rough. It had been bad twenty years ago, but it had gotten worse. Much worse. There were vehicles at the curb that were up on cinder blocks, and not for repair. Several vehicles had been stripped to the frame. There was a dumpster blocking half the street, while trash of all types littered the grounds. Many of the first-floor apartments were vacant and had boarded windows. Several of the upper apartments had people and laundry hanging out the windows. Clusters of people blocked the entrances to the residential towers. Several of the row apartments were charred by fire, but still appeared to be inhabited.

There was a backboard and hoop installed on one of the utility poles, where a group of young men were playing basketball. The van had to come to a full stop to avoid hitting any of the youths who defiantly remained in the street. After a minute of waiting, Chaz blew the horn. Joe glanced over at Chaz as the van inched forward.

Suddenly, out of nowhere, a hand slapped against the driver's window, startling Chaz and the passengers in the middle seats.

"What you old fools doing here?" Demanded an ebony-skinned man about 30 years old, wearing a checkered jacket. "I'm talkin' to you, old man!" He slammed his hand on the window again, anger on his face. "Don't you look away from me."

Chaz looked at Joe. Joe looked at Harry, seated behind Chaz. And Harry looked to Vern. Then Vern said, "I think he's talking to you, Chaz."

Chaz turned his attention back to the man at his side window. Chaz lowered the driver's window enough so that he could talk to the man with the checkered jacket, but there was not enough opening to let him reach in.

"You talkin' to me?" Chaz did his best to imitate Robert De Niro's character in *Taxi Driver*. "You talkin' to me?" he enunciated with a Brooklyn accent.

The man outside the van just stood there, surprised that any of the old-timers would have the guts to even answer him. "Are you fools crazy or just lost?" he asked, looking to the youths around him for an audience. "Better yet, why don't you just get out of that sissy ass van and we'll talk on my turf. Hear me?" He growled theatrically.

Again, Chaz looked at Joe, Joe looked to Harry, and Harry to Vern.

Vern swiveled his head in all directions. "One at the nine o'clock, and six at noon." Vern assessed. "What do you think?" The four men all nodded at the same time.

Both passenger side doors opened first, allowing Joe and Vern to exit the van. As Joe walked up to the front corner of the van, Vern rounded the rear of the vehicle, surveying the area.

The intimidating figure in the checkered jacket stepped away from the van and started to reach inside his jacket. "What the f...," but before he could finish his thought, the two doors on the driver side flew open. Instantly, there were three automatic pistols and one snub-nose revolver pointed at the man.

"So," his eyes bulged and bounced from man to man. "I take it that you men are lost. Uh...I can give you directions, and you can be on your way. Just let me get these kids out of the street for you." As everyone stepped aside, the van drove past, and cautiously continued down Towers Road.

Chaz' hands were vibrating on the steering wheel. Nobody said a word for the next ten minutes, until they were well out of Precinct Twelve.

It took another twenty minutes for the van to arrive at Houghton Park, where they pulled up next to a vacant picnic shelter.

"This should do," Chaz suggested. With no people in the immediate area, Chaz placed the box on a table and started unpacking items.

"Was that really necessary, Chaz?" Joe asked. "Someone could've gotten hurt back there."

Chaz heaved a sigh of relief and nodded. "Yeah. I'm glad that they used their common sense and moved. They definitely could've gotten hurt."

Joe just shook his head and helped Chaz unpack the box.

"What do you have here?" Vern asked as he picked up the device that looked like a pistol with a scope and a six-inch plastic bowl at the end of the barrel.

"That's a parabolic mic with a 20-power monocular. It'll pick up and record conversations up to 300 feet away," Chaz explained.

Then Harry added, "I have one of those, too. A great little gadget to have handy."

Chaz instructed as he placed the headphones on Vern's head to demonstrate. "Put the headphones on, plug the cord into the bottom of the pistol grip, and then switch it on."

When Vern followed the final instruction, his head recoiled, and he yanked the headphones off. "Damn near blasted my eardrums out!"

"Sorry," Chaz said meekly. "I should have told you to turn the volume down before switching it on. When you aim the device toward your subject, you can turn the volume up to the desired level. You can zoom in on the visual and monitor the conversation. It synchronizes the audio and visual for recording."

Vern swung the device in the direction of the next picnic shelter and followed Chaz' instructions. "Look at that. I can't believe it! So clear and you can even pick up a whisper."

"If you want to record the video and the audio just push the two buttons on the left side. You can record only video, or just audio, or both," Chaz explained. "And if you want to review what you recorded, you have to turn it off before you remove the SIM card." He ejected the SIM from the base of the grip as he spoke. Chaz then slipped the card into the slot on his laptop. "Here's what Vern recorded."

The video image bounced about and was amateurishly shaky, but the voices were clear. The video showed a young couple seated on one side of a picnic table at the next shelter, maybe 200 feet away. Their backs were to Vern, but it was clear what was going on as the audio played. "Ah, ah, ah," the voice panted. "You got it baby," whispered a male voice as the woman's shoulder closest to him, moved up and down rapidly. "Ah, ah, keep it up, Honey."

Then the screen went blank. "...and here is how you delete recordings you don't need," Chaz instructed.

"OK, what else do you have that would be useful?" Harry asked.

Chaz looked at Harry and smiled. "This is for you Sgt. Harry. I bet you don't have one of these," he said as he lifted what looked like a walkie-talkie out of the box. He raised the antenna, turned the dial on, and then started fiddling with another dial, which scanned various frequencies. There was nothing but modulating static. Then he asked Joe, "Can you call Mike and see if he can be at the meeting on Tuesday?"

"Now?" Joe asked.

"Sure. We'll wait."

Joe walked to the far end of the pavilion. He dialed Mike's home phone.

"Hello," Chrissy answered.

Joe responded, "Hey Chrissy. Is Mike around?"

"Sorry Dad. He went to the store. Anything I can help you with?"

Vern and Harry huddled close to Chaz as they listened to the voices. Then Chaz turned the volume up so that Joe could hear Chrissy as she spoke.

"Wait a minute, Chrissy." Joe looked at the three, smiling at the other end of the shelter. "I'll call Mike later. Bye." Joe ended the call. Then he questioned, "You were listening to my call?"

"Not only that, Joe. Look here," Chaz beamed as he turned the display screen to Joe.

"What?" Joe's jaw dropped. "My cell number, Mike's home phone number, his address, and the names the phones were listed to."

"So long as the one phone is within 100 feet," Chaz clarified.

"Aren't these the kind of eavesdropping devices that Jamie said required warrants?" Joe asked. "Is all of this stuff in that same category?"

Chaz reached into the box again and retrieved a few other gadgets. "Joe, to be as serious as a heart attack, let me ask you one question. What would you do to find out who killed Sean?"

Joe was stunned. He thought a minute before answering. "Chaz, I would go to hell and back to collar that guy. But what you are proposing here… I wouldn't want to drag anyone else down that path."

"In for a penny, in for a pound. What difference does it make?" Harry asked. "That is the way we've always been. But in the past, it has always been to help someone else."

"Now we're going to bat for one of our own, Joe," Vern stressed. "And nobody had to force me to get on board that train."

"Besides," Chaz joked, "how many times have you told us to 'Go to hell'? Now it's our turn. 'Go to Hell!'" he demanded as he picked up the box from the table. "If you liked the last one, wait till you see what these can do." Chaz took the lid from the box and scooped up a handful of small square objects, the size of dice. "These are all video cameras. Not like the ones that Best Buy sells. Oh no," he emphasized, as he held what appeared to be a quarter-inch length of an ink pen refill with two fine wires extending from one end between his thumb and forefinger. "No. This is the world's smallest commercial video camera. Have you ever heard about, or seen, a Teddy Bear Nanny Cam? Well this is the pupil of the bear's one eye."

Harry had to move closer and bring his specs down to his nose to see the camera. "Now, I don't have anything like that Chaz. You got a spare one I could have?"

"I've got a box full of these things in various sizes. Can you imagine what we can use these for? All you need to make them operational is a power source. Even something as small as one of those hearing aid button batteries."

Although impressed with Chaz' gadgetry, Joe was deeply overwhelmed by his friends and their support.

"Maybe Chief Amico's boys have a few of these scattered around the projects," Vern mused.

"What are you talking about," Harry asked. "What makes you say that?"

"Well, I recall Freddie saying that the uniforms in 12 stepped up their patrols in the Freedom Proj. He also said that all shifts in the Narc Bureau are riding the dealers hard in there. Well, if that's true, how come nobody came to back us up? Sure, they might have people undercover, but Freddie said patrols. Somebody should have seen us driving through there!"

It was a good question, Joe thought. "I'll have to bring it up to Freddie or Big Will and find out why we didn't see any police activity there. Where's the cavalry when you need 'em?"

Chaz disagreed, "I don't know if that's a wise course of action, Joe. We weren't supposed to be there. Remember? I think that something like that just might rub Big Will the wrong way."

"You're right, Chaz. But one way or the other, I'll get an answer to that question," Joe promised.

CHAPTER 20
Tuesday, April 16, 2019

APPEASEMENT AND APPROVAL

THE TUESDAY MORNING Coterie breakfast went as planned, minus one member, who was out of town. As done several times before in recent meetings, Mike Morgan was invited to sit in.

Chaz had already returned from the restroom, and all sat waiting impatiently for Lavon to bring the orders.

Big Will opened the discussion. "You guys have had the whole weekend to formulate some plan of how we go about investigating the connection between Sean Morgan and the Freedom Boyz, or to rule it out. Come up with anything?"

Vern, Harry, and Joe looked toward Chaz. "Captain Will, we have looked at the matter up close, and believe that the best course of action is to conduct surveillance to collect evidence that the Narcotics Bureau can use. Drop it in their lap and let them start making arrests. Once they have suspects in custody, you can join the interrogations, as your homicide investigations parallel their drug investigations." Chaz waited expectantly for a response. "What do you think?"

Big Will leaned back in his seat, crossed his arms and reflected for a moment, glancing from one person to the next. "Do you guys really believe that you are up to doing this kind of work again?" he asked in a most serious tone.

Joe, Chaz, Harry, and Vern looked briefly at one another, and all bobbed their heads in agreement.

"No doubt," Harry answered.

"Absolutely," Vern echoed.

"I personally showed them how to use the surveillance equipment that we have available," Chaz announced. "I think they're up to it. I know I am."

Joe was almost overwhelmed by the support. He set his jaw and stated, "My friends not only have my back, but they stand shoulder to shoulder." His words were rewarded with a round of smiles.

Satisfied, Big Will turned to Mike. "I know that you have the day job in Communications, but do you think you'll be able to put in some time with these guys?"

"Try to keep me away, Will." Mike replied with steadfast determination.

"Joe," Harry called across the table and nodded toward Mike, "the kid could be our ears on the radio."

Joe answered, "I've already had that conversation with Mike." Then with a second thought he turned to Big Will, "That is, if you think it's a good idea."

"We're going to need all the help that we can get. But remember, I'm going to be held accountable for you guys. So, no going rogue. Try to fly under the radar. Don't ruffle any feathers. You're only doing surveillance, so you shouldn't be coming in contact with anyone. When it comes down to the Freedom Boyz, it's only observe and document. That's all. Agreed?" Big Will insisted.

"Oh yeah." "Uh-huh." "Absolutely." "Sure, Big Will," they responded in turn.

"Alright then," Big Will affirmed. "Did you guys come up with any specific plans?"

"We did look at some aerial photos of the Freedom Housing Project, the towers and row houses, and all the public parking areas," Joe informed Big Will.

"I brought some stats that you might be interested in." Williams had duplicate copies of police reports that he passed around. He leaned over the reports and began pointing to details. "In the confines of that housing complex, consisting of 512 city-owned and operated rental units, there were 3 homicides, 29 assaults, 5 rapes, 19 burglaries, 37 stolen vehicles, and 4 arsons last year. And those are just the crimes that were reported."

"Sounds like that place hasn't changed much," Harry commented glibly.

"And of the 29 reported assaults, three were police officers responding to calls in that hell hole. Not to mention several police vehicles vandalized."

"So, what you're saying is that when we're in the Freedom Proj, we should be careful," Vern interpreted.

"Extremely careful," Williams emphasized. "Two-man vehicles and always two vehicles together. We have to back up each other, even though there are regular patrols going through there, and as I understand, several unmarked narcotics cars are working that area."

Harry looked at Joe. "I guess that answers that question."

"What question?" Big Will asked.

"Oh, it was nothing," Joe answered. "I just asked Harry before if he knew how many cops are working that area at any given time. Sounds like a lot," he answered sarcastically.

"There should be enough backup there if anything goes sideways. But they can't be everywhere, so help might take a couple minutes. That is why I want you in pairs of vehicles." Williams emphasized.

"You want us to use our own vehicles?" Chaz asked.

Williams thought for a moment. "Good question. I think I can requisition a couple vehicles from the impound lot," Big Will proposed. "But just for surveillance purposes."

Chaz asked, "Can you also get a couple sets of night vision scopes? That would be a big help. I think that we should start with some nighttime reconnaissance. Maybe situate a couple cameras so that we don't have to physically be on the premises to observe any activity. What do you think about that Big Will?"

"As long as the cameras are placed in public spots and only view public areas," Big Will directed.

"When do you think we should start…," Vern's question was interrupted by Williams' phone.

"Chief of Homicide, Williams," he answered, and quickly added. "Freddie. I wasn't expecting you to make this meeting."

"How did you know it was me?" Taylor asked.

"By the 561 area code on my caller ID. So, how's the weather in Boca Raton? And don't make me jealous."

"Let me tell you, BW. You're not missing anything. Two feet of snow and Angie almost got frostbite laying on the beach," Freddie joked.

"And how is Angie?"

"Good. Thanks for asking. She is taking a nap right now and I had time to call. Thought that I might catch you all at the Round Table."

"That's good to hear. What can I do for you?" Will asked.

"Oh, I just called to see how the Coterie operation is going. Anything I can help you with?"

"Not at the moment, Freddie. But when you get back, we could use the structure chart of Freedom Boyz gang, and photos if you got 'em."

"Consider it done. I should be getting back Sunday night."

"Want me to pick you up at the airport again?" Williams offered.

"No thanks, BW. I left my truck at the Park-N-Ride as it was only a couple days, but I appreciate the offer."

"So, you'll be back for next Tuesday's meeting on the 23rd?"

"Yeah. I'll be there," Freddie confirmed. "The guys can bring me up to date on whatever they're doing."

"It won't be much. I told them that they can place a couple CCTV cameras as long as they monitor them remotely. They'll probably set them up tomorrow or Thursday night."

"So, by next Tuesday we should have something to look at?" Freddie asked enthusiastically.

"Most definitely," Big Will stated firmly.

"Well good luck, BW. And tell the guys I send my best wishes. Angie is awake. She's calling me. So…"

"Okay, Freddie. Go make a snowman." The conversation conveniently concluded as the breakfast orders arrived.

CHAPTER 21

THE USED CAR LOT

MIKE HAD JUST arrived at his office when a call was transferred to his extension. "Communications, 9-1-1. Lieutenant Morgan," he announced.

"Mike, this is Will. How is the rest of your morning schedule shaping up?"

"It's wide open, Chief. What do you need?"

"First off, when there is no need for protocol, call me Will. Secondly, I would like you to help me pick out a couple vehicles for the Coterie. You got the time?" Will asked.

"Of course, Will. Anytime you want."

"Can you meet me at the Police Garage in an hour?"

"I'll be there," Mike agreed.

The next call Will placed was to the Chief of Detectives. As soon as the receiver was lifted, before Chief Smyth could even utter his name, Will began, "As I promised, Howie, you are the first to know. I have instructed that restless bunch of retirees to conduct surveillance, and surveillance only. Who knows? Maybe they may even come up with some useful information. But here is why I called," Williams continued, "not just to update you on what their activity will consist of, but to requisition a couple junkers from the impound lot for them to use. I mean, you don't want them to use their own vehicles that the city would then be responsible for. Would you?"

Now that the Chief of Detectives had his moment to speak, he cautiously answered, "We're not talking about actual police cars, are we?"

"No. Hell, no. These would be vehicles that the City had towed in for various reasons and have taken title to. These are the cars that the garage would auction off, but likely no one would pay much for."

"And it won't cost the Department, or the City, anything?" Chief Smyth questioned skeptically.

"Not a penny. And when they're done with the cars, they can be returned to the garage and included in the next auction or sold for scrap," Williams explained.

"I don't see anything wrong with that. Sure. Borrow a couple of those wrecks. But I'm reminding you, Will, you keep me informed of what they're doing."

Will heaved a sigh of relief after hanging up. Smyth never inquired about registering the vehicles or insurance, which Will had already thought about. He expected he could use undercover temporary plates and have the wrecks covered by the City's self-insured policy. Hopefully it would never become an issue, but Will would cross that bridge later, if he had to.

It was 11 o'clock when Will began pacing back and forth outside the Garage Manager's office. A few minutes later Mike arrived.

"What are we doing here?" Mike asked as he greeted Will.

"We're going shopping. I already cleared it with the Chief of Detectives and the Garage Manager. Walk with me out to the yard. We have to pick out three vehicles that we can use."

As the pair walked up and down the rows of vehicles and twisted chunks of metal that used to be vehicles, they came to an agreement. "I like that '84 Buick Electra in the second row." Will said.

Then Mike nominated, "That 2008 Dodge minivan in the main aisle with all the trucks. A banged-up fender, but the alignment looks OK. It also looks like it could be roomy enough for a couple guys to move around in."

And the last choice was made by Williams, "That '05 Caddy Escalade, the maroon one. That looks like it would blend into the area. Needs a little touch-up work. Clean the interior. Add tint to the windows in all the vehicles. I'll talk to Vinny, the shop supervisor."

"Anything else you need me to do?" Mike asked.

Before proceeding to Vinny's office, Will asked, "Can you call your dad and have him bring Chaz, Harry, and Vern down here at 4:30?"

With a nod, Mike returned to Headquarters while Chief Williams went to visit the shop supervisor.

"I have a favor to ask, Vinny."

"Whatever you need, Will."

"There are three vehicles I have out in the yard, and I need to have them cleaned up, running, and window tint put on." Then Will handed Vinny a paper with scribbling. "These are the ones. Can you do it?"

The supervisor looked at the paper, then peeked over Will's shoulder, trying to find the cars. After a moment, he agreed, "I can have those done for you by tomorrow."

Williams scratched his head and pressed for a more accommodating answer. "I was really hoping for you to say that you could have them done by the end of today. You know, like 4, 4:30?"

Vinny wrinkled his face and shook his head. But then his eyebrows arched into a resigned look. "I remember that thing you did for me. You'll have those cars ready at 4. I'll pull a couple techs off other work orders. We'll get it done, Will. The Commissioner with have to wait for his oil change."

Will put out his hand and said, "Thanks Vin. I knew I could count on you. Oh, and could you put untraceable, undercover, temp plates on those vehicles?"

As Vinny proceeded to shake Will's hand, he felt a folded paper in his palm. "Thank you, Will. But that's not necessary."

Will smiled. "That's for lunch my friend." With a wave over his shoulder, Will walked out of the office.

CHAZ'S van arrived at the Police Garage promptly at 4:30 with four occupants. Williams waved for the van to pull over to the entrance of the garage near the fuel pumps. "Have I got a surprise for you," Big Will beamed. "Follow me," he said as he strode into the main aisle of the garage, finally stopping at the rear of the Dodge minivan.

"What's up, Big Will?" Joe asked, surveying the cars around him.

"Here you go, Joe," Big Will said as he tossed a set of keys. "You look like a van man, Joe."

Will turned to Harry and motioned with his thumb toward the Buick. "It may look old, but I understand that it accelerates like a rocket and rides like a boat. And as I recall, '84 was the last year for the Buick Electra before it became the Park Avenue."

Turning to address Vern, Will said, "Here are the keys to that 2005 Escalade. I had one like this many years ago. This one's a little rough, but it'll go through anything." It wasn't a boast. Will knew his cars.

Joe was stupefied, "What are these for, Big Will?"

"Surveillance. And only surveillance."

"Just for this investigation?" Chaz asked. "Can we make any changes to them?" he pressed.

"What changes would you want to make?" Williams asked, a little surprised.

"Each of these vehicles should have cameras installed so that we can park them where we have the best point of view. Then we can monitor from off-site."

Big Will was quite pleased with that suggestion. "Observe and record from off-site? Knock yourself out. I don't think minor alterations like that would hurt, as long as we can do it quickly."

Chaz was rubbing his hands in anticipation, seeing the possibilities.

With a grin, he announced, "If you guys drop the vehicles at my house, I'll be able to work on them tonight. For sure I'll have them ready for service by tomorrow night."

"That would be great if you could do that, Chaz," Big Will agreed. "Today is Tuesday, so you think by Wednesday night you'll be able to roll out the observation vehicles?" Then with hopeful anticipation he pressed on. "Do you think we may have something to view at our Friday meeting?"

"There's only one way to find out," Vern answered. "Let's get these vehicles to Chaz' house so he can get to work."

"I don't have anything planned for tonight, Chaz." Harry offered. "I'll give you a hand," His gravelly voice carried a spark of excitement.

Joe and Vern also volunteered to pitch in. Anxious to get the vehicles outfitted, the parade of cars departed the Police Garage within minutes.

IT was just after dinner Wednesday night when the Coterie assembled at Chaz' residence, while there still was sufficient daylight to work with. Even Big Will showed up, having finished his shift.

Chaz had a double-wide driveway that led past the side of his house to a two-car garage situated behind the house. The driveway now resembled a used car lot.

Joe asked Big Will, "How did you get the cars approved so fast? We only talked about it yesterday, and by the end of the day you had us pick up three vehicles."

"It was a matter of urgency, Joe. I simply spoke with Commissioner Howes and told him of our needs, and he approved it. After that, I just called in a couple small favors. And that's how things get done."

The group made a final inspection of the vehicles. They had been outfitted with multiple miniature cameras installed at the top of windows on all sides of each vehicle. There were also cameras installed in the roof liner of each vehicle over the rear seats so that a full view of the front seat could be viewed and beyond, out the windshield. If you didn't know where to look, it would have been nearly impossible to spot the cameras.

Big Will was impressed with Chaz' work. "I had no idea that you knew how to do all this stuff. Had I known, I would have used your talent while you were still on the job."

"That's the last thing I would have needed, Big Will. More pressure." Chaz then turned to his counterparts. "What do you guys think? Okay?"

Each nodded and praised the work. Joe then asked, "Now how do we monitor the cameras in the vehicles?"

Chaz opened two laptop computers and demonstrated how the cameras mounted in each vehicle would display. "The split screens of each monitor can record each view of the vehicle's six cameras and can display a full screen rotation of the cameras, or fix on just one," he explained. "Because each vehicle is large enough to easily accommodate four passengers, I suggest that we park one vehicle at the north end of the central parking lot and another vehicle at the south end of the lot. That way we can view the pedestrian traffic at four of the towers. We can also see which people are going to which vehicles."

Big Will added, "When Freddie gets back, he will get us the photos they have of known members of the Freedom Boyz. Once we have those photos, we can start matching them to the video we get."

"So, when do you think is the best time for us to drop off the vehicles?" Vern asked.

"To minimize the foot traffic in the parking lot and prying eyes of tenants, I think we drop the first vehicle about 2 a.m. and the second one about 3 a.m." Chaz suggested. "It will take only two people for the placement of vehicles if done one at a time."

Joe proposed, "I can make it at that time." Then asked, "Who else?"

Chaz said, "I can do it with you, Joe…," but was cut short by Vern.

"No. I'll go with Joe, Chaz. You have to get a full night of sleep because you'll be manning the monitors tomorrow. Besides I don't know squat about computers, but I can drive."

Big Will approved of the plan. "We just let the vehicles sit there. Let the residents get used to seeing them parked in the same positions. Like Trojan Horses. We do this right and we don't have to risk any of our guys being spotted or confronted."

"Exactly," Chaz confirmed. "That won't happen again."

Williams asked, "What do you mean again?"

Chaz responded, "You know, we won't have to go to the vehicles again and again to change the batteries. I've powered all the cameras off their car battery. I also included a GPS unit in each vehicle. Just in case they get stolen, we'll be able to get them back."

"Oh. Good idea, Chaz." Big Will walked from one vehicle to the next, expressing his confidence, "I knew that the Coterie would make a comeback. If we can get some damning video on enough of these scumbags, Narcotics can make their arrests, and there's a decent chance that one or two will roll over. Once those perps start talking, hopefully we'll crack a couple homicides! Maybe one will be Sean's."

CHAPTER 22

Planting Vehicles

The maroon Escalade pulled up and parked on the street in front of Joe's apartment building.

As Vern was walking up to the building, Joe exited looking at his watch. "Quarter to two. Nice timing, Vern," Joe greeted the retired sergeant. "Although, I think we're going to have to make a stop before we deliver the van."

"Why? We have a full tank of gas, don't we?" Vern questioned. "What else do we need?"

"I was looking at this van. It's a 2008 and looks pretty damn good. Too good. We have to do something about that. I think a stop at the Sanitation Department Garage can cure that," Joe suggested. "We have to dirty up these vehicles and make them a little less attractive."

It was already 3 o'clock when the two vehicles were finished being splattered with mud, coated in dust, and the interiors had been littered with an unbelievable assortment of trash.

"That should turn off anyone shopping for a vehicle to snatch," Vern said, appraising their work. "So, how are we going to do this?"

"I figure we'll plant the van first. You follow me into the center parking lot. I'll park the van in the best position I can find near the south end, where we can observe the entrance to the Evelyn and Florence Towers. Then I'll walk between the towers, past the row houses, and you can pick me up in the south parking lot."

"And then we're both in the Caddy?" Vern asked.

"Yeah. Then you drive back to my apartment. I'll get my car and follow you back there. Then you can park the Escalade at the north end of the center lot, where the cameras have a view of the Catherine and Deborah Towers. I'll pick you up in the north lot and drive you home," Joe explained. "As long as we get this all done before daybreak, Chaz can check the computers and we can get some sleep."

Vern ran through a checklist with Joe, "You have your cellphone? A walkie-talkie from Chaz? And a flashlight?"

"Check, check, and check," Joe answered.

"And you're packing?"

"Always," Joe replied patting his jacket pocket.

"Okay," Vern said with a nod. "Let's do it. You take the lead. I'll have eyes on you until you leave the parking lot, then I'll come around the other side and pick you up."

The plan went as scripted. Joe parked the van in the first row closest to the high-rises, between a new shiny white Cadillac CT6-V with gold trim and an older Kia that obviously hadn't been moved in a month. The vehicle was situated with a full view of the front entrances of Evelyn and Florence Towers. As soon as Joe walked away from the van and disappeared into the shadows between the buildings, Vern quickly drove to the rendezvous point where Joe was waiting.

A half hour later the pair were leaving Joe's apartment on Parkside. Joe, in his own car, followed Vern who was still driving the dirtied Escalade. It was just after 4 when Joe pulled over to the curb on Towers Road in a shaded spot that offered a full view of the north end of the central lot. Through the binoculars, Joe carefully watched as Vern found an open spot in the second row from the Catherine and Deborah Towers. This was a good vantage point, as the Escalade sat higher than the other vehicles. The cameras had an unobstructed view of the entrances to both complexes.

Joe's walkie-talkie crackled with a moment of static, and then clearly received Vern's report. "Joe. Just locked the vehicle. Leaving the north end of the parking lot," Vern's voice was steady as he recounted his progress.

Joe continued to visually monitor Vern's movement until he blended into the darkness between the towers. Once Joe lost sight of Vern, he drove to the north side of the row houses to wait.

As soon as Vern was engulfed by the dark void between the buildings, he heard a sound from the shadows. It was just the sound of gravel being walked on, but it rang alarm bells in his head. Before he could extract the walkie-talkie from his pocket, a tall silhouette of a man appeared. Vern could not see his features, but he recognized the voice.

"You lost old man? What you doin' on my turf?"

Then Vern caught a slight glint of errant light reflecting from the chrome finish of a snub-nose revolver.

The man advanced closer to Vern, the pistol now clearly visible. With the confidence of power in his hand he demanded, "Empty your pockets old man. Do it! Now!" He leaned forward aggressively as he barked his order.

Instinctively, Vern had taken a sideward stance. He leaned back slightly on his back leg and sprang forward. His leading foot struck the man's wrist causing the gun to fly in the air. No sooner had both feet returned to the ground than his entire body spun around, sweeping the man's feet out from under him. As soon as the man's back slammed to the ground, Vern's right foot swung down, his heel crushing into the robber's groin.

The man yelped in pain, grabbing his crotch. Vern's leg chopped down again, landing a second kick squarely across the miscreant's left kneecap. The man yelped again and swore, sobbing as he tried to drag himself away.

Vern hopped spryly to his feet, found the chrome plated snubby .38 and stuck it inside his waistband. A minute later he emerged from the north side of the towers where Joe was nervously waiting.

"Where were you, Vern? You should've been here two minutes ago. You had me worried."

"There was some unfinished business that I had to take care of," Vern proudly announced. "You remember that good-for-nothing that threatened us the other day?"

"Yeah. You ran across him?" Joe asked in amazement.

"Well, he's still not much of a criminal. Even with this," Vern exclaimed, as he carefully pulled the chrome plated gun from his belt and placed it on Joe's dash.

A look of shock washed over Joe's face. As he started to put the car in gear he commanded, "We'll get him. Which way did he go?"

Vern threw both hands up, signaling for Joe to wait. "We don't have to go after him now. He'll be around this viper pit. He must live here. Besides, Big Will told us not to make contact with anyone. Zero contact," Vern chuckled. "We can get this guy anytime we want."

"You got a good look at his face?" Joe asked.

"No. But he shouldn't be too hard to find. He'll probably be the only one hobbling around here with a cast on his left leg. Not to mention that we'll have his prints on the gun. It feels like the first night we worked together, Joe. Remember?"

A smile spread across Joe's face as he drove away from the Freedom Housing complex. "I forgot that you are a black belt in that Kung Fu."

"How many times do I have to tell you guys? It's a cross discipline, Muay Thai and Taekwondo." Vern frowned and shook his head.

ALTHOUGH Joe was exhausted, he couldn't sleep for more than three hours. By 9 a.m. he was on the phone calling Chaz.

"Hello," a woman's voice answered.

"Oh, this must be Kitty. Is Chaz home by any chance? This is Joe Morgan."

"Yes, he is. He's in that back room playing with his toys. That's all he does lately. I'll get him for you, Joe." After a brief pause, he was shaken by the familiar bellow, "Chaaaaaaz. One of your cop buddies is on the phone."

Joe thought she could have spared his eardrums if Kitty had just lowered the phone before she called for her husband. "Thanks Kitty," Joe returned with a loud voice.

A moment later Chaz picked up the extension in his workshop. "You can hang up now, Kitty," Chaz instructed his wife. "I'm sorry I didn't get the phone quicker, Joe. But I was, uh, indisposed."

"Didn't mean to call so early, Chaz. But I was curious if you looked to see if the cameras were working?"

"Don't worry about getting me up. I usually get up around six. Sometimes earlier. This morning I was up at 5:30 and started reviewing the video from the cars that you and Vern set up. Talking about Vern… did he have some problem over there this morning about 4:23 a.m.?"

"As a matter of fact, he did. After we dropped the second vehicle off."

"The Cadillac Escalade?" Chaz asked.

"Yeah. After he left the vehicle he was walking back to where we were supposed to meet and…"

Chaz jumped in, "He was accosted by someone. And then there was a fight. Well, kind of an altercation that lasted only 43 seconds."

"Vern didn't say exactly what happened, but I suspect that he handled himself okay." Then Joe added, "He didn't have a mark on him. In fact, he disarmed the guy of his gun. Now that we have it, and we can give it to Big Will so he can have it run through ballistics."

"The infrared was able to pick up Vern between the buildings," Chaz boasted. "Some really great video. Exciting, too."

"Yeah," Joe groused. "I'm sure Big Will is going to be enthralled. Was there anything else that was significant on the video?"

"There were a couple young men who were walking through the entire parking lot checking out the cars. They were very interested in our van. They had their faces pressed up against the windows, but that's all they did. I guess with the dark tint on the windows they didn't see anything that interested them."

"It's a smart move you made installing those cameras, Chaz. We didn't have to sit in the van all night and worry about two clowns like them."

"And later, about a half hour ago, those two came out of the Evelyn building with this other guy who was draped in gold chains. They left in the luxury Cadillac that was parked next to the van. We got the plate number."

"Great work, Chaz," Joe complimented. "Why couldn't the surveillance be this easy when we were on the job? Can you imagine how much more we could've gotten done? Well, what do you think, Chaz? Should I call Big Will and let him know what happened so far? Or should we ride out one more night and tell him at the Friday Round Table?"

"I don't see what harm Thursday night would do. Besides, nobody got hurt. Well, none of our guys."

Joe agreed, "Let's go one more night. Then we can drop it in his lap at the Round Table."

THURSDAY night was more like a boys' afternoon out, as Chaz invited Vern, Harry, and Joe over for beer, pizza, and surveillance videos. They arrived early in the afternoon. The main computer had a 24-inch monitor and was displaying the views from the cameras in the Escalade, while a laptop showed the action of the van's cameras. Each screen managed a half dozen camera views.

The new Cadillac luxury sedan that departed at 8:34 a.m. returned at 12:40 p.m. The car was driven by the man laden in gold and accompanied by the two individuals that were earlier observed looking through the vehicles in the parking lot. By their body language, and the way they positioned themselves on each side of the driver as they exited the vehicle, it appeared that they were bodyguards of some sort.

"Did you see that?" Harry asked. "Can you play that back again?" He pointed to the van's view of the Cadillac, which was now parked several spaces away. Harry lowered his glasses onto his nose. "Back it up about 10 seconds, and watch the guy lean into the rear seat area."

Chaz reversed the video and then hit forward.

"There. See!" Harry jumped to his feet, leaning into the laptop. "He has a pistol in the small of his back. You can see it as he leans forward into the rear seat area behind the driver's seat. Mr. Gold Chains there is standing to the side, overseeing everything."

The three men backed away from the vehicle when a fourth person began to emerge from the rear seat of the Caddy.

Then the Coterie members began to howl with rib splitting belly laughs, when a pair of legs eased out of the rear seat, the left leg having extreme difficulty with its full cast. He was still wearing the checkered jacket.

"I take it that's your guy?" Joe asked Vern. "That big oaf tried to mug you?"

Vern could hardly answer he was laughing so hard. "He tried his best… for about 8 seconds."

"Do you think he filed a crime report at Twelve?" Harry cackled. "I can see it now. Officer, I want to report a crime. I was attacked by an eighty-year-old man, a foot shorter than me, a hundred pounds lighter than me, and he stole my gun!"

"Yeah," Joe added. "And he'll want to apply for the Crime Victim's Assistance Program for loss of income as a robber."

The group roared even louder as they watched the three assist the much taller man as he hobbled into the Evelyn Tower building.

The rest of the afternoon was spent watching a boring, couple hours of inconsequential events. The only highlights were: a domestic in a Chevy; a man working on his car while procuring parts from another parked vehicle; and an apparently crazy guy dancing around in an open housecoat, one slipper, and a shower cap. Nothing else. What was most notable in the videos was what they didn't see. No police patrols.

CHAPTER 23
Friday, April 19, 2019

FESSING UP

JOE, HARRY, VERN, Chaz and Mike were seated at the Round Table when Big Will arrived.

"We already ordered, Big Will. We ordered your regular steak and eggs, over easy, and rye toast," Chaz stated, looking pleased with himself.

"Well? How did it go?" Big Will asked. Then he noticed the men looking to each other sheepishly, as if to find a volunteer to respond. "Uh-oh." Williams sensed. "Cameras not working?"

"Oh no," Chaz said proudly. "They worked perfectly. The daylight video and even the infrared night vision. Perfect."

"Then what's the problem?" Big Will demanded as he examined each of his friends. "Nobody got injured, did they? Or did one of you smash up one of the surveillance vehicles?"

Everyone shook their heads negatively. "No. Everyone is fine," Joe affirmed. "And so are the vehicles."

"Are we going to play guessing games here?" Williams asked. "What happened? I know something went wrong. Just tell me," he urged.

All eyes turned to Joe. "Well, there was one small wrinkle," Joe said. "It's better to just show you." And he nodded to Chaz.

Chaz placed the laptop on the table, had the video set to Thursday, 04/18/19, 04:23 hours, and he pressed the play button.

Big Will watched as a diminutive older person walked into the darkened area between the two apartment buildings where he was confronted by a much larger person. Even with the night vision of the camera, the distance and position of the people prohibited any clear identification. Big Will continued to watch and witness the smaller person overwhelm the larger one. A smile came across Williams' face as he viewed the meager man pick up an object from the ground, as the other fled the scene with a severe hobbling injury.

"It's wonderful to see the underdog come out on top. So, what is wrong? You couldn't find the victim?"

Vern beamed. "No, I'm here." He declared flatly.

Big Will's face became a mixture of confusion and wrath. "I specifically told you guys that this was strictly surveillance. No contact."

"I only contacted him briefly. But he never contacted me," Vern explained with a dry chuckle.

"And Vern did recover this," Joe advocated, as he placed a paper bag on the table and slid it over to Williams.

Big Will looked inside the bag. His eyes widened. "Is this what you picked up from the ground? He was armed?"

"He was armed for a minute," Vern smiled.

Harry chimed in, "This could be the break we're looking for. When the Lab examines the gun, they should be able to find prints. Then we'll know who this moron is. If we can find that out, then maybe he'll give us Mr. Gold Chains and his associates."

Now Big Will just looked confused. "What are you talking about, Harry?"

"You'll see when you play this," Chaz said as he slid a thumb drive over to Big Will. "I've cut and pasted the important clips of video, so you don't have to sift through hours of crap. It would've helped immensely if we had the photos to compare to these four guys in the video."

"We would've had them if Freddie was here," Big Will agreed. "But he'll be back Sunday. I'll see him Monday morning and I'm sure that I can get those mug shots and other photos to you guys by Monday afternoon."

Harry took another sip of coffee. "So, what about this weekend? You want us to keep up with the surveillance?"

Big Will weighed the evidence obtained and the potential identification of suspects, to the risk. "Alright. Stay the course. But NO contact with those people," Big Will warned sternly.

"Not unless it is absolutely, no choice, unavoidable," Vern vowed.

"Anything else you guys want to tell me?" Big Will asked.

"No," Joe replied. "However, Big Will, I do have one question. Did you get a chance to interview that other driver at the hospital?"

"Donalson?" Williams questioned. "It's been two weeks now that he's been in a coma. My fear is that he won't pull through. Or if he does, the head trauma is so severe that he won't remember a damn thing. Or... he'll just be a breathing vegetable."

"Oh yeah, another thing," Chaz grabbed Big Will's attention with his curious expression. "When I sat through all those hours of video, not once did I see a police cruiser go through the parking lots. No marked units whatsoever."

"I'll look into that, Chaz," Big Will promised, "and I'll drop off this gun at the Lab as soon as I get back to HQ. Vern, I want you to file a report of Attempted Robbery. List the suspect as John Doe for the time being."

"As soon as I leave here, I'll go to 12 and file the report, Big Will."

Williams thought for a moment. "You don't have to tell them what you were doing there at that time of morning, or that we recovered a gun, or that we have video."

"Please tell me that I can report that I kicked his ass." Vern begged.

"Sure," Big Will agreed. "That will document his injury for a later iden-tification."

THE first stop Chief Williams made at headquarters was on the third floor, the Forensic Laboratory.

"Hey Chief," welcomed the Senior Lab Tech. "What can I do you for today?"

Williams smiled and laid the paper sack on the counter. "Henry, I need a full examination. Ballistics, prints, history. The whole shebang!"

"And I would imagine you expect me to drop everything I am working on because you need this ASAP?" Henry guessed with a wry grin.

Chief Williams loved trading barbs with Henry. "Well, yesterday would be better, but I'll settle for ASAP."

"Will do, Chief," the Senior Tech answered as he logged the weapon into the Lab. "Here's your evidence receipt slip, Chief."

As soon as Williams returned to his office, he checked his computer for messages and reached for the phone.

"Precinct Twelve. Sergeant Scott." Stated the voice answering routinely.

"Hey Sarge. This is Chief Williams. Is Captain O'Neil in?"

"Yes sir. But he's on a call right now," Sergeant Scott explained. "Do you want me to take a message for the Captain, or would you rather hold?"

"I'll hold," Williams replied.

He waited a full four minutes for the Captain to take the call. Finally, he heard, "Captain O'Neil."

"Thom. Will Williams. Hope I didn't catch you at a bad time."

"No. Not at all, Will. What can I do for you?"

Williams was a bit vague when he asked, "You have regular patrols running through the Freedom Housing?"

"No. Why do you ask, Will?" Thom requested.

"Well, my guys will be looking to locate a witness in one of my cases and I just wanted to make sure that there would be units in the area if needed," Williams explained.

"Our patrols have been instructed to stay out of that one block area at the behest of the Narcotics Bureau," Thom stated. "I guess they have an ongoing investigation in that rat hole. My men only go in there if they receive a call. Otherwise we stay out. Don't get me wrong, they hang in the area in case they're called, but we don't want to ruin any other unit's operation."

"Thanks, Thom," Will said. "Oh, do you know who contacted you from the Narcotics Bureau. Maybe I'll call them and see what they have going."

"I don't know exactly who called us. It was a week or so ago. But I can tell you that it was a request via phone, not a written request."

"Thanks Thom. I'll let you know when my guys are in the area."

Will's next call was answered by Chief Ric Amico. "Chief of Narcotics Bureau."

"Good afternoon, Ric. Will Williams," Big Will announced.

"What's up Will?"

"I was speaking with Thom O'Neil at the Twelfth. He informed me that your guys have something going at the Freedom Project. Can you tell me what it is?" Will asked.

"No. Nothing that I am aware of. Why?" Ric inquired.

"Oh, nothing, really. We were going to serve a couple witness warrants over there and I checked with Thom, you know, to make him aware that we'd be around, and he said that he thought your squad was doing some work there. That's all," Williams tactfully explained.

"No," Ric responded. "You need any help?"

"No. We're good. But thanks."

Now Big Will had more questions than he cared to ponder. But they all needed to be answered. Then his concern was sidetracked by a call from area code 561.

"Hey Freddie," Big Will answered. "How is everything in the land of palm trees, sand, and drinks with little umbrellas? Don't tell me. Let me guess, Sunny and 85 degrees."

"Hey, right back to you, BW," Freddie responded. "Actually, it's been raining the last three days. Angela and I had to stay inside the whole time.

With this heat, it gets so humid when it rains. I can't wait to get back up north."

"So, you called looking for weather sympathy?" BW asked.

"Naw. I was curious about what happened since last Tuesday's meeting," Freddie replied. "The last I heard when I called on Tuesday was that you and the group were having breakfast, and you mentioned that Chaz was going to set up some type of surveillance at the Freedom Towers. How'd that go?"

"Pretty good," Will stated. "I secured an Escalade and a minivan from the impound lot and Chaz rigged them up with cameras. We had one small glitch though, and I only found out about it this morning."

"What happened?"

"It seems that during the early hours on Thursday while they were trying to sneak the cars into place, someone tried to mug Vern." Will said.

"Is Vern okay?" Freddie queried.

"Vern? Oh, he's alright. The mugger? Not so much," Will giggled. "But they got the cars in place and the cameras are working fine."

"BW, I wish I were there to help. But I'll be back home on Sunday night, so if you need anything…call me. I'll be available all day for you on Monday until I go to work at 11.

"Oh, by the way," Will interrupted, "don't forget to get us a package of the Freedom Boyz mug shots and whatever surveillance photos your squad may have. If you can get those to me Monday morning, I'll get them to Chaz," Williams reminded Freddie.

"Absolutely, BW. I didn't forget. As a matter of fact, I had a couple of my guys put that package together while I was gone. I'll call and make sure it's done. You'll have the package Monday." Freddie assured.

THE buzzer rang in apartment E-318. Bax answered, "Yo, whassup?"

"We got her here, Bax," reported the voice from the lobby of the Evelyn Tower.

"Bring her up," he commanded.

A couple minutes later a tall, well-proportioned man escorted a middle-aged woman to the entrance of E-318. She couldn't help but notice how the door was heavily protected. It had a sheet of steel reinforcement and numerous cameras positioned down the hall. There was no need to ring a bell or knock on the door. As soon as a person approached E-318, they were being monitored. Either the door would electronically open, or there would be the sound of additional locks engaging.

Bax stood approximately 10 feet from the door as it opened for him to welcome the visitor. He was proud to exhibit his lavish apartment and the gold jewelry that he wore. "Ms. Donalson, I had Lenard bring you here so that I could express my sincere feelings regarding your son, Tyrell. He has been a good friend, and I was so concerned when I heard that he was in a car crash. I haven't been able to go and see him because they only let relatives in. Have you visited him? How is he doin'?"

"I've been up to see him twice," she answered. "They only let me see him for ten minutes at a time. He's still asleep. You know, unconscious."

A slight smile formed as Bax handed Ms. Donalson an envelope. "Here. This might help with cab fare the next time you visit him. And there's something there for you, too."

The woman peeked into the envelope and was amazed to see a thickness of $20 bills. "Oh, thank you Mr. Bax. Thank you!" she exclaimed.

"I know you're going through some bad times now. So, the next time you go to see Tyrell, if he's awake, tell him that I am concerned for him. And tell him that he should get all the rest he can. Not even talk. Not to anyone. Just rest. Okay? And there is a phone number I wrote down on a piece of paper in there where you can reach me. Call me when he wakes up. Okay?"

"I surely will, Mr. Bax. Thank you," Ms. Donalson gratefully replied.

"As a matter of fact," Bax suggested, "I think it would be good for you to see how Tyrell is doing this afternoon. I can have Lenard drive you up to the hospital and he will wait for you while you visit him. Then Lenard will take you home. How would you like that?"

Although not expecting to visit her son that afternoon, Ms. Donalson tightly grasped the envelope and responded, "That would be ever so kind." With a last nod of appreciation to Bax, she exited apartment E-318 with her escort.

CHAZ checked the cameras. All were functioning correctly. He was anticipating increased activity, as it was a Friday night, so he invited the Coterie for another video party. Joe, Harry, and Vern were called, but only Joe and Harry were able to stop by.

"This is getting to become a routine," Joe suggested.

"Do you mind a routine?" Chaz asked.

From 8:30 p.m. to 11:30 p.m. the three intermittently played cards as they viewed the two computer screens. They watched as the cameras automatically switched from daylight mode to night vision. Periodically there would be people entering or leaving the five-story apartment buildings, going to or from their vehicles, but there was nothing exciting. Nothing unusual. Not, at least until after Joe and Harry had left. Then, just before midnight, Chaz watched three men as they moved from vehicle to vehicle throughout the central parking area. They used flashlights to look inside each vehicle. They didn't try to open the doors or do any damage. They just kept moving from vehicle to vehicle. It occurred again at 2 a.m., but despite his best efforts, Chaz fell asleep at 2:35.

CHAPTER 24

Who is Anjanae?

WHEN Chaz woke, he quickly noted three things. First, the date and time stamp on the video of the laptop indicated that it was 8:44 a.m. on Saturday. Second, there was no reception of video from the Escalade at the north end of the lot, or from the van at the other end. Third, he had a painful kink in his neck from sleeping in a seated position.

Of course, he attended to the most important problem first. Anticipating this possible situation, Chaz had a contingency plan. With a couple strokes of the keyboard, the computer commands switched the power leads to a bank of backup batteries that were placed on the floor behind the driver's seat of both vehicles and covered with debris. The screen of the computer lit up with the views of the six cameras in the Escalade. The problem there was that the main battery under the hood had likely died. Chaz also had a remedial plan for this. He would have AAA come to charge the battery. The lack of pictures from the minivan was yet another problem. All systems appeared operational and the battery was still at full charge, but there was still no picture. This would require an on-site inspection.

The last problem Chaz addressed was his stiff neck.

THE buzzer rang in Joe's second floor apartment. He pressed the speaker button. "Who is it?" Joe asked.

"Will Williams," came the reply. The door was unlocked, and a moment later Will was met at the top of the stairs. "I have to start working out again," Big Will huffed.

"Let me guess," Joe said sarcastically. "You were in the neighborhood and just thought you'd drop in?" Joe led Will down the hall to his apartment. "Coffee?" Joe offered.

"No thanks. I just needed someone to talk to. Someone I can trust," Big Will confided.

"About what?" Joe asked. "Obviously, you're not looking for life coach guidance."

"On second thought, I will have a cup of coffee. Black, please."

"Of course." Joe suspected that Williams had questions. Serious questions or else he would have just called. "That's the good thing about the Coterie, we all know how each other takes their coffee, well, except for Vern who drinks tea," Joe wandered off topic.

"And that's why I stopped over today. I'm not sure how one of our guys takes his coffee," Big Will acknowledged.

Confounded by the cryptic response, Joe questioned, "Who are you talking about? Me?"

"No. Whatever gave you that idea? I'm talking about Freddie."

The answer astounded Joe. "Exactly what are you talking about?" he asked as he poured two cups of coffee. He slid one cup across the table to Big Will.

"I suppose that there is some logical explanation, but there are just a few things that don't add up with him," Big Will asserted. "Like a couple weeks ago when Freddie didn't make it to that Friday breakfast when Mike first joined us. Remember? He told me that he worked late and had a morning meeting with Ric Amico. He said that he was dead tired and went right home to sleep. I found out that none of that was true. He wasn't even home."

"You went to his house?" Joe queried.

"Yeah, but not because I was checking on him. I had that information about Sean that I wanted to give him as soon as I could. I thought he could follow up on it. Later that day he called me to say that the meeting with Chief Amico was called off and he spent the day helping a friend. What friends does he have that are more important than our group? And at a time like this?" Big Will asked suspiciously.

"And that's what all of this is about?" Joe said. "So, Freddie has other friends outside our circle."

"But there's more," Big Will insisted. "Do you recall last week when we were in the planning stage for the surveillance at the Freedom Projects? Wasn't it Freddie who stated that the routine patrols in Precinct Twelve were increased in that area? Wasn't it also Freddie who assured us that the Narcotics Bureau was putting the squeeze on activities in that area?"

"Sure, I remember him saying those things."

"Well, that's all bullshit! In fact, the exact opposite is true. I spoke with Thom O'Neil at 12, and he said that his people were asked to stay out of the projects because Narcotics was conducting an ongoing operation. Then I spoke with Ric Amico who informed me that his Narco guys had nothing currently going at the Freedom Towers! So, what the shit?"

Joe was at a loss for words. He simply shook his head and shrugged his shoulders. "So, what do you propose?"

"I have no idea, Joe. That's why I came to talk to you." Big Will submitted. "You always see things different from me. What do you think we should do?" Big Will reversed the question. "If he doesn't want to be helping in this effort...okay. But don't lie to us. Christ, he could be putting some of our guys in harm's way, thinking that there is backup out there when there ain't."

"So, you think he's what? Lazy? Dirty?" Joe pressed. "Or could it be that one of the other guys in the Narco Bureau is up to no good? Maybe Freddie has a rat-bastard in his squad?"

"I don't know. I really don't know," Williams repeated with a sigh of disappointment. "But we should find out before someone gets hurt." He then announced his final issue with Freddie, "And it seems like he's never here when we need him."

"You can't blame a guy for wanting to be with his wife, Big Will. It's not his fault she wants to stay in Florida. Quite frankly, if my wife had wanted to stay in the warm weather, I'd have been right there with her. I don't see why he just doesn't retire and move there, like half the retired guys do."

"Do you think this is an issue that we bring up at the next meeting?" Williams asked. "Or should one of us address this directly with him?"

"Well aside from not being forthright on a couple things, he hasn't hurt anyone or broken any laws...," Joe scratched his head. "I'm just upset if he's not supportive of our efforts to find Sean's murderer. Come to think of it, he couldn't even come to the funeral."

Big Will dropped his huge hand onto Joe's shoulder. "I feel let down, too. We'll just let it ride a while and see what happens. Okay?"

CHAZ was waiting outside when the AAA tow truck arrived. He slipped the driver a couple twenties and instructed him with the plan.

Once the tow truck stopped near the Escalade, Chaz would get out and walk down to the van. In the meanwhile, the tow truck driver could then unlock the Escalade to access the interior and release the hood. By the time Chaz had checked out the van, he expected that the driver would already have replaced the battery.

The AAA driver stropped his truck at the rear of the Escalade. Chaz quickly handed him the keys and exited the tow truck. Before the driver could get to the front of the Caddy, Chaz was gone. As he weaved through the rows of vehicles heading toward the south end of the parking area, he observed that several of the vehicles had been vandalized with spray paint. When he reached the planted van, he noticed that all the windows had been spray-painted, and the side of the van had been tagged with "FB4EV-ER" graffiti. With a second look at the rest of the parking area, it became apparent that there was a common thread to the vandalism. All the vehicles that had their windows obliterated with paint and tagged with the markings were vans of one sort or another.

Without checking the van further, Chaz hurried back to the tow truck where the operator stood by with a perplexed expression.

"Battery's changed?" Chaz asked as he approached. "What's wrong?" he demanded.

"There is no battery here to change," the tow truck operator replied, pointing toward the open engine compartment.

Chaz looked at the front of the Escalade. The grill was damaged with marks from a pry bar. The hood was sprung open, the battery cables had been cut, and the battery was missing. "Damn it!" Chaz shouted. "Let's get out of here...now!"

Without a moment's delay, the tow truck sped through the parking lot, exited onto Towers Road, and fled the projects.

Once in the safety of his own workshop, Chaz called Joe to advise him of the development.

"Are you okay?" Joe inquired.

"Yeah, I'm just pissed off. That's all, Joe," Chaz complained. "I fell asleep around 2:30. And when I just played back the video, I saw the three people walking through the parking lot and stopping at each of the vans that were vandalized. I should have played the video back before I left, damn it!"

"Well at least we know what happened to our surveillance vehicles," Joe offered as weak consolation. "But now we have to figure out why those bastards did it, and where we go from here."

"Do you think that they spotted you and Vern when you dropped the vehicles off?" Chaz questioned.

"No," Joe responded firmly. "We did that early Thursday morning, Chaz. If anyone had seen us then, they would have hit those vehicles sooner. Why wait until the weekend? Besides, if they'd seen us drop those vehicles, they would have known which van to target. They wouldn't have had to hit all the vans in the lot. I don't know how, but maybe they were tipped off."

"You have a point there, Joe. They hit all the vans in the parking lot, every single one," Chaz confirmed. "I think we all should get together somehow to figure out what we do next. This isn't something that can wait until the Tuesday meeting."

"Let me make a couple calls, Chaz. I'll get back to you soon," Joe advised.

BAX and his two bodyguards were making their daily rounds, checking on the activity of distributors, when he received the call.

"Yo. Ya got th' man!" he answered the phone. The only part of the conversation the pair of personal protectors in the front seat could hear was the animated voice of their boss.

"Tomorrow night? Yeah. Good," Bax nodded as he listened. "That's the same, seventy-five grand. The same as always." After a longer pause, Bax shook his head dismissively, "Don't sweat it, man. As long as we been doin' business, it's always been just you and me. Nobody else knows who you is." Bax nodded energetically, "Uh-huh. And that's the way it's gonna stay, as long as you keep up your end with the information and makin' the deliveries. Okay, m'man." It appeared an agreement had been reached. "Okay. See you then. Same time, same spot." He ended the conversation with his signature sign off, "Cool."

The driver kept looking forward, while the front seat passenger looked over his left shoulder for instruction.

"Hey Bax, that the call you was waitin' for?"

"Back to the Tower," Bax directed. "As soon as we get back, I want you to get things moving. We need everyone at work on the fourth floor by eleven tomorrow night. It's payday, again!"

"Is there anything else you need?" Lenard requested.

"Yeah. I said it's payday. You know what that means?" Bax waited for a response from Lenard. When there was none, Bax announced, "Tyrell is not here no more, so that makes you my Second." Lenard nodded but still didn't speak. Bax continued, as if he felt he needed to dumb it down, "That means when I go to pick up the goods, you drive. And I want you packing heavy. Guns up the ass, man."

This was the moment Lenard was hoping for. Official recognition and a promotion. "You can count on me, Bax. I will always have your back."

"Have the SUV ready at nine tomorrow. And like when Tyrell was running the protection, I want two escort vehicles."

Lenard let a small smile crack through his stern facial expression. "Got you covered, Bax!" Lenard affirmed.

"And while we's speaking about Tyrell, did you hear anything from his Mom? She was supposed to call."

"No, Bax. But I will contact her as soon as we get back."

"Yeah. See how the poor boy is doin.'"

JOE sat at his kitchen table sorting through a stack of papers covered with his scribbling, a pile of printouts from the Department, a single business card, and his phone. Joe stared at the mountain of work and reflected on his conversation with Big Will. He weighed the years of trust he had with each member of the Coterie. With his phone in hand, he sat motionless for several minutes trying to decide which call to make first. Then he decided.

"Precinct Twelve. Desk Sergeant Scott," was the greeting.

"Scotty. Joe Morgan, here. How have you been?"

"Oh, just fine, Sir. Haven't seen you since…" Then he remembered when it was. "Ah, what can I do for you, Sir?" Sergeant Scott quickly changed the subject.

"I was just wondering. Have you received any notification of the Narcotics Bureau running an operation in your Precinct in the past month or so?" Joe inquired.

"Yes sir," the Desk Sergeant replied. "I took the message myself and posted it on the bulletin board in the Briefing Room. That was over at the Freedom Housing Projects."

"So, the patrol units were instructed to step up their passes through there or were they requested to stay out of the Projects?" Joe asked.

"Oh, we were requested to stay out. The Narcs didn't want our marked units to spook the players they were after." Scott explained. "Each of the platoon Lieutenants would have the information posted on the bulletin board, and should have notified the patrols to skirt the area unless taking calls there. Yeah. I haven't heard anything since posting that note."

"And how long ago was that request made?" Joe prodded.

"I guess it was two or three weeks ago. And I don't know what the operation concerned or if it's still ongoing. Do you want me to call and find out?"

"No. That's okay. I'll be talking with them shortly. But do you recall who notified you of their operation?"

"I don't recall specifically. I know it was one of their shift supervisors. It probably would have been their Day Shift Supervisor, Lt. Thomas. Yeah, it had to have been him because I was working the desk on days, and I recall that the call came in late in the morning."

"Thanks, Scotty," Joe concluded the call.

His next call was to Big Will. He explained the incident Chaz reported to him. "What do you think, Big Will? Chaz doesn't think that this was a random act. He suspects that the Freedom Boyz may be on to us. He also thinks that we should all get together for a meeting."

"I don't know how the Freedom Boyz would've gotten wind of us being there. Nobody else in the whole Department knew exactly what we were doing. Not the Precinct, Narcotics, or…," Williams stopped abruptly. "You don't think that someone from the Police Garage could have overheard any of what we were planning? Do you?"

Will looked confused and he pondered the possibilities. "Vinny?" He thought out loud. Then he suggested, "Freddie?"

Joe interrupted, "No. It couldn't be. He's been in Florida for the past week. He has no idea what we've done so far. You are really getting paranoid with Freddie's absence."

"We did talk with him on the phone at last Tuesday's breakfast, if you remember." Will jarred Joe's recollection. "And a couple days ago I had a brief conversation with him."

"Did you tell Freddie anything specific that we were doing?" Joe asked.

"No. Of course not. It was mostly small talk about the weather, and I told him about that episode with Vern, how he was almost mugged. We had a good laugh over that. But I don't recall saying anything specific," Big Will reported. "But getting back to your question about getting together, yeah, I think it's necessary. But let's not meet at the Towne, or any other place where there might be cops stopping by. We need someplace more secluded. More private."

"I know just the location," Joe declared. "I'll set it up and notify the others." As promised, Joe made a succession of calls to secure the meeting place for 6 p.m., and advise the others of the emergency meeting, time and place.

Now there was one final call to make.

"Chuck Mason," stated the voice answering the call.

Joe's voice was soft and deliberate. "Chuck. You told me that I could contact you if I needed anything."

"That's right, Cap. Anything! What can I do for you?"

Joe went directly to the point, "Here's what I need," and Joe provided a couple names, addresses, phone numbers, and whatever other information he had pertaining to the two individuals. "Can you do it?" Joe asked.

"No problem, Cap. Give me a couple days and I'll have it all for you."

"LUCKILY, it's not a Wednesday night or the hall would be packed," Joe informed Harry, who was the first to arrive.

"What the Hell, Joe?" Harry's voice nearly echoed. "How'd you come up with this place?"

"I called my friend, Father Sullivan, and asked if anyone was using the Bingo Hall in the basement of St. Catherine's church. He was more than obliging. We will have all the privacy we need."

The others arrived, each on the heels of the other - Vern, Big Will, and even Mike. They pushed two folding tables together and began situating the folding chairs on both sides when, as usual, Chaz arrived last. He began making a straight line to where the group was gathered. In perfect synch, five arms raised up and pointed to the far corner where the restrooms were located. Chaz made an abrupt left turn and marched to the men's room.

"The reason we're here tonight," Joe began to explain, "is because our surveillance vehicles have been compromised. Or so it seems. I gave you a brief overview when I spoke with you earlier, so you all know what happened. No need to cover that ground again. But I think it would be prudent if Chaz could bring us all up to speed on the current status of the vehicles."

Chaz leaned onto the edge of the table. "Everything was working fine for two days. Last night the Escalade went down when the battery was stolen. I managed to get it back online using a backup battery, so it is still operational. The van is still operational, although all the windows have been painted over. We have no view. I was on site this morning and felt that it would be impossible for any of us to go there and make any repairs or changes."

"Chaz, do you think we should continue with these pieces of crap?" Harry asked.

"We have good cameras in each vehicle, and they have provided good intel and evidence for the short time they've been working. I say we stay the course. Whoever did this thinks they have sidelined the Escalade by cutting the cables and removing the battery. Let them think that, Harry," Chaz answered. "The Escalade is still producing pictures and video. Unfortunately, it's at the north end of the lot and it seems most of the Freedom Boyz activity is at the south end. Before it went down, the van captured a lot of activity at the Evelyn Tower. That's where we need eyes."

"How do you propose we do that, Chaz?" Big Will questioned. "We can't just walk up to the van and start scraping the paint off the windows. It would take too long and it would single out our van from the rest."

"Absolutely right on both counts, Big Will," Chaz allowed. "But if we had someone who could blend in with the neighborhood and strategically scrape off just enough paint to allow the cameras a view, that would take no time at all. And remember, we still have the Buick Electra in reserve."

"And I still have my own surveillance van we could use," Harry offered.

"One step at a time," Big Will advised. "Which one of us do you think best blends into the neighborhood?" Williams queried. "The six-foot-six black guy, who everybody in these projects knows is a cop? Or maybe one of you old white guys?"

Then Mike raised his hand as if looking for permission to make a suggestion. "I have someone in mind. She's a Detective, a Sheriff's Deputy who I went through the academy with. We've kept in touch through the years and at reunions. I know she's done some good undercover work. You want me to ask her?"

Harry questioned, "A woman?"

"An African-American woman Deputy," Mike clarified. "And she can take care of herself."

"Who is she?" Big Will asked.

"Anjanae Adams. Ever hear of her?" Mike tested the group, as he looked from person to person, finally stopping at Big Will. Nobody said a word. "And that's my point. She's from out in the sticks and has been assigned to the southern part of the county. Nobody up here knows her. You want me to call her, or do you want to go through regular channels...which could take a week?"

Big Will examined the possibility. "First of all, we don't have that kind of time to waste. Then, do you think she would want to help us? Besides, do you know her that well that you could just call her directly?"

Mike smiled as he removed his phone from his shirt pocket, pressed the button for contacts, scrolled down to A. Adams, and then pressed the dial button. As the phone rang Mike said, "I'm sure she'll be willing to help. She's a good cop and one helluva..."

Then the call went directly to the mailbox with a generic message. "Please leave your message. The subscriber will call you back."

The group teased Mike, with Harry leading off, "Hello, Deputy Dawg?"

Mike ignored them and left his message, "Anjanae. This is Mike Morgan. I have a really big favor to ask. Can you call me back ASAP? Thanks."

"You call someone and ask for a big favor on a message machine, and you think they'll call back?" Vern chided. "That's not...," but before he could finish his sentence, Mike's phone rang.

"Hello, Anjanae?" Mike switched the phone to speaker.

"Yes, Mike. How have you been? Haven't seen you for a couple years. That is, until I was at the wake. I'm so sorry, Mike." Anjanae's voice was warm and welcoming.

"Thanks, Anjanae. And thanks for calling back so quickly," Mike said smirking at the older men around him. "But I have a predicament I think only you could help with."

"Oh, really?" she questioned with a seductive tone.

"No, nothing like that, Anj. In a way, it has to do with Sean's death. There's an investigation and," at that point Mike took the phone off speaker and walked away from the group. A few minutes later he returned and had their undivided attention. "When do we need her here?" he asked.

Chaz suggested, "Whenever she can make it. The sooner the better."

"Mike put the phone back up to his ear. "Did you hear that? That is wonderful. Thank you ever so much, Anjanae." Mike ended the call and announced, she'll be here in an hour and a half. It's quite a drive."

In the meanwhile, in order for the Coterie to finalize their tactics for getting Anjanae in and out of the parking area, Chaz had to run home for a few pieces of equipment. Harry also returned home to pick up his own surveillance van.

It was shortly after nine o'clock, the sun had just set, when Anjanae arrived at St. Catherine's Bingo Hall, amid great anticipation.

Harry was flabbergasted as she descended the stairs to the basement hall. "There's no way we're going to send someone who looks that cute into a place like that."

Big Will also had his doubts as he towered over her. "You definitely will attract attention if there's any of those gang members patrolling that lot. Isn't that what you said they did, Chaz?"

Anjanae turned to Big Will, reached up along his back to a spot under his shoulder blade and pinched as hard as she could with her thumb and forefinger, bringing Williams almost to his knees. "Don't let my size fool you. I can take care of myself. Now, what's the job at hand, fellas?"

Chaz proudly displayed his devices. "Do you know how all these work?" he asked as he inventoried the equipment. Four walkie-talkies, one ear-comm, one phone interceptor, and one parabolic mic with recorders."

Vern eagerly pushed through the group to be near Anjanae. "Where did you learn your pressure points?"

As the plan was designed, at eleven o'clock Anjanae would drive the '84 Buick through the central parking lot, park it in the closest open spot near the van, and lay low in the car.

Vern would be partnered with Joe and stationed in the south parking lot, within striking distance in case Anjanae or any other member needed help. Harry would park his van on the edge of the central lot where he could view the Buick and the entrances of the two Tower buildings at the south end of the lot. Once Harry observed where the gang's security patrol came from, he would notify Chaz, who could watch them remotely using the cameras in the Buick and the Escalade. If possible, Harry could utilize the parabolic mic to eavesdrop on the guards from a safe distance.

Once the guards' route was observed and timed, they would wait for the second round to be made. Mike, in full uniform, was paired with Big Will who had his unmarked city Tahoe equipped with lights, siren, and police radio. They would be positioned just off the property on Towers Road to act as the backup unit if needed, but only if absolutely necessary. Big Will did not want this to appear to be an official police operation and have it blow up in his face.

The main objective was to have Anjanae get to the van, remove a minimal amount of paint from the windows, install the phone interceptor, and get away undetected.

An hour later the three lot guards, whom Chaz witnessed a night earlier, started to make their second round, periodically stopping to look into vehicles.

Anjanae slid over the back of the Buick's front bench seat and snuggled into a ball on the rear floor. She pulled a blanket over her head and waited for an all-clear sign from Chaz.

The three guards spread out and meandered through the lot working their way northward. Once they passed the van and Buick, Chaz alerted Anjanae through her ear-comm, and the others via walkie-talkie, that the coast was clear.

Harry then drove slowly in the opposite end of the lot to distract the guards.

"Anj. It's clear to exit now," Chaz guided her as she slipped out of the Buick. With the poorly lit lot, her small frame barely created a shadow as she moved between the parked cars. When she arrived at the driver's side of the van, she opened the door, reached in and plugged the adapter cord into the power outlet. "Okay Chaz. Step one is done," she announced into her ear-comm. Gently she locked and closed the driver's door, and went to work with a razor blade to scrape the paint from the top of the specific windows until she heard Chaz' voice.

"You got it. Clear view on driver's side."

She then worked her way around the vehicle, clearing a spot on the rear window, and then the passenger side middle window. Just as she was about to reach up over the hood of the van, an intense spotlight shown down from the roof of the Evelyn Tower. As soon as the light fixed on the petite figure, the three goons were diverted from checking out Harry's van. They split up, two walked down one aisle, while the third started running down the next parking lane nearest the van.

"What's that light?" Anjanae shouted.

Chaz ordered, "Anj. Get out of there." On the walkie-talkie he urgently directed, "Harry. Block the two SOBs in the next aisle. Don't let them get near her."

Big Will was in the Tahoe with Mike, as they waited impatiently and listened to the excitement on the walkie-talkies.

To avoid the spotlight, Anjanae slid under a nearby truck. She then rolled from one vehicle to the next while the spotlight moved about, searching for any movement. Chaz was nearly frantic as he demanded updates.

The PI surveillance van revved its engine and went full bore down the adjacent parking lane. The two characters jumped out in front of the van displaying weapons, expecting the van to slam on the brakes. At the last moment of indecision, they realized that it wasn't slowing at all. The first man dove out of the path of the van, ending up sprawled half under an old Lincoln, watching the passenger side of the covert vehicle as it flew by. However, he did manage to get off two shots from a handgun, which reverberated between the buildings and scared the hell out of Chaz.

All the activity swirled together in a three-second burst.

"What's happening? Who's shooting?" Chaz yelled.

A split second later, Harry announced, "I'm OK! I'm checking for her." A moment later the second yard bird was treated to a flying lesson as he sidestepped the vehicle on the driver's side. Harry's timing was perfect as he kicked open the driver's door. It swung open with such velocity, combined with the vehicle's speed, and connected so precisely with the entire right side of the man, that the impact propelled him over the top of a panel truck.

When Big Will heard the crackling gunshots as they echoed through the projects, he knew the situation had turned dire.

Mike grabbed the walkie-talkie and alerted, "We're going in." As Big

Will turned on the engine and was about to engage the overhead lights and siren, Mike shouted and pointed to the end of the row houses. "There she is." A slim outline of a crouching person darted out from the darkness and into Big Will's headlights. Mike sprang out of the passenger door and drew a bead on the area from where she sprang. Big Will just shoved his door open, leaned out, and took a stance between the doorframe and the vehicle. Both had fixed their weapons in a direction to provide defensive cover.

Anjanae shot past Will's open door, opened the rear door, and dove into the back seat. "I don't think anyone followed me," She reported. "I'm good."

Chaz was still demanding a situation report, "Talk to me. Someone!"

Big Will picked up the walkie-talkie from the seat and informed the other members of the Coterie, "Anjanae is in my vehicle. We're heading for the meeting point."

Vern then checked in. "We're on the south side of the towers. We're okay. Heading to rendezvous point."

Harry finally acknowledged, "I'll have to get a dent taken out of my door and fill a couple holes in the back of my van, but otherwise, I'm okay. I'll see you guys there."

Two blocks away, all the vehicles pulled into a closed plaza to account for everyone - the Tahoe with Big Will, Mike, and Anjanae; Joe's personal car with him and Vern; and finally Harry and his battlewagon.

"Now that's what I call a party, Mike." Anjanae giggled. You guys know how to get a girl excited." Then she looked toward Mike. "If I knew you guys did all this fun stuff I would have joined the PD instead of the Sheriffs."

"Enough!" Big Will ordered. "Things were going south for a few minutes there. We're lucky nobody got hurt."

"We're all okay," Harry assured Big Will. "And thanks, Anjanae. It was a lot of fun. Just like the old days. And..." Harry directed a side glare toward Big Will, "we didn't fire any shots."

Williams informed the group, "Now I'll have to check with Chaz to make sure he didn't have another heart attack. Then we'll see if this thing was successful or not." He looked at his watch. "You all go home. Get some sleep. I'll be in touch tomorrow." Then he spoke directly to Anjanae softening his tone, "We can't thank you enough. To give up a Saturday night on the spur of the moment, and then to go through this?"

Anjanae smiled broadly and stated, "Mike saved my life twice. This is the least I could do. On top of that, it was just going to be another boring Saturday night."

Will offered, "Well if there's anything we, and I'm sure I speak for the rest of this bunch, if there's anything we can do for you, all you have to do is ask."

"There is one thing, Will," she hinted. "I left my car at the church. Can I catch a ride?" she asked.

"Of course, little lady," he answered with a smile.

Her smile turned to a scowl as she imitated a pinching motion. "Little lady?"

Will threw his hands up as if surrendering. "Okay. I meant Dangerous Lady!"

CHAPTER 25

Eenie, Meenie, Miney, and Look Out Moe!

CHAZ WAS SO exhausted from the previous night's excitement that he was still asleep at 10 a.m. when the phone rang.

"Good morning," Chaz answered.

"Morning, Chaz," responded the familiar voice.

"Big Will. You guys scared the hell out of me last night."

"And for a few minutes it scared the hell out of me, too. I didn't mean to wake you, Chaz, but do you think you'll have time to check the cameras to get photos of those two that took shots at Harry? Maybe some photos of them as they were around either of the vehicles? Maybe we can ID them."

"I was wound up so much, I didn't get to sleep until four in the morning. After you left the projects, I did make a preliminary computer search and I'm pretty sure we have some good usable video. I also checked the phone interceptor and we got a handful of numbers for that time of night."

"Great!" Will declared. "They come back to anyone we know?"

"Sorry, Big Will. I didn't get a chance to run them. It was getting too late. When I did get to bed, I just laid there looking at the ceiling. When I finally did start to doze off, I had to…"

"I know. Go to the bathroom?" Williams guessed.

"But now that I'm up, I'll start back on the computer. Give me a couple hours. Okay?"

"So, how did we do overall?" Will asked.

"The Escalade is still transmitting video from all four sides. The van is getting video from the rear and both side windows. Luckily, it's backed in, facing the entrance of the Evelyn Tower, where most of the activity is taking place. It looks like that is where the spotlight came from and where those guards came from. The Evelyn Tower."

"And what about the Buick?" Williams asked.

"There is a dash cam that is operable and both side window cameras. But what is really great is that Anjanae was able to connect the phone interceptor and it's registering phone numbers."

"So, that's the thing that we heard in the park when Joe called Mike?"

"Oh yeah, Big Will. We also have the parabolic mic, voice and video recorder. But that's hand operated, and we have to get someone close enough to use it."

"We can't go through another night like last night," Will responded. "Let me think on that, Chaz and I'll get back to you. Mind if I stop by later?"

"No. Not at all. How about after one o'clock? That will give me enough time to review the video."

THE eleven o'clock mass had just concluded. Joe was half-stepping with the crowd as they exited the church. Joe recalled that his phone had vibrated twice in his pocket as he waited in line for communion. Finally, he was able to slide his phone from his pocket. The first phone number on the caller ID was Chuck Mason, although no message was left. The second was from Big Will, who left a brief message: "Just received call from CMC. Donalson is out of the coma. I'm going there now." The time of the recording was Sunday, 11:40 a.m.

It was almost half past noon by the time Joe pulled into the hospital parking garage and another ten minutes before he arrived at the ICU ward on the fourth floor. Joe walked past the nurse's station and went directly to where Big Will was talking with a middle-aged African American woman.

"Joe, this is Mrs. Donalson, Tyrell's mother." Will made the introduction.

"I just spoke with her and she said that Tyrell woke up while she was visiting, and he started talking. But apparently, he didn't make sense. There's a doctor in with him now."

"So sorry that your son was injured so badly, Ma'am," Joe stated.

"What was Tyrell saying that didn't make sense?"

"Thank you for your concern, Mister. But I could hardly make it out. He just kept repeatin' 'dump truck,' or 'dump the truck.' He wasn't makin' any sense. I really don't know, Sir. But if you don't mind, while we wait for the doctor, I have to make a call."

Joe asked Will, "Did you talk with Chaz yet?"

"Oh, damn it!" Williams said, as he looked at his watch. "I was supposed to meet with Chaz today after one, but then I got this call."

"Which I would consider more important," Joe granted. "Did we get any good video?"

"Yeah, and the phone thing that records the numbers is working," Big Will bobbed his head. "I'd say that it all worked out okay. I checked with Precinct Twelve this morning and guess what? Nobody called 9-1-1 to report gun shots or anybody being hit by a car."

"Imagine that," Joe laughed. "Nobody knows nothing, as usual."

Just then the door opened and a doctor emerged. "Well, Doc?" Big Will urged. "Can we talk to him?"

The doctor shook his head. "Sorry Officers. Mr. Donalson is semi-conscious, weak, and heavily medicated. I'm afraid you'll have to come back. He was rather agitated, and I gave him another sedative to settle him down."

Mrs. Donalson joined the doctor and the officers. "Can I go back in there again to see Tyrell?"

"As I was just telling the officers," the doctor explained. "Your son is in no condition for visitors."

"But I was just talkin' to him."

"I understand," the doctor said. "But he's sleeping now."

Big Will looked at Joe and rolled his eyes. "How much sleep does he need? He's been sleeping for two weeks."

Then Mrs. Donalson sighed, "I guess I'll have to call Mr. Bax back and let him know Tyrell ain't talkin' again."

Big Will nearly grabbed the phone from the woman's hand. "Who did you just call?" he asked.

"Mr. Bax," she replied nonchalantly, as she showed him the folded paper with the phone number and two names, Bax and Lenard. "They're Tyrell's friends. Mr. Bax axed me to call him when Tyrell was able to talk. So, I did, and I spoke with Mr. Lenard. I told him that Tyrell is awake and talkin' again. He said that he would tell Mr. Bax."

"If you want, Mrs. Donalson," Chief Williams offered, "I have to speak with Mr. Bax anyway. I'll give him a call, and you won't have to be bothered. And if he wants to visit, did you tell him what room Tyrell was in?"

"Yes, I told him room 420. That is quite kind of you, Sir," she answered as she looked up to Will. She handed Will the paper with Bax's phone number and said, "Please tell Mr. Bax 'Thank You' for me. He's such a good friend of my Tyrell."

"I most certainly will relay that message to Mr. Bax, Ma'am."

As soon as Mrs. Donalson was out of sight, Chief Williams turned to the doctor and requested, "Can we have Donalson moved to another room as a security precaution?" He then turned to the officer who was stationed outside Donalson's room, 420. "Notify your duty officer. I want a second officer guarding this prisoner. Until he's arraigned, he gets NO visitors at all. That includes relatives."

CHAZ was excited when Big Will and Joe finally arrived. "C'mon in," Chaz greeted both men as he ushered them through the kitchen.

Joe led the procession down the hall to the workshop. "I know the way, Chaz."

Big Will had been at the house recently to examine the vehicles in the driveway but had never been in the inner sanctum. "Holy crap, Chaz. What is all this stuff?"

"It's my hobby," Chaz answered. "But here's what I wanted to show you." Chaz pulled out a couple of chairs from the workshop table and gestured for the men to sit. "These are the photos I printed from all the video we took last night." There was a stack of approximately 20 pictures. They showed two men near the van as they began spraying the windows, two young men wielding firearms in front of Harry's van, several persons prying open the hood of the Escalade and walking away with the battery, and a couple photos of the local lot guards talking on their cellphones. All the photos had time and date imprints. Chaz then presented a computer-generated list of phone numbers that had been 'trapped' by the interceptor, which also listed the number that had been called or the phone that initiated the call.

"This is remarkable, Chaz." But after a moment, Joe countered, "I still think it's not enough for Narcotics to make arrests or get search warrants."

Big Will looked through the photos. "When Freddie gets back, he said that he'd get the entire gallery of Freedom Boyz arrest and surveillance photos. That will be tomorrow. Once we get those photos, we can start identifying who these people are."

"And that will be enough for arrests?" Chaz asked.

"Yeah, but only on the minor charges that these photos support," Will answered. "Petit Larceny, Misdemeanor Vandalism, and maybe a couple other minor bullshit charges. Nothing that is worth shit when it comes to interrogation. There's no leverage here."

"We'll have one Felony Assault and Weapons Possession on the gimp that attacked Vern, but I don't want to place all our hopes on him," Joe opined. "No. We have to get a couple guys on some good solid charges."

"Like Murder?" Big Will prompted.

"And how do you propose to do that?" Chaz asked.

Joe looked at Big Will. "From your years of experience, when does Homicide usually get its best breaks?"

"When somebody eventually talks, it's usually a disenfranchised friend, a disgruntled partner, or someone looking for a deal," Big Will detailed.

"So, we need to hear someone talk. Believe me, they're already talking. Just not to us,'" Joe replied.

"And?" Williams prodded.

"We're going to have to eavesdrop," Joe concluded.

"Remember the Professor at Community College emphasizing that those things require court orders, warrants?" Big Will reminded Joe. "If you hear anything good, it can't be used in court to prosecute the case."

"I know that," Joe responded. "I think if we listen to what these scumbags are talking about amongst themselves, find out who knows what, then we'll know who we have to find charges for. Then we can squeeze them to make deals with the information we know they have."

"Well, we can't just sit around the parking lot like we did last night," Chaz said. "They're pretty much on to us. Although we still have some good cameras operational."

Joe scratched his head. "Chaz, how far does that plastic dish thing for listening work?"

"About 300 feet," Chaz figured. "Maybe I can boost the power a bit depending on the location and conditions."

"And how far is it between the towers on the north end of the parking lot, and the towers on the south end of the parking lot?" Joe questioned.

"I see where you're going," Joe interceded. "If we found an apartment we could set up in on the north end, like a south window on a middle floor of the Catherine or Deborah buildings, we'd have a straight, unobstructed path for listening to anyone outside the Evelyn or Florence buildings."

"And how do you propose we find someone who will let us use their apartment. Go knocking door to door?" Chaz offered sarcastically.

Big Will sprouted a curious smile. "Joe, call Mike and see if Anjanae might be willing to play 'house.' I'm sure that we can find some funds to compensate her for her time. In the meanwhile, sit tight. I'll be back by three. And Chaz, get to work on making that machine better."

Roz watched Lenard on the monitor as he pounded on the door. As the door swung open, she immediately shushed him. "Shhhh. Quiet, Lenard. Bax is taking a nap. He's going to be up late tonight. You know, you should be getting some sleep too."

"Roz, I gotta talk to him right away. He's gonna really be pissed if you don't get him up. He's gonna want to hear this," Lenard urged. "Please wake him up."

A few minutes after Roz disappeared from the room, Lenard heard Bax grumble loudly from the next room, "This better be good!"

Once Bax entered the room Lenard announced, "Tyrell is awake and talking."

"What?!" he shouted. "I thought he was dying. What do you mean he's talkin'? To who?"

"I don't know, Bax. His mother called a little while ago and told me that she was visiting him, and he was talking to her. Then she said that the police were there."

"Goddamn it, Lenard! Why didn't you call me earlier with this information?" Bax demanded.

"I did, Bax, but your phone went right to voicemail. I called three times and left messages. So, that's when I came over and Roz got you up."

"Alright. Alright," Bax relented. "First things first. We need to see who Tyrell is talking to. Then we have to stop him from talking anymore." Bax glared at Lenard. "You know what you have to do?"

"But what about that delivery tonight?" Lenard asked.

"I just told you, idiot. First things first!" Bax jabbed his finger into Lenard's chest. "Tyrell would know what I was talking about, and he wouldn't ask any stupid-ass questions. So, do you want to stay my Second, or do I have to bring someone else up?" Bax raged.

"No, Bax. I got it."

"And get it done soon, because we're leaving here at nine. With or without you," Bax threatened.

IT was just a few minutes after three when Will returned. "We're all set."

"With what?" Chaz asked.

"With apartment 325. It's on the third floor, vacant, and it's all ours as long as we need it," Big Will proclaimed.

"How'd you do that so fast, and on a Sunday?" Joe asked.

"As it turns out, Sharleen's brother-in-law works for the City's Building Maintenance Department. He got ahold of the building manager for the Catherine building and told him that he needed an apartment for a couple out of town relatives. He set us up with apartment 325."

"I guess working for the City does have its perks," Chaz laughed.

"Joe, did you get ahold of Mike? Can Anjanae help us again tonight?" Big Will hoped for a positive reply. "Even if only to get us into the apartment to set up."

"I heard back from Mike just before you arrived. She's in. But she says that she can't stay all night. She has an afternoon shift tomorrow."

THE afternoon detail had arrived and relieved the two officers that stood on opposite sides of the hall at room 420. The Head Nurse tried to explain to the man who claimed to be Tyrell's brother, that he was not able to visit because Tyrell was sedated.

"You can call back in the morning," the nurse suggested.

He was having none of her explanation. Hysterical, he demanded, "Tyrell is the most important thing to me right now. I gotta see him? I gotta!"

The commotion at the nurse's station drew the attention of one of the officers just a short distance down the hall. The officer approached the irate man, "What's the problem, Sir?"

"My brother, Tyrell. I really gotta see him!" Lenard said to the officer. "My mother was up here earlier and she said Tyrell was talking to her. Can I just have a couple words with him? Please?" he whined. "I just have to talk with him for a minute."

Compassionately, the officer considered the request. "Wait here. I'll go and see if he is awake."

The officer walked down the hall and entered room 420, where he planned to call Chief Williams to clear a visit for Tyrell's brother, Lenard. Lenard nervously followed. When both men entered the room, it became apparent to Lenard that there was no one in the bed. As the officer turned, he caught a glimpse of a knife. When he began to draw his pistol, Lenard dove at the officer, rapidly thrusting the knife several times.

A moment later, the officer collapsed, and Lenard grabbed the officer's automatic from the floor. He opened the door to leave, when he was confronted by an officer who had exited room 421 with his weapon drawn.

The second detailed officer stood blocking the entrance to room 421. But in the split second when the door of the room across the hall had opened, three images immediately registered with the officer: Lenard standing with a gun in his hand; the officer lying on the floor with a knife protruding from his chest just above his vest; and a pool of blood on the floor. The officer opened fire with a burst of three shots. Lenard fell as fast as gravity could pull him down.

"I need a doctor!" the officer yelled as he yanked the gun from the suspect's hand. He then pulled his portable from the holder at his hip. "Detail 16-Adam. I have an officer down! Need the Precinct Duty Officer, Shift Supervisor, and Homicide at CMC fourth floor!"

Hospital personnel scrambled down the hall and rushed into Room 420. A moment later the officer heard "Car HB-1, Chief Williams responding," along with the other requested units.

BIG Will responded to the call at the CMC. Once it was determined that the injured officer had not sustained life-threatening wounds and that the suspect was deceased, the Chief of Homicide ordered his afternoon shift detectives to take command of the homicide investigation and keep him informed. Big Will stayed at the hospital until his detectives arrived.

Williams then returned to Chaz' residence, where Anjanae was already briefed and waiting.

"I had no idea that we'd be working together again so soon," Anjanae greeted Will with a smile as he entered the workshop.

"Bodies stacking up. Cops assaulted and stabbed," Big Will summed up the situation. "Joe, I don't know if this is worth it."

Joe's response was somber. "Apparently the murders and the assault have a connection with the Freedom Boyz. And we suspect a connection with Sean's murder. We have to find that connection, Big Will. There's no two ways about it. These are your cases."

"Yeah, I know," Big Will agreed. "But it should be a job for the Homicide Bureau. Not the Coterie."

"Remember how we got here, Big Will?" Chaz asked. "He's one of our own, and the Department was getting no results. We have to follow through with the surveillance. We need to get the evidence the Department needs for arrests. After the interrogations, we can back off."

"Are you up to this Anjanae?" Will asked.

"Hell yeah!" she answered.

It was just after dark when Big Will, under cover of a new moon and outfitted in jeans and an oversized dark hoodie, accompanied Anjanae into the Catherine Tower. They found their way to apartment C-325, opened the door and found a nearly empty flat. Except for a table and three chairs in the kitchen and parts of a bedroom set in an adjoining room, it was a blank canvas. They quickly unpacked the equipment from the duffle that Will had carried up the three flights of stairs.

"How long do you want to stay tonight?" she asked Will.

"Eleven, perhaps. Certainly not past midnight," he responded. "I have to be in the office early tomorrow, because of that shooting at the hospital. Actually, I should've gone into the office tonight."

"Will, if you want to go to Headquarters for a couple hours, go ahead. I'll be okay here. The door is locked, and nobody knows we're here," she said. "Nothing happens on Sunday nights."

"You mean, like nothing happens on a Sunday afternoon at a hospital?"

Will looked at his watch. Nine forty-five. He considered her offer and decided. "Alright. I'm going to hurry down to Headquarters, get the initial reports on the injured officer and the shooting victim, and I'll get things lined up for tomorrow. I'll be back by 11, 11:30, the latest," Will promised.

"No sweat," she assured. "All I'm doing is taking video and sound recordings tonight, so that Chaz can make adjustments tomorrow. Just a trial run."

As soon as Will departed, Anjanae dragged the table to the south-facing window. She then opened the window about a foot from the bottom and set up the tripod with attached parabolic mic just above the sill of the window, next to the table. She ran an adapter and extension cord to a nearby outlet and pulled up a chair. Making subtle changes in direction she recorded and made notes in the log starting with "9:50p: Equipment set up. No activity." She then hunkered down and kept watch on the entrance of Evelyn Tower. She observed several people entering and exiting the building. Then she transcribed her observations in the log. "10:30p: Two men came out of Evelyn and began to patrol the main parking lot. Monitored conversation as they were talking on portable radios."

The taller of the two men stopped periodically to check the interiors of various vehicles and communicated with the other, "Boy, Lenard is gonna catch hell from Bax when he gets back."

"How come Lenard missed that meeting? He was supposed to be the point man," the other shorter, stockier man questioned as he walked along the opposite side of the parking area.

"Don't feel bad for Lenard, Moe. He's the one that screwed up. It's probably going to cost him his position at the top. You know what that means for us? Another shot at the Number Two position."

Moe responded nervously, "I don't know if I'd want that job. Bax has been going through Twos like dirty socks. You can have the next opening. I'll stay with the outside security."

The taller guard quipped, "The way Bax is goin' through right-hand men, he ain't gonna have any hands left."

It was almost 11:30 p.m. when Anjanae considered shutting down the operation so she'd be ready to leave when Will arrived. On a whim she decided to watch the entrance until he got there.

At 11:45 p.m. she made her last entry: "Three vehicles drove across the lawn and blocked the entrance of the Evelyn Building. Audio and video obtained."

What was recorded was a white Lincoln Navigator escorted by two black Chevy Suburbans that stopped at the front entrance. Several people armed with assault rifles emerged from the Suburbans and assumed positions cordoning off the entrance, while two others carried what appeared to be backpacks into the lobby.

Although the exterior lighting had been disabled, the foyer lights were sufficient to show the features of "Mr. Gold Chains" who stood at the entrance and checked the contents of the canvas bags as they were brought inside. The video was able to capture two of the plate numbers and the faces of four heavily armed men. As best she could count, each of the two men carried two backpacks at a time into the lobby, each making five trips. Quite noticeably overseeing the operation, "Mr. Gold Chains" motioned for the shorter of the lot guards to step forward.

"Where is Lenard? He ain't answering any of my calls," he demanded angrily.

"I don't know Bax. He never came back here. I thought he was gonna meet up with you."

"Moe, you tell him to get his ass upstairs as soon as he gets here. And if he don't show up by a half hour… well then, I want you to come up to the fourth floor. Understand?" Bax barked in clipped tones.

Moe paced feverishly back and forth, hoping, praying that Lenard would show up.

It was almost midnight when Big Will returned. "You missed all the action," Anjanae chastised.

"What happened? What did I miss?" Will asked eagerly.

"It looked like some kind of drug buy. I mean, a lot of drugs," Anjanae emphasized. "There had to be a half dozen guys armed with AKs and "Mr. Gold Chains" seemed to be running the show."

"Shit!" Big Will exclaimed. "I'll have to wait to see Chaz tomorrow before I can view the video or listen to the audio."

"I'm turning everything off." She quickly removed the SD card from the listening device and handed it to Big Will. "And here's my log and notes," Anjanae said, handing over her notebook. "Now, if you'll drop me at my car, I'll talk to you tomorrow and we can figure out what we have and where it will take us."

Will opened the apartment door, poked his head out, and made sure the coast was clear. Then with an exaggerated patronizing bow, stated, "Right this way, Dangerous Lady."

CHAPTER 26

―――

A FULL DAY OF CHAOS

WILL WILLIAMS WAS known for his resilience. He had spent most of his day off responding to a homicide "Call In" at the CMC. He had followed that with hours of "volunteer work" with the Coterie, which dragged into the early hours of Monday. Regardless, Will still managed to arrive at work before his entire day crew.

"Good morning, Chief," greeted the Desk Sergeant on the first floor.

"So that's what they call this," Will replied sardonically.

As Williams stumbled off the elevator on the third floor and shuffled his feet along the janitor's newly mopped floor, Earl, the cantankerous custodian sized up the Chief's rumpled suit and asked, "Did your wife leave you, or did she just go on strike?"

The friendly banter brought a slight smile to Big Will's face. "I can see it's going to be one of those days," Will muttered loud enough for Earl to hear.

Once situated behind his desk and armed with a fresh cup of coffee, he plowed through the paperwork he had carefully prioritized last evening. Of utmost importance was the officer-involved shooting of Lenard Swaggert. Will had this marked #1 on his to do list, and in parenthesis wrote, "(connection to Morgan murder?)" The last notation of the several itemized on his list was "Call Chaz."

He was about to leave the office to go to the hospital to interview the injured officer and take another crack at Tyrell, when Freddie Taylor materialized at his door. "Knock, knock," Freddie said.

"Not in the mood for a knock-knock joke, Freddie. However, it's nice to have you back. When did you get in?" Big Will asked.

"I got in late last night. There were some delays when I had to change planes at Reagan National, but I got some sleep on the earlier plane and almost a full night's sleep last night."

"You didn't have to come into the office this early," Will offered apologetically.

"BW, I knew you were waiting for these," Freddie reported as he handed a thick envelope of photos to Williams. "I could've called Chief Amico last week to have him put the package together for you, but I assumed that you want to keep the Coterie operation as much under the radar as possible. So, I had a couple of my detectives collect the photos for me. They weren't told what it was for," he assured.

"Thanks, Freddie. There has been so much shit going on."

"You mean regarding Sean Morgan?" Freddie questioned.

"Remember the guy with the stolen truck who was in the coma?"

"Yeah."

"Well we definitely have him tied to the Morgan homicide with that vehicle, and he is out of the coma now. As a matter of fact, I was just about to leave for the hospital to talk with Tyrell Donalson," Will stated.

"Do you mind if I tag along?" Freddie queried. "I have nothing going today and I'd like to ask him a few questions about the Freedom Boyz. Maybe we can both get some answers."

"I don't want to tie you up all day, Freddie. While I am at the hospital, I also have to interview the copper that was stabbed while guarding Donalson."

"What?!" Freddie gasped. "When did that happen?"

"Yesterday afternoon. You miss all the good stuff," Big Will noted with a raised eyebrow. "Then our group did some surveillance, and not only got some photos of the players, we have some recorded conversations."

"No shit?" Freddie exclaimed. "That was over at the Freedom Towers?"

"Yeah. The guys did good. After we compare these pictures to the video and photos we got, we should have enough to turn over to Narcotics for search and arrest warrants," Will declared, peeking into the envelope.

With that, BW headed for the door. "Come along, if you still want to, Freddie."

"Absolutely, BW. I got your six."

As they waited for the elevator, Will stated, "I'm going to have to run over to the police garage to fill up first. I didn't realize until I parked that I was on empty."

"Why not take my vehicle?" Freddie offered. "It's parked right in front."

"Sure. Why not," Will accepted.

On the twenty-minute drive through morning traffic, Big Will had sufficient time to bring Freddie up to date with the Coterie business.

Freddie listened intently to BW's update and his account of some near disastrous events. After following up with several questions, the conversation turned to more mundane small talk. "So did Ang fly home with you this time?" Will asked.

"No. She really likes the weather down in Florida. So much so, that I wonder if she'll ever come home. She's either on the beach or futzing around with her friends. Sometimes I wonder if she even knows that I'm gone when I'm up here," Freddie sounded a bit depressed.

"Well, if you ever retire and head south, I want first dibs on the Yukon," BW quipped, trying to lighten the mood. "What year is this?" he asked as he leaned over and looked at the odometer.

"It's a 2018. It's the extended version and has all the options that were available, all the bells and whistles," Freddie boasted. "Got it almost a year ago."

Just making out the odometer reading, Will noted, "That's some high mileage for a year-old truck. But I suppose I wouldn't mind, if it brought the price down a little."

Freddie did not comment on the high mileage. "I'll let you know, BW, but it doesn't look like retirement anytime soon."

When the pair reached the fourth floor ICU ward, Williams observed a gathering outside Room 421. "Excuse me," Will addressed the first officers he met. "What is happening here?"

One of the two uniformed officers at the door explained, "Internal Affairs is in with your prisoner, Chief."

"Who authorized that? And why didn't anyone notify me?"

Without waiting for an answer, Chief Williams barged into the room. Tyrell was sitting up in the bed and appeared to be fully aware of what was happening.

Excusing himself from Tyrell's bedside, one of the IAD Detectives walked over and quietly informed Williams, "We just got here a couple minutes ago, Chief. Mr. Donalson was mirandized and is considering giving a statement. He wants to know what we can do for him?"

"What we can do for him?" Williams questioned in a hiss. "I'd like to have a word with you both outside the room. Please." Big Will politely ordered more loudly.

As soon as the door closed, Chief Williams stressed in his harshest whisper, "I am the Chief of the Homicide Bureau. I have at least one homicide, and possibly more, that I am investigating that involve Mr. Donalson. My homicide investigation trumps any internal investigation you may have. Do you understand? Never undermine another of my investigations again."

"But Sir," the IAD officer countered respectfully, "there is an officer-involved shooting we have to investigate. Officer Warren Webster shot the suspect, Lenard Swaggert, who we understand stabbed Officer Bart Rhoney, as Swaggert was allegedly attempting to harm or kill Donalson. We need to corroborate these facts and find out why Swaggert would want to kill Donalson. That's why we were interviewing him."

"All well and good, Detective," Williams responded, reigning in his temper, "I want the same questions answered. When I get those answers, you will receive a full transcript of the interview. Is that satisfactory with you?"

As the two suits from IAD departed, Big Will entered Donalson's room again. More composed, he introduced himself. "My name is Will Williams, Chief of Homicide."

"I know who you are," Tyrell replied respectfully. "Everybody do."

"Then you know that when I come around asking questions, somebody died or is about to die. That's what I investigate. I am the only man who can make you a deal. You understand that, Tyrell?"

"Uh-huh," he nodded.

"From what the other two detectives told me, you're a smart guy and know how to negotiate for yourself. You want to talk deals?" Williams asked calmly.

At that point one of the uniformed officers opened the door and Freddie walked in to join Big Will. "So, you are Tyrell?" he observed. "I work with Chief Williams, and anything you tell him you can say to me," he instructed.

Donalson's face lost its spark of hope. "I know who you are, too. I don't remember anything. I'm not saying anything, except…I want a lawyer."

Unfazed, Williams sat in the visitor's chair and leaned toward the bed. "Tyrell. That friend of yours, Lenard Swaggert, came here to kill you. Can you tell me why? And your other friend, Frenchy Montour? They got to him already. He's dead. You can talk to us now, and we can work with the new charges."

"What new charges?" Tyrell quizzed indignantly.

"Once I walk out of here, your charges will also include Murder. The murder of Clarence Benson."

"Who is he?" Tyrell challenged Chief Williams.

"You might know him better as T-Bone. Now is the time for you to use your brain and say 'I'm gonna make the best deal I can for myself.' I know you have valuable information and it won't do you any good in a cell."

Tyrell looked at Chief Williams and then at Lieutenant Taylor. "I know my rights. You can't even ask me any questions. I want my lawyer. I have nothing more to say."

As Big Will and Freddie exited Donalson's room, the Chief stopped momentarily to speak with the two uniformed officers. "Until further notice, only medical staff is permitted in that room. I don't care if it's the Pope himself. He doesn't get in without my authorization. If anyone gives you a problem, have them call me or the PC."

Will and Freddie both stopped down on the third floor to interview Officer Bart Rhoney. It was intended more as a "Get Well" visit than an interview, as all pertinent facts had already been memorialized in numerous reports. There were already full write-ups filed by the Precinct Officers and Detectives who received the initial call, the Department's Shift Supervisor, as well as the Homicide Detectives who caught the case yesterday afternoon. All imperative information had been collected and filed in a dozen different places.

"Officer Rhoney, how are you doing?" Will asked.

"Good, Sir," the young officer answered. "I learned a very valuable lesson."

"And that is?" Williams probed.

"Never take any detail for granted. I thought yesterday was going to be a boring eight hours," the young officer lamented.

"Remember two other things and you'll be fine," Williams added without sounding condescending. "Peripheral vision, and don't trust anyone when you're in uniform."

Just then Big Will's phone buzzed again. Even Freddie heard it.

"It's Chaz," Will told Freddie, tapping the phone in his pocket as he stepped away from Rhoney's bedside. "He's called me at least a half dozen times. Four times since we got here. You know, there are some things more important in this world than his equipment. I'll get back to him as soon as we clear up this hospital stuff. Whatever his problem is, it probably can wait until tomorrow's breakfast." Pausing as he exited the room, Will asked Freddie, "You'll be there, right?"

BY the afternoon Chaz had given up on contacting Big Will and instead decided to reach out to Joe.

"Hello," Joe answered on the second ring.

Excitedly Chaz blurted, "We know who the main people are. We got video, pictures, and even audio recordings. Anjanae got what we needed!"

"Slow down, Chaz," Joe urged. "Let's take it one item at a time. We have photos?"

"Yeah Joe. Lots of photos. Well, actually its video taken by the planted vehicles and from the monocular video recorder. But there is so much video that a hundred stills can be made. We will be able to make positive IDs of the Freedom Boyz."

"Okay. What about audio recordings? What do we have?" Joe pressed.

"Well, we have the two yard-guards from the parking lot talking while they're sweeping the lot. They talk about Bax, who is the apparent leader, Baxter Brown that Freddie laid out for us a few weeks ago. This confirms it. Apparently, he goes through hired help like water. Then on the audio we found that they just received a huge shipment of drugs, and it's on the fourth floor of the Evelyn Tower. It's all there on video, too."

"Not only that, Joe, but I began checking the phone numbers that we logged on the phone trap. Almost all those are burner phones. You know the prepaid throwaway phones. So, they have no names listed to those numbers. But it is possible to find out who bought the phones if they used a credit card. But that's probably too much to hope for," Chaz added.

"How many phones are we talking about?" Joe asked.

"Fifty. Sixty. And they have out-of-state area codes," Chaz reported.

"Out-of-state?" Joe questioned. "Where out of state?"

"There were a few phone numbers with area codes 703, 202, and most had a 404 area code."

"And," Joe prodded, "what geographic areas are those numbers assigned to?"

"Well in that order… Arlington, VA, Washington, DC and Atlanta, GA," Chaz detailed. "The strange thing is that all but one of these phones are being used locally. They're using them like walkie-talkies."

"And where is that one number that isn't local listed to?" Joe asked.

"It's a DC number, 202-912-9855. But it has a restricted listing. No information available."

"So, what Freddie told us is true?" Joe asked. "You know, about the structure of the Freedom Boyz?"

"So, it appears," Chaz agreed. "Joe, do you think you can get ahold of Big Will? I've been trying all morning. I left a couple phone messages and a couple texts. I want to get the photos that Freddie was supposed to drop off so that I can start matching them with the people in the video."

"He is probably swamped, Chaz, with that shooting at the hospital. I'm sure he'll call when he gets a chance."

Joe was still turning his mind inside out, trying to make a connection between Sean, the Freedom Boyz, and that damned note. Joe was torn as he mulled over the two possibilities: the phone numbers traced back to DC, and the doubt that Big Will had cast on Freddie. Then there was his recollection of Chuck Mason working for a DC agency. After an hour of not being able to fit the puzzle pieces together in his mind, he had no choice but to call Big Will.

Just as Chaz had complained, Joe's first two calls went straight to voicemail. He then sent a text message, but it too received no reply. Joe waited as impatiently as Chaz. Every few minutes he checked his phone, in case he had missed a response. While checking yet again, Joe noticed a voice message from Sunday that he had overlooked during the avalanche of activity.

It was from Chuck Mason and simply requested, "Call me ASAP. I have some of that information you requested."

Joe made several attempts to reach Chuck at the number that was on his business card, 202-912-9855 ext. 666, but could only leave a message in return.

BIG Will finally called at the end of his shift, almost 6 p.m. "Sorry I couldn't find time sooner, Joe. It's been one helluva day."

"I remember how it used to be," Joe said. "You certainly don't have to explain to me, Big Will."

"Thanks, Joe. I imagine that you're calling to see about that packet of photos Freddie gave me. He dropped it off this morning. I have it right here. You want me to swing by on my way home? Maybe you can take it to Chaz and see if there's anything useful there."

"That would be great, Big Will. Also, there's something else I have to tell you, but it can wait until you get here."

It was 6:30 when Williams pulled up in front of Joe's building. Joe had decided to save Big Will some time and waited on the front stoop.

"Here you go, Joe," Big Will said as he delivered the envelope. "You called Chaz to let him know?"

"Yeah. I'll be going to meet him right after you leave."

"What's this other thing you needed to talk about?" Big Will questioned.

"Do you remember Chuck Mason? Used to be in my Bureau until he resigned."

"Yeah," Big Will answered with a leery tone, "and you're being generous. He was forced to resign. He was a dirty cop."

"His motives were good. But ends don't justify the means," Joe conceded. "Well, he showed up at Sean's wake."

"I didn't see him there," Big Will said looking a little surprised.

"No. He didn't come in. He waited to talk to me out in the parking lot."

"Typical of the coward that he was," Will noted. "So, what did he want?"

"Nothing actually. He only wanted to extend his sympathy and asked if I forgave him for his screwups. Then he thanked me for allowing him to resign," Joe explained.

"Hmmm," Will grunted. "Did he say what he's doing now?"

"Uh-huh," Joe acknowledged. "That's why I wanted to talk to you. Chuck is apparently working for some federal agency. He stated that he could help. So, I reached out to him and asked him to check out a few things. Now I'm not so sure about him."

"Now you bring this up? Joe, you should have asked me about him sooner. You say he just showed up in the parking lot at the funeral home? Why did he wait so long since he last spoke with you? And if he's working in Washington, how did he hear about Sean? What agency did he say he worked for?"

"All great questions. I wish I would have gotten those answers. It's no excuse, but I suppose I was at a weak point and was looking for whatever help I could get," Joe reasoned. "So, my question now is, do I reach out to him again?"

Big Will sat on the top step, resting his forearms on his knees and dropped his head to think. "You know Joe, I find that it is quite a coincidence that he shows up a couple days after Sean is killed and that stolen vehicle was burned. You say he asked you if you forgave him… but did you ask if he still blamed you for bringing him up on charges in the first place?"

Instead of answering Will's questions, Joe hesitantly added, "One other thing, Big Will. Chaz told me that this phone number, Chuck's phone number, showed up several times as incoming calls to Baxter Brown's phone."

Big Will rolled his eyes in disbelief. "You gotta be kidding me. And you want to call him back?" Then with a moment of inspiration he added, "I'll tell you what you should do. Yeah. Call him back. Get him to meet with us. I have some questions for him. And for Christ's sake, don't tell him that we had this conversation!"

After Big Will departed, Joe felt conflicted between confiding in Big Will and possibly betraying someone whose assistance and trust he had sought. In the end, he couldn't escape one thought…what if Big Will was right?

Joe spent the next half hour making calls, leaving voice and text messages.

CHAZ said that it was not too late as he greeted Joe at the door.

"Big Will would have come himself," Joe explained as he handed Chaz the envelope from Big Will. "He has a lot of loose ends to tie up."

"Well as long as we got the photos," Chaz shrugged. "Let's see what we have here," Chaz said, sliding all the material from the envelope onto his work bench. There had to be a dozen copies of suspects' rap sheets with attached mug shots. Then there were several stacks of photos taken during various surveillances. On the back of each suspect's photo were the date of observation, suspect's name, and locations of the photo. Accompanying that material was a line and block chart that detailed the operational structure of the Freedom Boyz.

Chaz and Joe spent the next three hours viewing video, comparing photos, and making notes in preparation for the next meeting of the Coterie.

CHAPTER 27
Tuesday, April 23, 2019

"WILL DO, WILL."

THE COTERIE SHUFFLED into the Towne Restaurant by 9:30 a.m. All members arrived at about the same time. Joe carried a folder, as did Big Will. Spreading the materials on the table near the end where Williams and Morgan sat, the group waited for the chair at the opposite end of the table to be occupied. As usual, they had to wait for Chaz to return from his trek to the men's room.

Lavon had already been by to confirm that there were no changes to the regular orders, when Big Will informed her that they'd only be having coffee and Danish this morning. Eventually, Chaz returned.

"Now that we're all here, a full complement of charter members, except for Howie Smyth, and guest Mike Morgan sitting in, we can proceed," Joe suggested. "I think it would be beneficial if we summarize the events and findings that have arisen since Sean's murder."

Harry seconded the suggestion with a gruff chuckle, "Yeah. Sometimes I don't remember things exactly as they happen. An' besides, some people weren't here all the time." He looked across the table to Freddie to acknowledge his presence.

Freddie added, "It certainly would be good to have a full briefing so that we all are up to speed and on the same page."

"Okay," Big Will agreed. "So, here's the whole ball of wax. As you know, on March 16ᵗʰ Sean was run down by a hit-and-run driver. Initially it was suspected to be an accident, but witnesses and physical evidence indicated that it was intentional.

"Much later we learned, at least my Bureau did, that a member of the Freedom Boyz, Clarence 'T-Bone' Benson, was shot to death sometime on March 17th, the day after Sean was killed. Rumors on the street spread like wildfire that T-Bone was taken out because he killed a cop's kid. But I'll get to that in a minute.

"On March 19th," Will continued, "an unknown subject passed a threatening note to Joe Morgan's parish priest to give to Joe." Will looked to Joe, and resumed after a confirming nod.

"The stolen vehicle Benson was driving was found burned-out on March 21st, twenty miles out of the city," Will stated as a matter of fact. "Obviously to destroy any evidence and dump the vehicle where it was unlikely to be connected to the hit-and-run.

"On the 27th, Joe came to us for help. We decided to take a different approach than the traditional police investigation, and instead of looking for a suspect, who we believed was dead, we chose to pursue a motive."

Harry looked down the table to Joe. "He knew who the best investigators were. And we would give 110%."

"Okay," Williams agreed. "After a little introspection and scratching the surface, we were unable to find a clear motive as to why anyone would want to harm Sean. Even though we found that young Morgan was dabbling in marijuana sales, with a substantial monthly gross for a high school kid, and I received a call confirming that Sean's supplier was a member of the Freedom Boyz, there was no clear motive for him to be killed," Big Will concluded. "And when we examined the possibilities that Joe or Mike could have been the intended targets… we found that Mike may have had some personal disputes and a bad relationship that has long ended, but nothing would add up to a motive for this. And that brought us to Joe. It was his car that Sean was driving. The murder occurred in front of his residence. But was he the target? We were unable to find any direct evidence of such motive. In fact, the following will specifically tie the Freedom Boyz to this murder.

"By April 5th, we had another two homicides that my Bureau logged in. Two more homicides possibly connected to Sean Morgan's," Big Will's voice slowed to a connecting speed. "My detectives identified the two John Does we had in the morgue as Gus Trumble, a vagrant with past gang ties, and Clarence 'T-Bone' Benson, a known member of the Freedom Boyz gang found shot to death at the end of Dutton Street. It is believed that he was the driver that struck Sean Morgan, or so the rumors on the street lead us to believe." Big Will looked at each of the other members for any contradiction. "The only item that significantly linked these two homicides is a set of tire tracks of one dual-wheeled truck that was conclusively identified at both scenes - the location where the burned-out stolen car was found, and at the end of Dutton Street where the body of Benson was found. So far, everyone follows?" Williams asked.

He continued, "Also at this time, there occurs a car chase where two vehicles flee from patrol units. Both are reported stolen, and as the good Lord assisted, both stolen vehicles collided with each other, putting the two drivers in the hospital with serious injuries. They were Tyrell 'T-Man' Donalson and Maurice 'Frenchy' Montour. Both verified as members of the Freedom Boyz gang. Most importantly, the vehicle Donalson was driving was a dual-wheeled F-350, forensically identified as being at both aforementioned crime scenes, and registered to him."

Williams then referred to his notes. "On April 9th, Freddie and I were able to conduct the initial interview of Frenchy Montour. He clammed up and we thought that we'd return later and take a second shot at him. Unfortunately, someone thought that he just might talk, so they silenced him. The other guy, Donalson, who we believe is a more likely person of interest, remained in a coma. Could not be interviewed."

"So, during that period when I was in Florida, neither one of them cooperated at all?" Freddie asked.

"No," Big Will admitted. "Even when you and I went to interview Tyrell on the 21st, the day after another Freedom Boyz member named Lenard Swaggert tried to kill him, Donalson refused to talk and demanded his lawyer."

"Now comes the good part," Chaz blurted out.

"Yes. The good part," Big Will indicated as he looked at Freddie. "This is the part you missed, Freddie." Will went on to itemize their findings. "The Coterie, with the little-known expertise of Lt. Chaz Bohen, put together a plan of surveillance and evidence collection. They performed amazingly well." Big Will turned his commentary toward Freddie. "During the course of their surveillance they managed to secure photographs, video, and some audio recordings of the gang members that you provided photos of, Freddie. The line and block organizational chart you gave us helped immensely to identify the players."

Raising his hand, Mike asked, "Just how much more of this investigation are we going to have to do before the Department takes over?"

Williams was a little taken aback by the tone of the guest. "WE will do what WE have to, to get the evidence that WE need, so that the Department can proceed with proper arrests. That is our goal Mike. Don't lose sight of that. Besides, I think we are pretty close to that hand-off point. Here's what we have."

Will sorted through the material in front of him and handed several photos to Chaz. "On April 14th, you, Vern, Joe, and Harry were out for a Sunday drive. Please tell me what happened, and if you recognize anyone in these photos?"

"You know what happened, Big Will," Chaz said as he leafed through the photos and selected three that showed "Mr. Checkered Jacket." "This guy threatened the four of us and demanded that I get out of my van."

Vern, Harry and Joe looked at the photos and corroborated Chaz' account of the incident.

Williams smiled again. "Very well. The four of you will have to file charges against this 'Mr. Checkered Jacket' - who we have identified as Gerald Anderson, a member of Bax Brown's security guard - for Menacing, Harassment, and Attempted Robbery."

"And what about my next encounter with that scum bucket?" Vern pressed.

"I was getting to that, Vern. You have already filed charges at Precinct Twelve against this character as a John Doe. Those charges of Attempted Robbery and Criminal Possession of a Weapon will have to be amended to include his actual name and further identification."

"Gotcha, Big Will," Vern acknowledged. "I'll take care of that immediately."

Then Harry asked, "What about the damage to my surveillance van?"

With an even broader smile, Big Will turned to Harry. "I'm getting to that Harry." Will picked up four photos from the center of the table and passed them around, until they ended up in Harry's hands. "Do you recognize any of these people regarding an incident on Saturday, April 20th?"

"Yeah," he responded excitedly, "these are the two people who shot at me and damaged my van. You can see the guns in their hands in these pictures. Where'd you get the photos?"

Chaz announced with pride, "That is from your dash cam I downloaded."

"Yeah, that's them! One dented my driver's side door, and the other shot at me and then shot up the back of my van."

"Great," Williams pronounced. "You are officially a victim of Attempted Murder, Reckless Endangerment, Harassment, and Property Damage. You'll need to file the appropriate complaint forms for the arrest warrants. We've identified these guys as Modell 'Moe' Dewitt, and Robert 'Slinky' Johnson. Both are residents of the Evelyn Tower, apartment E-318."

"Isn't that the address Tyrell Donalson used on his truck registration and UUV report?" Joe pointed out.

"Bingo, Joe!" Big Will exclaimed. "This evidence, along with the attached crime reports - which you all will have completed and delivered up to my office by one o'clock - will be presented to the Chief of Detectives and the District Attorney for arrest and search warrants. I would like to give a special thanks to Freddie who provided us with the information from the Narcotics Bureau to expedite the identification process. If it hadn't been for him, this whole process could've taken weeks longer."

As the group applauded Freddie, Chaz interrupted, "Big Will. We really don't have time for breakfast if you need all these reports done by 1 p.m."

"What's the urgency?" Vern asked. "We can get the paperwork to you later in the afternoon."

"No," Will countered. "I need the paperwork ASAP, if we're gonna get search warrants signed this afternoon. I've already contacted Howie Smyth, and he has agreed to have the DA in his office at 2 p.m. After the presentation of our work by Freddie and me, our detectives, both Homicide and Narcotics, will walk through the warrant applications. I think we'll be very busy tonight."

"Why, Will?" Mike asked. "What's the big rush?"

"Chaz brought to my attention that the video he reviewed this morning indicates that there was a huge number of drugs delivered to that building by the Freedom Boyz last night. Those drugs have to still be in there somewhere. With these warrants, we should have the basis to search just about the whole building. Like I said, it's going to be a busy night."

Mike nudged Joe, "I'll have to call Chrissy with the good news and to let her know that I'll be getting home late tonight."

"Ah, about that call, Mike," Will interceded, "I will make that call for you, and for anyone else who has to notify someone. I will deliver your message that you're gonna be working late, because as of this moment we are on full lockdown for the remainder of the day. Everyone has to place their cellphone in this box, which I will guard with my life. Otherwise, nobody is to communicate with anyone outside the Coterie. I don't want the Department to blame any of us if there is a leak. For additional security, and to make sure this all remains secure, we will be paired up for the day. Harry and Vern, get your paperwork done. Chaz and Joe, likewise. Freddie and I will stay together, as we have to make that presentation to the Chief of Ds at 2. Mike, I cannot order you to stay away from all communications, since you're the Commander of the Communications Division. But what I have to do is demand your personal cellphone and request that you monitor all radio calls in Precinct Twelve."

"Will do, Will," Mike responded.

FREDDIE Taylor appeared a bit aggravated with the fact that he was off-duty and had just completed a long night on duty, but he was still on the clock. Will had arranged with Ric Amico to have the time spent this day count as Freddie's next evening shift. Lieutenant Lempke had volunteered to cover Taylor's next tour of duty. "So, BW, you're going to hold my hand all afternoon?" Freddie asked sarcastically.

"Let's just agree that we're holding each other's hand, Freddie. I don't want anyone to accuse me of calling the reporters, and you will be my witness. Especially if it steals the spotlight from Howie," Will chuckled. As the clock moved past the noon hour, the Coterie deadline was quickly approaching. Chaz and Joe reported in first, followed by Harry and Vern.

It was exactly 1:59 p.m. when the secretary in the Chief of Detectives' office announced the arrival of Chief Willie Williams and Lieutenant Alfred Taylor. When she opened the door to Chief Smyth's office, Will and Freddie were met by the hopeful faces of Assistant District Attorney Matt Reynolds, Police Commissioner George Howes, and Howie Smyth. It was a tightly controlled meeting. Within forty-five minutes the evidence had been presented, questions were asked and answered, and the applications for warrants were officially endorsed by the DA's Office.

By the closing of Tuesday's business hours, a City Court Judge had signed all warrants. Before the Chief of Detectives could proceed with the execution of what was dubbed "Operation Castle Down," he secured the floor plans for the entire Evelyn Tower and provided copies to all units for briefing. Big Will had arranged for Chief Ric Amico to have his unmarked units stake out the perimeter of the Freedom Towers Housing Projects. Any gang member exiting the area was to be identified and detained for questioning.

At 4:40 p.m. Narcotics Detectives Santucci and Stafford pulled over an older Ford sedan that ran a stop sign at Towers Road and Fillmore. The vehicle accelerated as soon as the flashing lights came on, but the two male occupants must have used some better sense and pulled to the curb, a couple blocks from the projects. The driver fidgeted with his cellphone, as the two plainclothes officers approached the vehicle with guns drawn. The driver froze before completing his call.

"Out of the car," Detective Santucci ordered. "Hands on the roof!" As the officers performed a preliminary pat-down, they discovered that the driver had a loaded .380 in his waistband. He was quickly facedown on the ground and cuffed. The passenger was also searched and cuffed. A quick once-over of the vehicle's interior found another handgun under the passenger seat and a briefcase packed with various glassine bags of suspected cocaine.

The two suspects were placed under arrest and interrogated in the rear seat of the unmarked car. As instructed, the officers broadcasted on Tac 5, which was their car-to-car frequency. "Command. This is Car 44. We have two perps detained two blocks from the castle," Stafford reported. "You're going to need to talk to these guys right away."

As directed, the officers sped off to the command center, which had been set up in the second floor auditorium of HQ.

Detective Stafford introduced the pair to Chiefs Amico and Williams. "This is Donald Gray, who is on parole, and is found in possession of a loaded .380 revolver. The other was the driver of the car, Moe Dewitt, also charged with Criminal Possession of a Firearm. Both will be facing some serious time with the amount of drugs they had in their possession."

Amico looked at Williams, "You want to inform them, or shall I?" Ric asked.

"Have at it, Ric," Williams granted.

"Gentlemen, I have no time to screw around, so I'm only asking once. Which of you wants the deal of a lifetime?"

They both attempted to raise their hands but were restrained by their wrists cuffed behind their backs. "I'll tell you what you need to know!" yelled Gray.

Not to be outdone by his companion, Dewitt yelled even louder, "Shut up! I know more than you, I'm Bax's second-in-command! Damn it. I knew I never should've taken that jump."

Will then suggested, loud enough for all to hear, "Ric, you take that one in the conference room for ten minutes and I'll take Dewitt into the interview room for ten minutes. Whoever gives the most useful information will get the deal. And I will make it sweet. I promise." While the two command officers interrogated the pair, Lt. Taylor continued making the authorized notifications.

Within the next fifteen minutes the command was fully apprised of where Baxter Brown could be located, that half of the fourth floor was dedicated to drug processing and storage, and that there were as many as ten heavily-armed guards who were more afraid of Bax Brown than of the police. This information was relayed to all primary units by text message, not transmitted over Tac 5.

CHAPTER 28

OPERATION CASTLE DOWN

AT 6:15 P.M. THE afternoon shifts of Precinct Twelve and adjoining precincts were put on standby. Detectives from Major Case, Burglary, Robbery, and Special Investigations units were assembled in the auditorium of Headquarters to be briefed. Commissioner Howes delegated operational command to Chief of Narcotics, Riccardo Amico and Chief of Homicide, Willie Williams, as they were the senior officers who had secured the warrants. Chief Amico requested that Lieutenant Taylor also join the command officers at the "Castle." The Chief of Detectives would man the Command Center at HQ. Together they arranged for the Fire Department to have sufficient apparatus on call and positioned at a firehouse a mile from the Freedom Towers. EMS was notified to have several of their ambulances stationed nearby as well. The power company was instructed to have service technicians available to interrupt service to the Castle when requested.

At 6:40 p.m. Chief Smyth ordered "Operation Castle Down" to commence. All SWAT Team members responded first by moving-in-force to surround the perimeter of the Evelyn Tower. Will, Ric, and Freddie accompanied the heavily armed force as they made their entrance through the front doors and a rear utility door. Immediately, three members of SWAT cleared the way to the basement boiler room, where power and water to the building was cut.

On the third floor, Bax remained calm as he viewed his monitors to see the police units rolling in over the lawn, through the parking lot, and surrounding his apartment building. Then the monitors went dark. He knew instinctively that the elevators would also have been disabled. He quickly called to Roz, "Get the baby to the safe room. I'll be there in a few minutes." He then stuck two handguns into his rear pockets and picked up his cellphone. One button activated an intercom call to all guards. "We're being hit. Stand your ground. Nobody gets up here. NOBODY!" he ordered. Then he pressed another button that connected to the fourth floor. "Dump it all. Throw it outta the windows if you have to."

By that time, the main SWAT force had cleared the first floor and evacuated the few legitimate residents before moving up the two stairwells at opposite ends of the second floor. No resistance was received as they cleared the second floor, although it took time for the next wave of uniformed officers to remove the legal tenants who were cowering in their apartments.

It took a good ten minutes before a SWAT team could breach the third-floor stairwell door at the north end of the hall. The fortified door had to be cut off its hinges and pried open. Two flash-bang grenades were thrown down the hall, and the echoing explosions were met with return automatic fire. CS grenades were then used. The beams of the flashlights angling through the smoke-filled corridor added to the confusion. Through the cloud of gas, coughing and vomiting could be heard, along with footsteps running toward the stairwell at the south end of the hallway. As the fleeing suspects unlocked the several bolts and bars that secured the door, a second SWAT team waited on the stairway and landing. The suspects flung open the door and let a burst of rounds fly blindly into the stairwell. Two officers returned fire, until the opposing gunfire ceased. Gas-masked officers dragged three limp bodies from the hall and yanked them down the stairs to the next landing, where other officers cuffed the suspects and attended to their wounds. Once the third-floor hallway had been secured, the SWAT officers broke windows at the ends of the hall to ventilate the area. When the air was sufficiently clear to breathe again, the uniformed officers relieved the SWAT team, setting up defensive positions so SWAT could proceed to the next floor. Again, the doors to this level were heavily fortified and had to be forcefully breached with a cut-n-pry tactic. The intel they had obtained stated that there were no regular tenants on the fourth floor. Any activity on this floor was likely illegal and should be considered a high target risk and hostile.

As soon as the first armor-clad officers rushed through the open door, the guards that were posted outside the drug lab threw down their rifles and handguns. They had heard the gun battle minutes earlier and realized that if the police had made it up to this floor, there would be no help for them on the way. Without waiting for instruction, they automatically assumed a kneeling position with hands locked behind their heads. In fact, two of the surrendered guards assisted with the entry into the rooms off the hall, instructing the occupants to give it up. Sixteen people were taken into custody without a shot fired on the fourth floor.

Bax Brown had ushered Roz and her infant into a closet with a false wall on the backside. After pushing past the hanging clothes, he put his full weight into the furthest end of the closet wall, opening a passageway into another room. The eight-by-fifteen-foot room was virtually bullet proof, having walls lined with 3/8-inch plate steel. The inside of the safe room had minimal furniture and a modest supply of food and beverages. There was also a narrow set of stairs connected to the long length of wall. The stairway extended up to a hatch in the ceiling that opened into a closet floor in the apartment above. Although primitive, the safe room proved to be quite effective. The police eventually forced an entry into the luxury apartment, but found no trace of any occupants other than the still warm, half-eaten, dinner on the kitchen table. Their search uncovered holes in various walls of adjoining apartments that were covered by wall hangings and flags, or blocked by bookcases on casters. Each escape route was followed and searched, but to no avail. The officers were perplexed by how the apartment door could have been so substantially barricaded from the inside, yet nobody was found within.

Once all levels of the building had been secured by several teams of officers, the SWAT commander allowed the Bureau Command Officers to enter and inspect the premises.

On Tac 5, Chief Amico advised Chief Smyth at the Command Center, "The Castle is secure. Twenty-three suspects in custody. Six of the suspects transported to CMC. One suspect deceased. Homicide is on scene. Send the Evidence Unit in."

Chief Smyth asked, "Are all officers okay?"

"Yes sir," Will reported. "As soon as the forensic team gets up here, we will come back to HQ to assist in booking and begin immediate interrogations."

"And the prime target?" Chief Smyth inquired.

"Sorry sir," Williams lamented. "Somehow he eluded us. We have no idea how he escaped. Our source swore he was on the premises. But somehow in the past forty-five minutes he disappeared."

"Okay, Will. Wrap up your end on-site and I'll see you when you get back," Smyth acknowledged.

Joe, Vern, and Chaz knew that as retired officers, effectively civilians, they were not allowed to participate in the execution of the warrants. But when they heard Big Will announce that he was returning for the questioning, they knew that they could observe, and possibly assist, behind the two-way mirrors of the interview rooms. They waited patiently at headquarters for the Bureau Command Officers to return.

While detectives were photographing the entire third floor, or as much as they could in the dark conditions, Big Will, Ric, and Freddie climbed the stairs to the fourth floor to examine the drug prep rooms and take a count of the packages of drugs that were still stored and not yet destroyed. The beams of their flashlights swung back and forth cutting through the darkness as they climbed the stairs.

"Damn stairs," Will complained as he reached the landing just below the fourth floor, huffing and puffing. "You'd think that they could have turned the power back on so we could use the elevator." No sooner had he uttered those words and reached the fourth-floor entrance, than the lights went on throughout the building.

Chief Amico directed the officers lined up in the stairwell behind him, "Make another sweep of that third floor. Check every inch of wall, floor, and ceiling. That son-of-a-bitch has got to be in here somewhere!"

Walking from one section of apartments to the next, careful not to disrupt any evidence yet to be documented, the three commanders moved quietly and deliberately. "I've never seen so much dope," Will stated with amazement.

"Yeah. It's a great haul," Freddie declared. "Reminds you of the 1996 raid at the Stratford Arms, huh, Chief?" Freddie referred to Chief Amico. "You made the biggest bust we ever had in this city."

"Well this isn't too shabby, Lieutenant. You did a good piece of work with setting this one up," Amico complimented.

Big Will stopped, looked at both of them and shook his head. "Shhhh!" Will ordered. Then in a whisper he said, "Someone's in the next room."

Big Will led the way with a Colt .45 in his powerful hand. Ric crept forward at Will's right side, also with his weapon at the ready. Freddie was a couple steps behind.

As the trio tiptoed into the room, they heard the sound of a heavy piece of wood landing against a wall. Then, from a nearby closet, came the sound of short shuffling footsteps, as if someone was moving into a standing position from the floor. The door of the closet began to creep open, until a sudden burst of energy erupted. A sizable black man laden in gold chains lurched forward with a pistol in his hand. He hesitated momentarily as he glanced at the faces of the three plainclothes men, but as quick as a snake, jerked his arm upward. He shouted, "You bastard! You're going down, too," as he fired two shots from his pistol.

Before he had a chance to pull the trigger a third time, Big Will bent into a crouch and got off two head shots. The man staggered backward into the closet and fell through the opening in the floor. He heard a woman scream as the body tumbled down the staircase. It was only then that he felt a burning in his upper right arm. "Damn. I've been hit," Will exclaimed as he turned to Freddie. But the Lieutenant was clutching the upper portion of his chest just below the left collarbone. Freddie's mouth moved, as if to speak, but no sound passed his lips as he crumpled to the floor.

On Tac 5, Chief Amico called, "EMTs come to the fourth floor! Officers down!"

"What the hell happened?" Freddie asked as his eyes fluttered wildly. Wheezing, he rolled back and forth in pain.

Ric Amico knelt down by Freddie's side and answered, "You caught one in the shoulder. But you'll be okay. Paramedics are on the way."

"And the target?" Freddie asked.

"We found Baxter Brown, Freddie. We got him."

"Is he dead?" Freddie asked.

"Sure is," Ric declared.

Freddie managed a wide smile before losing consciousness.

CHAPTER 29

First In Is First Out

THE BOOKING PROCESS took half the night, even with the extra Booking Technicians called in for overtime.

After processing, the prisoners were moved to holding cells on the fourth floor, and an assessment was made of each prisoner as to the value of his intel potential. Based on these rankings, they were taken one at a time to either Interview Room 1 or Interview Room 2. So began the process that went well into the morning hours. The enlightened administration had done away with the word "interrogation."

With the authorization of Chief Williams, Joe, Chaz, Vern and Harry were allowed to monitor the interviews of suspects in either Room 1 or 2. Both viewing rooms offered the anonymity of two-way mirrors.

The high priority suspects were brought in and detectives from Homicide and Narcotics worked jointly to conduct the interviews. A very dark-skinned man named Gerald Anderson was escorted into Interview Room 1 and assisted into a seat at the center of the table's length, facing the wall with the two-way mirror. The prisoner had a difficult time finding a comfortable position because of the cast on his leg. Vern and Harry recognized him immediately. Two detectives sat facing the subject with their backs toward the mirror, and an additional detective sat at each end of the table.

The Narcotics Detective, Jon Bain, took the lead as he announced, "Today is Wednesday, April 24th, 2019 and the time is 01:10 hours. Present are Detectives, Bain, Murphy, Sardina and Donovan. The subject to be interviewed is Gerald Anderson. He is currently in custody on charges of Felony Possession of Drugs with Intent to Sell, Felony Criminal Possession of a Firearm, Felony Assault on an Officer, Felony Attempted Murder, and he also has outstanding warrants for Burglary and Grand Larceny. Sir, you have the right to remain silent. You have…"

"Blah, blah, blah," Anderson interrupted Bain. "I know my Miranda Rights better than you. So cut the shit. I know I'm going to sit my ass in jail tonight. So, just ask your stupid questions that I'm not going to answer and take me to a cell where I can get some sleep."

"We'll try to accommodate you as much as we can," Det. Bain replied. "But first I need to know how long you have worked with or for Baxter Brown, aka Bax Brown?"

"Never heard of the guy. Does he have anything to do with shoes? Like Buster Brown?"

"That's cute," Bain smiled. "And are there any drugs you are addicted to that we should be aware of in case there is a medical emergency? Withdrawal? When was the last time you ingested any narcotic substance?"

"I take a lot of the little white pills. Aspirin, I think they call them. They're good for pain. Like you pains in my ass."

Exasperated, Det. Bain looked to the other detectives at the table. "Anyone have any questions?"

"Yeah, just a couple," Homicide Detective Bob Donovan answered. "Mr. Anderson, how long have you had this Colt .38 caliber snub-nose?" he asked as he tossed a photo across the table. It was an evidence photo of a chrome plated 2" Colt Cobra revolver. "And who did you get it from?"

"I have no idea what you're talking about. I didn't have any gun when I was arrested tonight," Anderson claimed.

"You are absolutely correct," Donovan agreed. "The reason you didn't have that revolver with you tonight is because about a week ago, an 80-year-old retired cop kicked your ass, broke your leg, and took the gun from you."

"That little runt got lucky," Anderson ranted. "He didn't fight right. He was only kicking. What kind of man does that? You should fight with your fists."

"And how old were you in 2008? Eighteen?" Det. Donovan asked.

"No. I was nineteen. Why?" he answered with a smirk, happy that the subject was deflected from him getting beat by an old man.

"Because you are being charged with Murder. You are the person that closes our cold case," Bob returned the smile. "In 2008 you robbed a little bodega over on North Thames Street. That chrome plated snub was the gun that killed Officer Taylor. Ballistics proves it."

"You ain't pinning that on me! That was the other guy's gun. I only took it after he was shot by the cops. I went out the back door and wasn't even there when that cop died!" Anderson screamed. "That was my brother you guys killed that night. I just took his gun as a souvenir. I didn't kill nobody." Realizing that he had said too much, Anderson began pounding the table with his fists and banging his cast into the leg of the table.

Det. Bain stated accommodatingly, "Now you can go to your cell to get some sleep." He then looked at the other detective. "We have to check the names of the two holdup men who were killed in that robbery."

Vern and Harry could not contain themselves, giggling like schoolboys when seeing a bully trip over his own shoelaces. Vern's tapping on the backside of the mirror drew some irritation from a couple of the detectives. From the interviewer's side of the mirror, their muffled voices could be heard shouting, "Wait 'til Freddie hears this!" Harry cackled. Vern added, "I wish Joe was here now."

The next several hours brought few new revelations about Sean's murder, except that a number of the Freedom Boyz claimed that Bax ordered T-Bone to shake up the guy driving the car. Bang him up, is the term that was used. Nobody thought that Bax wanted him dead. The other thing was, it was done as a favor for one of Bax's business partners. Someone pretty high up, that Bax owed a favor to.

Even though Vern and Harry, in one room, and Joe and Chaz in the other, took copious notes, every interview was documented on audio and video recording, so they could review whatever Big Will thought might be important. At 5 a.m. they decided to call it a night. They had all the next day to piece together any significant information and to prepare for the Friday Coterie breakfast.

Noon on Thursday rolled around way too fast. The incessant ringing of the phone woke Joe and annoyed him.

"Hello," he grumbled.

"Oh, Chuck. I've been trying to reach you."

"Yeah," Chuck replied apologetically. "I was involved in a undercover thing and, well you know how that goes. But I got all the information you wanted checked. I have to warn you. You may not want to hear it."

Still dazed from a lack of sleep, Joe asked, "Like what? How bad can it be?"

"Hey Cap, this is not the type of stuff you just drop on someone over the phone. I'll be back home…or what used to be home, later tonight. Maybe we can meet in the morning?"

"Perfect," Joe declared. "We just had a big raid along with Narcotics and we broke up a major drug operation and seized more than six million dollars in street drugs. Unfortunately, Will Williams and Freddie Taylor were both shot. But neither injury is life-threatening."

"That complicates matters a bit," Chuck hinted. "So where do you want to meet?"

"A group of us old codgers get together at the Towne Restaurant. We'll be there at 9:30."

"Excellent, Cap. I'll be there."

After hanging up, Joe had more questions. He wondered if he said too much, or not enough. The next morning would tell.

WILL Williams was kept overnight for observation as a precautionary measure, but he was being released Thursday afternoon. Before leaving the hospital, he had to make one stop.

"Freddie?" Big Will asked softly as he entered the room.

Lt. Taylor was propped up in the half-elevated bed. "BW," Freddie acknowledged. "I see you got a broken wing." Freddie referred to Will's right arm in a sling. "And seeing that you're in street clothes, I assume you are going home. Happy to see that, BW."

"Thanks, Freddie. But I had to stop in to see how you were doing. So... how are you doing? How do you feel?"

"Good. Really," he reported in a soft voice. "I guess the bullet was through and through, but it chipped some bone from a rib it struck. That bone chip lodged in a major artery. The doctor said that if that bone chip didn't get stuck in the artery, but just sliced it, I wouldn't be here today. He says that I should be out of here within a week. I suppose I should be counting my blessings."

"And we're blessed that you pulled through.," Big Will stated. "The Coterie hasn't lost a man yet."

"I'm sorry, BW, but my memory of that night isn't so clear." Then Freddie asked. "We did get him, Bax, didn't we?"

"Sure did," Will emphasized. "Had to blow his brains out before he could take another shot at us."

"So, we won't be getting any information from him about Sean's murder?" Freddie asked. "Damn. That's too bad."

BW agreed. "Hey, Freddie. Not that it's any consolation," Will changed the subject, "but in our cold case file for Junior's case, we made an arrest on the third guy that got away that night. Turns out he was one of the scumbags arrested in the raid. His brother, Lyle Anderson, was one of the deceased stickup men. We got the gun and the dirtbag made spontaneous admissions while being questioned. This will give closure, at least to his cold case file."

Freddie smiled, "It's karma. Everyone gets what they deserve."

"Sooner or later," BW agreed. "But for now, I'll just let you get some rest. I'll be seeing the guys tomorrow for breakfast. We'll save your seat." BW laughed. "You just get well."

"Thanks, BW", Freddie replied as he shook Will's left hand. "Tell the guys I can't wait to see them."

CHAPTER 30

The Sum of Good and Evil

Chaz, Harry, Vern, Joe, and Mike were seated at the Round Table waiting and hoping that Big Will would appear. Even Chaz was at the table before Big Will arrived, with his right arm in a sling, and the right sleeve of his jacket draped over his shoulder. He received a standing ovation that attracted the attention of all the other patrons.

You could almost see the embarrassment that colored his face as he raised his one good arm to quell the applause. He quickly took his seat at the head of the table. The only seat vacant was Freddie Taylor's. Once settled, Big Will delivered Freddie's message, "I saw Freddie before I left the hospital and he is doing fine. He's looking forward to joining us as soon as possible. Maybe in a couple weeks."

"And how are you doing, Big Will?" Chaz asked.

"I suppose you'll be taking a couple weeks off yourself," Harry added.

"No. I'll be back to work by the end of the week. Modified schedule of course, but I'll be back. There will be a few challenges though. I can't sign my name worth a shit with my left hand."

Lavon appeared at the tables and asked, "Can I assume that all the orders will be the same?" The group nodded and unanimously approved. Before heading toward the kitchen, she announced that she read about Lt. Taylor in the paper and offered, "I hope that he makes a speedy recovery. It'll be great when he's back with you guys again. Tell him that I'm praying for him."

"Yeah," Harry acknowledged. "At least this would be a step up from hospital food."

As soon as the slight laughter died out, Lavon left to place the orders, and Joe asked, "Did we get any useful information from the interrogations?"

"As a matter of fact, yes," Williams declared. "We know that Bax ordered 'T-Bone' Benson to hit the driver of your car. A kind of warning or punishment. But he hit the wrong guy." Will alluded to Joe, "We believe that it was supposed to be you, and we don't know exactly why. But we are certain that Bax didn't have this done for his own benefit. He ordered this for someone else."

"So, we're no closer than we were six weeks ago?" Joe questioned. "We still don't have a reason why this happened. No motive?"

Just then a barely recognizable figure with a full beard approached the Round Table. "Gentlemen," he greeted, with a two-inch-thick envelope tucked under his arm.

Joe stood and addressed the newcomer, "Boy you've changed since we last met. What's with the beard and curly long hair?"

"Like I said, Cap. I was on special assignment."

Joe then addressed the Coterie, "Fellas, you remember Chuck Mason?" The reception was mixed and subtle. "Have a seat, Chuck," Joe offered. "You guys may question why I asked Chuck to come here today. Well the fact of the matter is, that I asked him to do a little research on one of our own. Just as we checked into mine, Mike's, and Sean's lives."

"But that stayed in-house, Joe," Big Will protested.

"True, but I got the idea from you, Will." Joe surveyed the faces around the table. "Big Will brought up some questions about Freddie. Questions that were quite disturbing and that neither of us had answers for. So, I turned to Chuck for some research."

"Research?" Chaz asked. "What kind of research?"

"The kind that we can't do," Joe answered. "Even with local court-signed warrants."

Then Chuck jumped into the conversation. "I can neither confirm nor deny how this information was obtained, but suffice it to say, I got the information that you requested, Cap."

Big Will looked to each person at the table for their response to his asking, "Is this something we want to, or need to, know?"

Vern nodded yes. Chaz nodded affirmatively. Harry agreed. Joe said, "Absolutely," and Mike responded, "I have to know. If it's related to Sean, I have to know."

"Okay," Williams agreed, and turned to Mason, whom he obviously disliked and did not trust. On top of it all, Will certainly disagreed with Mason sitting in Freddie's seat. "What have you got?"

"The preliminary information Cap wanted to be verified, first off, was Lt Taylor's residence in Florida where he and his wife live." Mason slid the stack of papers out of the folder. And from the top pages read:

"Alfred and Angela Taylor co-owned a residence at 1234 Seaway Trail, Boca Raton, Florida. There is no mortgage outstanding. His wife, Angela, was a resident of the Rausch-Klackhorn Assisted Living Home in Boca Raton from December 2014, through January of this year, when she passed away. The cost of this care was approximately $8500 per month."

Big Will's jaw dropped, startled to hear that Angie had died. And it was more upsetting that Freddie continually lied to him about Angela not coming back north because she enjoyed the Florida weather and her friends. Now, even he began to demand answers. "What else?" Will asked.

"With the annual cost of over 100K for nursing care, I questioned how he could manage that on a Police Lieutenant's salary. So, I did a deep dive of his financial records. I found that Lt. Taylor, after using all insurance benefits, burned through his life savings by the beginning of 2016. Which coincidentally," he added, "is around the time he stopped flying to Florida and started to drive all that way."

"It was probably cheaper to drive," Vern suggested.

"And maybe it was some other reason," Chuck proposed. "Could this scenario be possible?" Chuck supposed. "Sometime in early 2017, Lt. Taylor stops a vehicle for whatever reason in the area of the Freedom Towers. It turns out to be Bax Brown. All Brown wants to do is to be cut loose, so he offers the Lieutenant a few grand, in cash, just to turn his back and walk away. It's just pocket money for Brown. But for Taylor, drowning in debt and needing to pay for his wife's care, he can't resist the offer. Then Bax has his hooks into him."

"We've known Freddie for what…thirty years?" Chaz asked disbelievingly. "He would never do that."

"Not Freddie," Harry vouched. "That's only supposition. You have any proof, Mason?"

Chuck leafed through a couple more pages from the stack. "Beginning in April of 2017, it seems that Lt. Taylor came into some money from somewhere. He deposited 110K into his savings account. In September of 2017, he purchased a 2018 GMC Yukon XL for $82,450 and paid cash. Then a couple months later he opened two offshore banking accounts, which at this moment have a combined total of $1.4 mil. Yeah, Sarge. It started as supposition, but money talks. And this money…is screaming corruption. He's probably a mule for Brown's organization, or worse, a partner."

Still distrusting, Chaz asked, "How come your phone number shows up calling Bax Brown several times last week?"

"Just placing a call to the subject, Brown. Whenever he picks up the phone on one of those calls, I had an open mic into his living quarters. Got some good intel from those calls," Mason reported. He pointed to the envelope, "It's all in here."

Big Will questioned Mason's assertion that Freddie had been driving back and forth to Florida, not flying. "But I picked him up at the airport a few weeks ago when he flew in from Florida," Will declared.

"He probably arranged for you to pick him up at the airport after he drove up and made his delivery. You, or any cop for that matter, picking him up at the airport would establish a reliable alibi that he was not even in town, in case something went south. He used you, Chief. I suspect he's been transporting drugs or other materials for Brown. But... it's only a theory."

"Come to think of it," Big Will winced with dawning acceptance, "I did notice that he had over seventy thousand miles on that new Yukon."

Then Joe asked, "So how would this all tie into the killing of Mike's boy?"

Chuck shook his head. "I don't know, Cap. I can get into people's businesses, homes, cars, but not into their heads. You'll have to talk to Freddie Taylor." Chuck then turned to look at Mike. "Maybe it has nothing to do with the drugs, but it does look like the two are connected somehow."

Then Joe queried, "So if this gang is responsible for Sean's death... and he was only killed because it was supposed to be me driving my car that night, how would I be connected to that gang? Why would they want to kill me?"

"Maybe Bax's right-hand man, Tyrell, will be able to clue us in," Big Will suggested. "Especially now that Bax is dead."

Lavon delivered the food, but the only person who had an appetite for the breakfast was Chuck. As he placed an order with the waitress, he passed several documents around the table. "Please excuse the redactions of the headers which contain agency names and data sources. This is all that I can risk showing you. And I can't leave any copies. You understand?" Chuck apologetically explained.

AFTER lunch, Big Will, Joe, and Mike went to the hospital for a follow-up interview with Tyrell.

"Remember me?" Williams asked.

"Uh-huh," Tyrell cautiously acknowledged. "More questions?"

"Definitely more questions," Williams confirmed. "Just so you know, this is retired Captain Joe Morgan, and his son, Lt. Mike Morgan. It was Mike's son that was killed a few weeks back."

Tyrell looked at the two white faces that were noticeably anxious to hear what he had to say. "And you want to know about that?"

"That's right, Tyrell. We know that you didn't drive the car that killed Sean Morgan, but you know who did," Will asserted. "And also, for your information, Bax Brown is dead. So, there is nothing he can do if you talk to us."

Tyrell bounced his head up and down. "Yeah. I know about it. But what's in it for me? Can we make a deal on some stuff?"

"What do you have in mind?" Williams questioned.

"I'll be getting outta here in a day or two. I don't want to go to a cell from here. I want a pass on anything I did in the past two months. Immunity on all that. You do that, I can tell you about that boy that was killed and a couple other bodies," he offered.

Big Will shook his head. "I think that's a bit too much to ask for. I'm sure that anything you'll tell us, we'll find out eventually."

Tyrell thought for a minute and then upped the ante, "Okay, I'll also give you a dirty cop. Is that worth it now?"

"Let me call the DA's office to see if they will do a deal like that," Will offered. "I'll let you know."

The two older men, and the younger man in uniform, moved to the waiting room at the end of the corridor where they had full view of anyone who entered or left room 421. Williams walked to the far side of the room and dialed the District Attorney's Office. He was on the phone for about ten minutes, pacing back and forth with his left hand holding the phone to his ear. He then made a second call, which was much shorter. Big Will returned to where the father and son were seated.

"Any activity down the hall?" Will asked.

"No. Nobody in or out," Joe reported.

"Good," he replied with a gleam of excitement in his eyes. "I don't want anything to happen to him. And I sure as hell don't want him changing his mind. The ADA will be here in a half hour."

The half hour seemed like an eternity, but eventually ADA Matt Reynolds arrived.

"Thanks for coming on such short notice, Matt," Joe greeted. "I can't remember how many times we made deals like this on other people's cases, but when it involves your own family..."

"I have the papers filled out. All we have to do is fill in a couple dates and get signatures. Are you sure this is what you want?" ADA Reynolds asked.

Joe looked at Mike before answering, "If this gets us to the bottom of things," Mike responded, "then let's get it done."

"Tyrell. This is Assistant District Attorney Matthew Reynolds. He has the authority to grant you immunity for the information you'll give. If required, for prosecution purposes, you will have to testify under oath, or the deal is off," Williams explained. "You understand that?"

With but a moment of reflection, Tyrell answered. "You keep your end of the bargain, then I'll keep mine. Yes, I will testify to what I'm saying."

ADA Reynolds printed March 1, 2019 to April 26, 2019. "You understand that the immunity for your actions only pertains to this period?"

"Yes, sir," Tyrell confirmed as he signed his name.

"Now tell me what you personally know about what happened to Sean Morgan," the ADA requested. "I'll be recording this interview. Is that alright with you?"

"Sure, as long as whatever I say for that period of time can't be used against me," Tyrell agreed. Once Reynolds nodded his consent, Tyrell continued, "Bax told me that I had to go out and check some addresses where I might find a tan older Buick, and he gave me the license plate. He said that I had to mess the guy up. Scare him really bad. He said he wanted the guy to suffer. Put him out of commission, you know?"

"And you found the car. You ran him down?" Reynolds pressed.

"Hell no!" Tyrell recoiled. "That's flunky work. I was Bax's Number Two. I got T-Bone to do it. And he screwed it up so bad."

"How did he screw it up?" Reynolds asked.

"He killed that boy, obviously." Tyrell paused to looked at Mike. "Sorry 'bout that, but T-Bone did it. Then when Bax saw it on TV, he jumped all over my ass. He told me to get rid of him and that car. So, I did."

"You killed T-Bone?" Reynolds asked calmly.

"Yeah, I did," Tyrell admitted. "That was so easy, man. That bonehead even picked where he was gonna be killed. Over on Dutton Street. That was the middle of March, right after T-Bone killed the boy. So, that's covered under the immunity, right?"

ADA Reynolds stated, "Mr. Donalson, we have an agreement. Anything within that time frame from March 1st to the present is covered. So, continue." Satisfied with the answer, Tyrell continued, "Bax also wanted me to get a note to someone at the funeral for that kid. With me being black and all, I couldn't go do it myself. So, I picked up a wino over on Elmwood. I drove him over to that funeral place and sent him in. He gave the note to a priest or a reverend, or something like that. Then I tied up that loose end, too."

"You mean killed him?" the ADA asked. "His name was Gus Trumble."

"Makes no difference to me what his name is. He was just a wino from the streets. But he wasn't feelin' no pain when he went. I gave him a hot shot, and he died with a smile on his face. That is also covered by that immunity, right?"

"So, you are admitting to two murders and an arson?" the ADA summarized. "Is there anything else you did during this period that you'd like covered under the immunity?"

"No. That's about it, for now. I mean, there's some small shit that I can't even remember, but I'll think about it," he answered smugly.

"Okay, Mr. Donalson. Chief Williams and these two other gentlemen now have questions for you," Reynolds informed Tyrell.

"I only have one question," Joe said. "Why did Bax want you to harm me?"

Donalson shrugged his shoulders. "I don't know. You'll have to talk to the Delivery Man."

"What do you mean the Delivery Man?" Big Will questioned. "Who is the Delivery Man?"

"You know. He's the one that delivers the payday to us. You know, the heroin, coke, pot. You know. Whatever we need. Once a month he makes the delivery."

"How do you know what he delivers?" Will asked.

"I told you. I was Bax's Number Two. I was his bodyguard whenever we went to pick up the drugs from the Delivery Man. I've been there for every pickup, every month, for the past two years. I know what we was getting."

"And the Delivery Man's name? His real name?" Williams pressed.

"That's not the way we work. Most people don't even know my last name. And especially with Bax. Uh-uh, Bax would never put his name out there." Donalson looked straight at Joe, "But I think it was the Delivery Man who wanted you messed up."

"So, how am I supposed to ask the Delivery Man, if you don't even know his name?" Big Will pressured Tyrell. "You know where I can find him?"

"No. But you should. He was with you the last time you was here, and tried to get me to do a deal. I wasn't gonna say anything with him here. It would get right back to Bax. But now that Bax is dead…"

Williams looked puzzled. "What do you mean, there was nobody with me except Lieutenant Taylor." Then Will paused with a stunning realization.

"Uh-huh. You getting the picture now?" Donalson asked Williams with a cocky grin. "The Delivery Man is the dirty cop. I didn't know he was a cop until you brung him into the room. I recognized him… and he recognized me. I almost shit my pants, man."

Big Will read Joe's expression and grabbed his arm. "Joe, don't go down there." But before he could say anything more, Mike flew out the door and headed for the elevators, with Joe and Big Will trailing close behind.

"Mike! Hold up. Wait!" Williams ordered.

The elevators were taking too long. His father and Will were closing in. Mike darted toward the nearby door to the stairway and disappeared. By the time the older men reached Freddie's room, Mike was standing along-side his bed with one hand on his gun.

"Why Freddie?" Mike cried. "Why did you have to kill Sean?"

Lt. Taylor recoiled to the furthest side of the bed. "It wasn't supposed to be Sean," Freddie whimpered.

Joe and Will arrived at the doorway to hear the rest of Freddie's twisted logic. "Your old man was such a goodie-goodie, a 'hero' that the other guys of the Coterie looked up to. He was nothing but a coward. A friggin coward!" Freddie shouted.

Joe stepped into Freddie's view. "All these years, Freddie. I thought you were my friend."

"How could I be friends with a coward like you, Joe. You got my boy killed. You held him up like a shield to protect yourself. You hid behind him. That shopkeeper told me what he saw. All these years, I knew what really happened."

"Freddie, Junior was already hit once when I got to the door. He was stumbling forward from his wound when he was hit twice more. I wasn't hiding behind him. I couldn't get around him. I swear. And that store clerk, he was hiding behind the counter. He didn't see anything until I shoved Junior out of the line of fire."

"Makes no difference now, Joe," Freddie railed, "You're still a coward! You got Junior killed. And right after his funeral, Angie had her first stroke. She couldn't take the stress and heartbreak."

"I'm so sorry Freddie. I had no idea you felt this way for the past eleven years. Hating me like this."

Big Will tried to lower the tension, "Freddie, I'm sorry about Angie. I didn't know she was so ill. None of us did."

"Do you know what it's like to watch you wife die a little bit every day? Waste away? Sink into an abyss of sadness and depression until the day she has a final stroke that puts her out of her misery? That's the misery I wanted you to feel, Joe!" Freddie snarled.

As Joe tried to move around Mike's left side to get face to face with this angry, broken man, Mike shifted his left side away from the bed to make room for his Dad.

At that very instant, Freddie mustered all the strength he could, gathered his pain and anger, and lurched toward Mike. Before Mike could make room for his father to slide by, Freddie grabbed the automatic from Mike's holster on his right hip.

Joe pushed past Mike, attempting to grab Freddie's hands. He dove over the bed rail and was amazed by the furious strength of a person of Freddie's age and condition. "No, Freddie!" Joe yelled. "No!"

The gun was pulled downward between the two men. A single shot fired, muffled between the two bodies. Both men slumped into stillness. Each moment was a terrifying eternity for everyone in the room.

Mike grabbed his father by his shoulders and pulled him as he laid across Freddie's body. "Dad!" he cried with horror.

Joe turned slowly, lifted himself to his feet, and looked at Mike with tears in his eyes. "I never knew, Mike. I never knew anyone hated me so much. I'm sorry."

Mike pulled his father close and wrapped his arms around him tightly.

Stunned, Big Will momentarily stood by helplessly. He then quickly stepped around the two and pried Mike's service weapon from Freddie's hand. Before he could check for vital signs, a handful of medical staff rushed into the room.

EPILOGUE

March 15, 2020

IT IS SAID that "All's well that ends well." Sometimes it does. But then, sometimes it's just too damn difficult to determine what "well" means.

Today, Sean Morgan is deeply missed by his family and friends, and is still fondly remembered as a star athlete and honor student at JFK High.

Retired Captain Joe Morgan now attends the Coterie breakfast every Tuesday and Friday with his friends. Lavon still teases him.

Lt. Alfred "Freddie" Taylor Sr. was not posthumously promoted, even though it was the custom for officers who died of injuries sustained in the line of duty. The story given to the press was that Taylor had succumbed to his injuries sustained during Operation Castle Down. This avoided the embarrassment of the truth. The press release cited the death of Lt. Taylor not as a hero, but simply as a casualty of the Police Department's succesful drug raid on the Freedom Boyz, and emphasized that it was the largest seizure of illegal drugs in the city's history. Even at his funeral, where a Police Honor Guard was provided, the circle of people that once considered Freddie a friend had diminished greatly. In fact, most people today would ask, "Freddie who?"

Tyrell "T-Man" Donalson did escape prosecution on the two murders that he confessed to after Sean's death. However, the immunity granted to him did not cover the two years prior to Sean's murder, which was the time period that Tyrell braggingly confessed to on multiple occasions. He was so proud to be Bax's Number Two, that his ego got the better of him. He is currently serving a 20 to Life sentence in a state prison for multiple drug convictions.

Unbeknownst to his fellow Coterie members, retired Det. Sgt. Harry Doyle had been keeping a journal throughout his career. He finally decided to write a book based on his exploits and his association with the Coterie.

Retired Staff Sgt. Vern Chosky is still instructing at his Dojo and has increased his enrollment, thanks to the recent publicity.

Retired Lieutenant Chaz Bohen has contracted with the Police Department to operate an in-house maintenance shop for their electronic equipment. He greatly appreciates the time away from Kitty.

Captain Willie 'Big Will' Williams is still Chief of the Homicide Bureau and is contemplating putting in his papers by the end of the year. Then he'll have no difficulty attending all the Coterie breakfasts.

Looking to follow in his father's footsteps, Lieutenant Mike Morgan took the promotional exam and placed number two on the list for Captain. Perhaps more importantly for the moment, he was unanimously voted into the Coterie as its first new member in 26 years.

Anjanae Adams had been promoted to Deputy Detective Sergeant by the County Sheriff. And equally important, she had also been inducted into the Coterie, making her the Coterie's first female member, and the first member from an outside agency.

Chuck Mason had unanimously been granted Honorary Membership to the Coterie. Without notice, he periodically appears for breakfast. The other members still do not know what agency he works for.

They are all doing well and regularly attend the Coterie breakfasts at the Towne Restaurant, as usual, in the corner reserved for the "Round Table." Often, they recount and embellish that night of their surveillance at the Freedom Projects. Chaz is still on water pills. And Police Commissioner Howes has hinted that he may retire. Over breakfast, the members are imaging how they could offer their service to a new administration…

About the Author

Dennis M. Adams delves deep through his many years of experience as an Army Intelligence Analyst, and a Detective with the Buffalo N.Y. Police Department, to create the characters of his debut novel, Motive. He holds a BS Degree in Criminal Justice from the State University of New York at Buffalo and resides in Western New York with his wife, Evy, and a greyhound. When not writing, Dennis operates his own practice as a Private Investigator.

Made in the USA
Middletown, DE
29 March 2021

36586304R00150